London on Fire

A Nathan Grant Thriller

Kenneth Rosenberg

Also by Kenneth Rosenberg

Chapter One

Just the sight of her sent a shot of adrenaline coursing through his veins. The three years since Nathan Grant last saw Natalia Nicolaeva only added to her beauty, like a rose coming into bloom. Where she'd previously had the glow of youth about her, she was now an unmistakably stunning, confident woman. What was her age at this point, twenty-four, maybe twenty-five? Nathan wasn't sure exactly, but Natalia had a charisma that set her apart. Her long, brown hair was tied back in a ponytail. She wore a white blouse under a short, fitted black jacket with black jeans and matching leather boots. Nathan had made the error of arriving a few minutes late, so Natalia was already waiting when he walked in the door. She rose from a table with a smile on her face.

"Nathan," she said. "It's been too long."

"I can only blame myself for that." He leaned forward to kiss her on the cheek. "Thanks for seeing me on such short notice."

"Of course! I hope you like Indian food. I've got about an hour before I need to head off for a client meeting." Natalia still had hints of her native Moldovan accent, but three years of studying in London had improved her English dramatically.

"A client?" he said. "I thought you were in law school?"

"Yes, well, I'm interning for a firm, but I don't want to bore you with that. Please, sit down!" Natalia motioned to the chair across the table and they both sat as a server arrived to hand them menus.

"Can I start you with some drinks?" asked the server.

"I wouldn't mind a Singha," said Natalia.

"Make that two," said Nathan.

"Sure thing." The server headed off to get their beers.

"So… how's life?" Nathan realized how painfully inadequate the question was. Here was a woman who'd stolen his heart three years prior, whose mere presence still rocked him to the core, and yet what exactly could he say?

"I can't complain." Natalia offered an equally lacking response.

"You must be graduating soon, right?"

"Six more months. Almost there."

"I'll bet you're top of your class."

"Not quite."

"Who's ahead of you? Give me some names. I know people who take care of these kinds of problems…"

Natalia laughed. "Don't forget, I can take care of myself."

"Oh, I know!" Nathan smiled in return, holding up both hands. "I remember that very clearly."

"What about you? Still running around with *the agency*?"

"No, no. I retired from that."

"Retired? You sound like an old man!"

"Fine, let's just say resigned. Moved on. That's more accurate anyway."

"What are you doing with your time?"

"I live in the south of France, in a quaint little village called Aureille. You should come for a visit."

"That sounds wonderful. My boyfriend has a thing for southern France."

And so, there it was. Nathan had half expected it. More than half. Why would a woman like Natalia be single? It was just as well, in any case. He'd never been particularly good at relationships himself. "Bring him along." Nathan tried to be magnanimous.

"If only. It's Ammon's first year with his firm. They hardly let him out of their sight."

"What type of firm is he with?"

"One of the big ones. Big money, long hours, no life."

"Is that what you have to look forward to in six months?" said Nathan as the server dropped two beers off at their table.

"Me? No way." Natalia lifted her beer. "That is not my future."

"Are you ready to order, or do you need more time?" said the server.

"I'll have the veggie korma with rice," said Natalia.

"For the gentleman?"

"Make it two." Nathan lifted his menu from the table and handed it over.

"Two veggie korma with rice. Anything else?"

"I think that will do," said Natalia.

"Coming right up." The server took the menus and moved off.

"What is your future, then?" Nathan picked the conversation back up.

"You know me. I'm a bleeding heart, always looking for a cause."

"Sure." Nathan realized that he didn't *really* know her all that well, if he was perfectly honest. They'd shared one adventure, chasing a very bad man across an island on the Adriatic Sea. He knew she could handle herself, and a weapon, as well or better than most of the Army Rangers he'd served with. She also had a very strong sense of right and wrong, a moral center. In that regard, her career choice made some sense. "Human rights?" he asked.

"That's the idea."

"I should have known you weren't in it for the money."

"I'll do just fine. Besides, I've got a little of my own stashed away. Sort of a retirement fund, you could say."

"Who are you meeting with today?" Nathan asked. "Or can you answer that?"

"No, it's fine. The firm I'm with was contacted by a woman who claims to have a story to tell, but she's a little skittish. It's a whistleblower kind of thing but I don't know the details. They want me to assure her that she's safe coming in."

"Is she?"

"I need more info from her to understand the contours of this thing. All she's said is that some influential figures are involved."

"It all sounds a little cloak and dagger."

"Indeed it does. Right up your alley, eh?"

"And they're sending the intern to do the dirty work?"

"I was the only one they could rope into the assignment."

"Let's hope you can reassure her, then."

When their food arrived, both of them dug in. Natalia kept her eye on the time as they chatted about more pedestrian topics, catching up on the previous few years. They weren't quite finished when her phone chimed and she picked it up to take a look. Nathan felt a pang of regret that the time he had with Natalia was already winding down. They'd had their hour together and now she'd go on with her busy life. He'd spend one more night alone in London before heading back to his wrecked house in the south of France. Nathan thought of all the work that needed to be done. There was fire damage and water damage, smashed furniture and broken windows. It was just as well that he would finally get going on it. Autumn was not far away, and he had no time to spare before the cold, wet weather began closing in.

Upon reading her text, Natalia quickly fired back a reply. "I'm sorry, Nathan," she said to him. "I've got to go."

"No worries, I'm just glad I got to see you." Nathan flagged down their server and asked for the bill.

"We could walk together. Which way are you going?"

"Whichever way you're going."

When the bill came, Natalia insisted on paying. The pair emerged onto Oxford Street and headed toward Marble Arch. Natalia kept up a rapid pace as they moved along the sidewalk. She tried to give off a casual air, but Nathan could tell that she was anxious.

"What's the story, Natalia? Is there more to this than you're letting on?"

"I don't know. My contact changed the meeting place. Something has her frightened."

"Where's the location?"

"Marble Arch Fountains, on the edge of the park."

"What do you know about this woman so far? Any background at all?"

"No, nothing. Just a first name. Bernadette."

"How did she contact you?"

"Through an encrypted app. At least she's being careful, right?"

"Are you sure you don't want some backup?"

"Thanks anyway. It was great to see you, Nathan, but it's time we parted ways. I don't want to spook her."

"I understand. I'll catch the underground. I hope you're able to sort it all out."

"Let's try to keep in touch a little better this time, huh? Maybe I'll take you up on that offer of a visit."

"I hope you do. You and Ammon both."

"We would enjoy it, I'm sure."

Reaching the tube station, Nathan saw Marble Arch itself across the road. He knew from prior experience that the fountain was just beyond that, though he couldn't see it from here.

"Thanks again for getting in touch." Natalia slowed her stride. "I'm sorry that I didn't have more time."

"No problem. Good luck with Bernadette."

Natalia leaned in to kiss Nathan on the cheek. "Safe travels."

Nathan inhaled the fragrance of her freshly washed hair. This Ammon person was a very lucky man. "Take care, Natalia." Standing on the sidewalk in front of the station, Nathan watched her as she waited briefly for a stop light before crossing the road and entering the park. Moving on past the tall, stone arch, Natalia disappeared from view. And so that was it, a brief connection, over nearly as soon as it had begun. There was nothing left for Nathan to do but move on. He entered the tube station and headed down the stairs. He'd only gone half a flight before he felt the overwhelming pull of concern. Nathan couldn't let it go, not like that. Maybe it was only curiosity, but he had to see how this meeting went down. Natalia Nicolaeva was not the type of woman who needed protection, but that didn't quiet the alarm bell in the back of Nathan's brain. What would it hurt to take a look? Keep an eye on things from a distance? Nathan spun back around and took the stairs two at a time, up and then out to the street. He crossed to the other side, but unlike Natalia, he didn't pass the arch to enter the park. Instead, he stayed on Bayswater Road, moving along the sidewalk until he stood at a railing that overlooked the long rectangular pool with a fountain in the center. On the left was a sculpture garden with Natalia standing beside it, periodically checking her phone. Nathan took a quick step backward so that a tree blocked him from view. From here he saw a carefully trimmed lawn, shady trees, and Cumberland Gate Road on the opposite side of the square, where black London cabs and red double-decker buses streamed past. The question that rang in the back of Nathan's mind was, did this Bernadette person fear for her reputation, or her safety? Was she worried about losing her job, or her life? That would all depend on what secrets she had to spill, and about whom. At the very least, Nathan wanted to get a look at her. He made a mental note of everybody in the park that he could see. A young couple were spread out on a blanket near the sculptures, having a quiet picnic. A mother pushed a stroller past the fountain before leaning down to point out some birds to her child. A jogger entered on one side and exited the other. The scene was tranquil. After a minute or two, Nathan saw a young female figure cross toward the fountain from the Hyde Park side and make her way around. She wore blue jeans and a pink hoodie, pulled up over her head, along with sunglasses over her eyes. Natalia moved toward her across the lawn until they met in the middle. After exchanging a few words, the pair walked a short distance and found a bench to sit on, side by side. Nathan did another quick scan. Nothing seemed at all out of the ordinary, with no suspicious characters following after the young woman. The only one paying them any attention at all was Nathan himself. He took one last look at them sitting on the bench. The emotion that flooded through him was pride, like a parent watching their child succeed in the world. Natalia could handle herself just fine. It was time to head home and let her get on with her life.

Turning toward the tube station, Nathan took a few steps, hands in his pockets. His flight wasn't until the following morning, which meant he had most of the day left to kill. No doubt he could find something to fill his time in the bustling metropolis that was London. Maybe take in a museum or two.

Nathan was considering his options when he spotted a sedan pulling to a stop on the opposite side of the park. A man in a black coat climbed out of the rear passenger door. He was tall and thin, with short dark hair, maybe thirty years of age. The man didn't pause or hesitate. Instead, he marched straight across the lawn toward Natalia and Bernadette, both of whom had their backs to the man. Nathan knew in the flash of an instant that this man meant business, only thirty meters away and closing. Nathan was sixty meters further, on the opposite side. The best he could do was to warn them. "Natalia!" he shouted, then leaped over the railing, dropping six feet to the lawn below before breaking into a sprint. Natalia saw him coming, but appeared confused. "Behind you!" he called out. By the time she turned around, the man was only ten meters away and pulling a pistol from his pocket. Natalia raised her hands in the air and said a few words, but the man lifted his gun, pointed it at the chest of a horror-stricken Bernadette and pulled the trigger once, then twice to make sure. Bernadette collapsed to the ground, the life draining out of her.

Nathan had closed half the distance when the man spotted him. He pointed the gun at Nathan's chest this time, then at Natalia, and back. Nathan slowed his stride and put his hands up. The only weapon at his disposal was his voice. If he could hold the man here long enough, and stay alive in the process, perhaps it would give the police time to arrive. "Whoa, whoa, it's all right, put the gun down," he tried, but the man turned and ran, back to the sedan still waiting on the edge of the park. He climbed inside and the car roared off into London traffic. Nathan looked to Natalia, holding one hand to Bernadette's bloodied chest. "I'm going after him," Nathan said.

"Nathan, don't!" Natalia called out, but there was no stopping him. On the far side of the park, Nathan flagged down a black

London cab but when it pulled over he didn't climb into the back like a normal fare. Instead, he walked around to the driver's side and flung the door open, then reached in to unfasten the man's seatbelt. Nathan grabbed the driver by the shirt and yanked him out of the vehicle, tossing him to the pavement. "Sorry buddy, it's nothing personal, but I need to drive." Nathan climbed behind the wheel, shut the door and took off. Which way had the sedan gone? He wasn't entirely sure and the car was no longer in sight. Nathan would need to take an educated guess. They'd be wanting to get out of the city center as quickly as possible. Nathan was no expert on London's roadways, but he'd stick to the busiest thoroughfares. That meant Edgware Road from here, he believed, heading toward the M1 Motorway. At the very least, he had a chance.

Nathan raced around the park and hung a left, swerving through traffic as he went and narrowly avoiding several pedestrians. Running over an innocent bystander would defeat the entire purpose of this ill-conceived pursuit. Somebody might get killed, Nathan would end up in prison, and the assailants would get away. He considered abandoning the chase altogether, but then he spotted the black sedan not far ahead. He couldn't very well give up now. They didn't know yet that Nathan Grant was on their tail. What was he going to do when he caught up with them? Run them off the road? It was worth a try, as long as he didn't get shot in the process.

With the pedal to the floor, the cab gave Nathan everything it had, moving around a city bus and then gaining on the sedan until their bumpers met, causing both cars to shimmy and shake. The impact was not enough to cause a crash, only enough to alert the killers that somebody was after them. Nathan reduced his speed, then punched it once more, and again, bouncing off their bumper each time as he tried to knock them off course. The rear window of the sedan exploded in gunfire, and then the cab's front windshield, with bullets whizzing past Nathan's head. He turned the wheel to the right as the two cars jostled and bounced, hoping he could get them to spin out, but then the sedan made a quick left turn.

"Dammit!" Nathan shouted to nobody in particular as he flew past the intersection. At the following corner, he made a left turn, and then another. By the time he'd relocated them down the side road, his adversaries were well ahead. Nathan came to a crescent lined with homes on one side and a park on the other. The sedan barreled along a footpath before exiting on the opposite side. Nathan followed, continuing past awestruck pedestrians, weaving after the sedan until it pulled to an abrupt stop in the middle of the road. Two men jumped out, the man in the black coat and a driver in a gray puffy jacket. Both held guns in their hands. Nathan slammed on his brakes and stopped some thirty meters away. He ducked low behind the dash as the shooting started, with hot lead tearing into the engine block and shattering the remaining windows. If they came just a little closer they could get Nathan point-blank and there was nothing much he'd be able to do about it. At any moment he expected to see them appear above him for the coup de grace. But then he heard two car doors close. The sedan was pulling away. Very carefully, Nathan peered over the dash. They were gone. The taxi was demolished, like something straight out of *Bonnie and Clyde*, but he was unscathed. It was a good thing these cabs had such heavy engine blocks. This one saved him.

Climbing out of the cab, Nathan saw spectators beginning to gather, astounded by what they'd witnessed and fearful of getting too close. Young mothers ushered their children away while a few people spoke on their phones, with others filming the scene for their social media feeds. Nathan heard the sound of sirens rapidly approaching. That meant it was time for the explaining to begin. Unfortunately, Nathan had very few answers to give.

Chapter Two

With no watch, no phone, no clock, Nathan couldn't tell how long he'd been locked inside this jail cell, lying on his back and staring at the ceiling. He didn't even have a window, which left him wondering whether it was night or day. He'd nodded off a few times and been fed once. The meal of porridge and tea suggested it was morning. They'd questioned him on arrival some hours before, and Nathan was entirely forthcoming. He even admitted to "borrowing" the taxi cab, insisting that the circumstances called for such a response. He couldn't just let these killers get away, could he? As Nathan sat in his cell it was apparent that the authorities would rather have handled the situation themselves. They didn't need some former spy going off half-cocked. That was no surprise, but he was beginning to wonder if actual prison time might follow. He didn't have his CIA bosses to help bail him out of this one in the name of international diplomacy. Somewhere on the outside, Natalia would be doing her best to help him. At least she had a working knowledge of the law on her side.

When the bolt next turned in the lock and his cell door slid open, two men stood on the other side. One was a guard, in uniform and holding a baton. The other man wore a gray suit with a narrow black tie. He was of average height and a little on the heavier side, with curly brown hair. He was fairly young, perhaps mid-twenties. In one hand, he held a brown leather briefcase. "Nathan Grant," the man said.

"That's right."

"I'm your solicitor, if you'll have me. Ammon Hanan. Can we talk?"

"Of course. Am I being charged with something?"

"Follow me." Hanan took a step aside to let Nathan enter the corridor. With the solicitor in front, Nathan in the middle, and the guard behind, the men walked to the end of the hall and into a small interview room, with a table and two chairs. The lawyer put his briefcase on the table before taking a seat. Nathan took the chair across from him while the guard closed the door and locked them both inside.

"I'll be honest, I don't normally handle cases like this one," said Hanan. "I'm taking it on as a favor."

"A favor to Natalia."

"That's right."

"She mentioned you when we met, before the chaos erupted." Nathan wasn't sure what he'd expected, exactly, when he'd pictured Natalia's boyfriend, but it wasn't this. Maybe it was because he knew that a woman like Natalia, with her own charm and beauty, could have just about any man she chose. Nathan had pictured her with someone, well, better looking. Ammon wasn't altogether unattractive, per se, but with his pudgy cheeks and fleshy lips… Nathan realized his prior assumptions were entirely superficial. Of course Natalia wouldn't choose a man based on his looks. She would choose him based on what was inside. That's who she was. For Hanan's part, he was being asked to represent this interloper, and likely pro-bono at that, to stay in Natalia's good graces. "I appreciate your taking me on, whatever the reasons," Nathan said. "Tell me, though, Ammon… Can I call you Ammon?"

"Of course."

"All right, what do you think are my chances of walking out of here without any charges?"

"That probably depends on what you can offer, in terms of cooperation. You were one of very few witnesses to the murder." Hanan opened his briefcase and pulled out a folder, placing it on the table before leafing through a few papers, stopping on what looked like a resume of sorts with Nathan's name at the top. "You stole a taxi and very nearly ran over numerous innocent bystanders. This all could have gone very badly indeed."

"Could have. I've never heard of charges being filed over what a man *could have* done."

Hanan peered at Nathan over the documents. "A cab driver was manhandled and, what do you Americans call it, car-jacked? His taxicab was completely destroyed. He may never recover from the emotional trauma, let alone the spectators who witnessed a gangster-style shootout on a public street."

"Don't forget, a young woman was murdered in broad daylight in a public park. I was only acting as a good Samaritan."

"Catching murderers is the job of the local authorities. If I were the circuit judge assigned to your case, I would find a way to keep you locked up at least until some sense could be made of the situation."

"If anybody can spring me, I have a feeling that you're the man."

"I would not get my hopes up. We'll do the best we can. I will request one thing of you. Unless the judge asks you a direct question, keep your mouth closed and leave it to me. Can you do that, Mr. Grant?"

"I can manage. Please, though, call me Nathan."

"In private, that is fine. In the courtroom, you are Mr. Grant."

"Of course. Tell me, though, did these men, these murderers... did they get away?"

"Sadly, they have not been apprehended as of yet. I would imagine it's only a matter of time."

"What makes you think so?"

"Mr. Grant, Nathan, you must come to terms with the fact that this is none of your concern. The police are well-equipped to handle it."

Nathan didn't like the sound of this at all. The whole thing was a mess. The only thing he agreed with was that he should have stayed out of it. If he hadn't felt some sort of misguided paternalistic concern for Natalia, he wouldn't have followed her over to the park in the first place. He would have hopped on the tube and learned about all of this later, in the newspapers like a normal person. This pair who'd murdered Bernadette were pros. If they hadn't been apprehended immediately, it was less likely with each passing minute that they ever would be. The question that bothered Nathan more than anything else was, why? Who was this Bernadette, and what damning info was she about to spill? Natalia likely knew more than she'd shared with him, but before Nathan could ask her, he had to get out of this jail. What he really ought to do, if he could swing it, was to head straight back to his quaint little village in southern France and stay there. He looked at his solicitor, Ammon Hanan. Nathan's immediate fate was entirely in this man's hands. "What's our next step?"

"I was able to arrange for an expedited court appearance. We will go before a judge first thing tomorrow morning."

"Another night in the slammer, then."

"Don't worry, Mr. Grant. The judge in this case is fair. He will hear us out, I promise you that."

Nathan nodded. "Can you tell me what time it is, at least?"

"Right now?"

"Yes, right now."

Hanan pulled up his sleeve to reveal a high-end chronometer, something he must have received as a gift from his family upon graduating from law school, or some other big life event. "Twelve-thirty in the afternoon. Only twenty hours to go. You think you can manage that?"

"Let's just make it the last twenty hours I have to spend in here."

"I'll do my best, but no promises."

"That's all I can ask."

A phone would have been nice, or a book. Anything to help pass the time. Being locked in a cell was just about Nathan's worst nightmare, the claustrophobia of it, the loneliness, the isolation. Twenty more hours. He would manage.

The following morning, after another breakfast of bland porridge, Nathan was dressed in his street clothes and summoned to court, escorted to a table near the front where he stood beside his solicitor. He spotted Natalia sitting in a gallery behind them along with a small crowd. She gave him a reassuring half-smile and a wave. He nodded in return. Ammon Hanan pulled out a chair for Nathan and then sat beside him. At a desk on the opposite side of an aisle were a man and a woman in business attire with a short stack of papers before them. The man was short and stout. The woman was sallow in the way that only a chronic smoker could be, with dark half-circles under her eyes. Nathan assumed these two were prosecutors.

"All rise for His Honor, Judge Malcolm Flagstaff," the voice of a bailiff called out and everybody in the room rose to their feet, Nathan included. From a door in the corner, a man appeared in a black robe fringed in white and purple. He was heavyset and wore a long white wig as he moved across the room to take his place behind the bench.

"You may be seated," the judge called out, and everybody took to their chairs once more. "This court is hereby called to order!" The judge took out a pair of glasses and perched them on the tip of his nose before looking over a page of notes. "Bail hearing for Mr. Nathan Grant, charged with assault, reckless driving and grand theft. Bail? What are you doing in my court today? With charges this serious? Denied!"

"But Your Honor!" Ammon Hanan called out. "Please, sir, will you give us a hearing?"

The judge peered over his glasses at the young solicitor, seeming to have very little patience for anything the lawyer might have to say. "Why should I?"

"My client has a distinguished record of service for the United States government, he is not a flight risk, and he was acting in good faith to track down a terrorist after a brutal attack."

"Not a flight risk?!" the male prosecutor called out. "Your Honor, please! The man is not a British citizen! If we release him, Mr. Grant will be on the next plane home, never to return."

At this outburst, the judge cried out in response. "Gentlemen! Must I remind you of the sanctity of this court? Please, one at a time. We will start with arguments from the prosecution."

"Thank you, Your Honor. The prosecution strenuously disagrees with the defense. Mr. Grant's record of service, as my right honorable colleague describes it, leaves us with more questions than answers. What was the true nature of his employment with the American government? Why is there no representative of said government present with us here today? Perhaps Mr. Grant is not being entirely forthcoming?"

"Please, Your Honor, let us not resort to wild speculation!" said Ammon Hanan.

"Order in the court!" The judge eyed Nathan Grant. "Perhaps the defendant can answer that question?"

Nathan looked to his solicitor and received a nod in return. "I was a soldier and a diplomat, Your Honor. I am now retired," said Nathan. Any mention of being an intelligence operative with the CIA was best left aside. This was something never admitted to, and it certainly wouldn't help his case.

"And what made you think you should go chasing after terrorists in a foreign city, of your own volition no less?"

"Instinct, I suppose."

"Instinct. I see."

"I witnessed a murder, Your Honor. I couldn't let the perpetrator get away."

"Hence the crux of our argument," Hanan chimed in. "If you don't mind, Your Honor, I will remind the court that Mr. Grant is the best witness that we have to the incident that occurred at Marble Arch yesterday. Nobody else got as good a look at the perpetrators as Mr. Grant."

"Your point, counselor?" said the judge.

"My point is, Mr. Grant's testimony will be hugely important to any case that the Crown may bring against the killers, assuming they are apprehended."

"Yes. So?"

"So, Your Honor, do you want a friendly witness or a hostile one? How do you think my client will feel being put on the stand if he's spent the previous months in jail? Do you think he'll be eager to cooperate? I should think, Your Honor, that my colleagues on the other side of this aisle should be happy to accommodate him." Hanan turned to the prosecutors, whose expressions gave away their discomfort. "Nathan Grant is not the priority in this incident, nor should he be. Mr. Grant was attempting to be a good Samaritan, that is all. It is the killers who ought to be the focus here."

The judge considered this argument, then looked to the prosecutor. "What say you to that argument?"

The male prosecutor slouched without comment. His colleague spoke up in her raspy voice. "The solicitor does make a valid point."

"Fine, then. Mr. Grant is to be released on his own recognizance under two conditions. First, his passport is to be held by this court. Second, he is hereby ordered to remain within the boundaries of the United Kingdom until this court determines that his services as a witness are no longer required. If Mr. Grant disobeys this order, this court shall initiate extradition proceedings to call him back, and the next time, I can guarantee you, he will not be released until we are full and well done with him. Am I understood?"

"What about charges, Your Honor?" Hanan pressed. "We request that they be dropped. Mr. Grant was only trying to do the right thing."

The disagreeable expression never left the judge's face throughout the entire proceeding. "Charges in this case will be considered pending a future hearing. How is that for a little bit of extra incentive? My decision in this matter will depend entirely on just how cooperative a witness Mr. Grant turns out to be. This hearing is adjourned!"

Nathan was struck by a flash of conflicting emotions. On the one hand, he was freed from the stifling claustrophobia of his small jail cell. In addition to that, if he testified against the killers, his own charges might be dropped. And yet... he was trapped here for the time being, no returning to his little cottage in Aureille. He wanted to raise his voice, to protest, but he knew it was utterly pointless. The decision was made and Nathan wasn't about to press his luck. Turning to look up into the gallery, he made eye contact with Natalia, who appeared to be relieved. As Nathan and his solicitor moved toward the aisle, they were met by the prosecutors on their way out.

"You are a very fortunate man, Mr. Grant, that your solicitor is so well connected," said the woman.

Nathan did not respond, but was instead ushered up the aisle and out of the courtroom. "What was she talking about?" Nathan asked his lawyer as they went.

"Nothing. Forget about it."

When they'd exited the room, Nathan stood with Hanan near a stairwell as the spectators' gallery emptied out. Natalia came down the stairs among the crowd. "That went all right," she said upon reaching them. She leaned toward her boyfriend to kiss him on the cheek.

"Apparently you can't get rid of me," Nathan said. "I'm officially barred from leaving the country."

"It could have been worse," she replied.

"If the two of you don't mind, I've got some work to catch up on," Ammon cut in. "The kind my firm pays me for."

Nathan didn't respond to this obvious dig. While he appreciated Ammon's assistance, he hadn't asked for it, that was between the two of them.

"Thank you, Ammon," said Natalia.

"Try to keep our friend here out of trouble, will you?"

"I'll do my best."

Ammon put a hand on Nathan's shoulder. "Let's get the paperwork sorted so we can all get out of here, shall we?"

After signing some documents at a front desk, Nathan got his belongings back, minus his passport. The three of them exited the building to the street, where Natalia kissed Ammon on the lips this time before he climbed into a cab and headed back to his office. Nathan stood beside Natalia on the sidewalk.

"You hungry?" she asked.

"Are you kidding? Starving. Jail time always has a way of doing that to me."

"Come on, then." Natalia looked at her watch. "Let's get a decent lunch into you."

Ten minutes later, they were settled into a booth at a nearby pub. Nathan flipped through a menu before ordering a full English breakfast and coffee.

"Sorry, mate, no coffee here," said a server.

Nathan's disappointment was palpable, but at least he was out, he had to remind himself. As Natalia had said, things could have been a whole lot worse. "Can you do a black tea?"

"Yes, we can. And for the lady?"

Natalia closed her menu and handed it across. "Chicken salad sandwich and a sparkling water."

"Right away." The server took the menu and walked off.

"No offense, but I think we could have done better than this place." Nathan took a look around at the scuffed tables and worn wooden trim, inhaling that familiar pub smell that came with decades of spilled beer.

"You could have spoken up."

"I'm sorry... it's fine. Thanks for helping spring me. I appreciate that. Ammon worked his magic."

"It was a good result, so far."

"The prosecutor made some comment about Ammon's connections. What was that all about?"

Natalia raised her eyebrows, not entirely comfortable giving an answer. In the end, she couldn't help but come clean. "The judge is a family friend. He and Ammon's father grew up together."

"Then why did he deny bail at first?"

"I don't know. Probably just performative. As soon as Judge Flagstaff was assigned to your hearing, we were pretty confident of the outcome."

"What if it goes to trial? Will he preside?"

"Let's just hope it doesn't go to trial."

"I don't like relying on hope."

"I understand, but we're in a tight spot here. We can't go chasing after answers to this ourselves. Any excuse and they'll lock you back up."

"But if the killers aren't caught, I can't testify against them. There will be no incentive for the judge to let me go."

"What are you suggesting, Nathan?"

"All I'm saying is that the men responsible for Bernadette's murder need to be caught, or I have no chance of getting out of here."

"It's not up to us. It's a matter for the police."

Nathan leaned back in his seat, trying to determine how best to phrase what he wanted to say. "I'm not very good at just sitting around and letting things play out. Besides that, I'm not currently working. I only have so much saved for retirement. I hate to mention such pedestrian concerns, but you do realize how expensive it is to stay in this city?"

"I'm sorry, Nathan, but you need to keep out of it. Period. If you need to borrow some money, we can try to work something out."

"I don't need to borrow money..." Nathan felt ashamed for even having mentioned that part of the equation, but it was all part of the reality of the situation. "How about this? We do a little research, that's all. Maybe help push things along as best we can."

Natalia didn't like this suggestion much better, but she didn't say no right away. "What sort of research?"

"Just poke around a little, that's all. We can start online, then maybe track down some sources, ask a few questions."

"There is no *we* here, Nathan. If you want to see what you can find online, that's fine, but I don't want you trying to interview any sources. That's not your role. You have no role, other than as a witness."

"And you're just going to sit on the sidelines? I know you too well, Natalia. This woman, Bernadette, she was murdered over what she was about to tell *you*."

"What I get up to is my own business."

"The Natalia I used to know would leave no stone unturned in her quest for justice."

"You don't know me as well as you thought, then."

Nathan tried to reconcile the vision he'd previously had of Natalia with the woman facing him. Perhaps it was true that she'd turned over a new leaf, but deep inside she was the same woman she'd always been. "Do what makes you feel comfortable," he said. "But at least answer some questions for me. Can you do that? Can you tell me your theory of why Bernadette was killed? What do you think she was about to tell you?"

"I don't know. She hadn't told me anything yet."

"There must have been something. Why did she set up the meeting in the first place?"

Natalia's flushed at Nathan's interrogation. "She sent us some emails claiming to have inside information about corporate malfeasance."

"Did you discuss contacting the police?"

"We never got that far. My sense was that she was trying to protect her identity. She didn't want anybody to know what she was up to, or where the information was coming from."

"Apparently, somebody found out anyway."

"Yes."

"And that's all you know?"

"Yes."

"It's not much." Nathan rubbed his hands together.

"Nope. Not much."

The server came back to the table and placed a small pot of tea along with a cup and saucer, a spoon, creamer and a bowl of sugar, in front of Nathan. For Natalia, he put a glass of ice on the table and then opened a bottle of mineral water, poured it until the glass was full and left the half-full bottle beside it. "Thanks," Nathan said before the server nodded and moved away.

"Bernadette wasn't her real name," Natalia confessed. "At least I don't think so."

"Why do you say that?"

"We only ever heard from her through one email account, but a search of that address yielded nothing. We don't have a surname. I really know almost nothing about her."

"What did the police have to say? Was she carrying any ID?"

"They haven't released anything yet."

Nathan poured some tea into his cup, blew across the top and took a sip. None of this was much to go on, yet. One mystery victim and two killers, vanished in the night. "I will need a place to stay while this whole thing plays out," he said.

"Ammon has a spare room. I could ask him…"

"No," Nathan cut her off. "I don't think that's a good idea."

"Why not? I'm sure he wouldn't mind."

"He's helped me enough already." Nathan took out his phone and searched for short-term apartment rentals. By the time the food came out, he'd booked a place not far away for the week. The cost was prohibitive, but he had to sleep somewhere and this was a better option than the hotel he was currently in. How long was this whole episode going to take? Sticking around until the men were apprehended and stood trial would bankrupt Nathan at these rates, but at least he'd bought himself a week to sort things out.

The server placed Natalia's sandwich on the table first, followed by Nathan's breakfast of fried eggs, sausage, bacon, tomato and baked beans, with toast. He inhaled the aroma of it before digging in. "Bon appetit," he said and took a bite of bacon. It sure beat cold porridge, any day of the week.

Chapter Three

Nathan stood on the sidewalk in front of a row of homes, all of them painted white, three stories high and connected one to the next up the block. Directly before him was a black iron gate, and beyond that a cement path leading through a small garden to a set of stairs. A series of street numbers was affixed to the wall beside the door. Thirty-Two A, B and C.

"Is this you?" Natalia asked. She'd accompanied him back to his hotel, where he'd checked out and brought his belongings to this new abode.

"I believe so. You don't need to hang around. I'm sure you have better things to do."

"Are you kidding? I want to check this place out. It looks pretty swank."

Nathan felt a tinge of regret. If he'd spent more than ten minutes searching the listings, no doubt he could have found something less pricey, but what was done was done. The location was in Shoreditch, just north of the financial district. If things weren't sorted out in a week, which seemed unlikely, he would try moving to cheaper digs further afield. Until then, this would do.

With his duffel slung over one shoulder, Nathan flipped up the latch and pushed open the gate. Natalia followed him through and up the front steps. A lock box was attached to the front door handle. Nathan dialed in the code, then pressed down on a switch to open the box and reveal a set of keys. "So far, so good."

Inside the front door, a stairwell led up past two other apartments until they reached apartment C on the top floor. Nathan used the second of two keys to open this door and let them in. He certainly couldn't complain about the apartment. It was small, sure, but homey. The main door opened into a living room, with a comfy couch, television, and two large windows. Directly across the street was a small park, and beyond that Nathan saw the gleaming skyline of the City of London spread out before him.

"Not bad," said Natalia. "I could get used to this view."

"It will have to do." Nathan moved into a small bedroom to his left that overlooked a central courtyard. He dropped his duffel on the bed and took out his laptop computer, then came back out and set it on a table in the kitchen, using a converter to plug the device's power cord into a socket along the floorboard. "In the grand scheme of things, being trapped in London is not such a bad deal. For a little while."

"I suppose..."

"You don't have to entertain me, Natalia. You must have plenty of other things you ought to be doing."

Natalia checked her phone messages. "I ought to be, but that doesn't mean I want to be."

"What are they saying at the firm about all of this? Any insights there?"

"They want me to come in for a meeting, ASAP."

"Go, then. I'll be fine."

Natalia eyed Nathan with concern. "If you need anything, you'll let me know?"

"Just try to keep me in the loop. I'd like to know what's going on."

"Promise me you're just an observer from now on. You've done enough already."

"I promise." Nathan said the words, though he wasn't sure this was one he could keep. "I'll walk you out."

Natalia nodded and the pair of them headed down the stairs and out to the sidewalk. "You would have been a lot better off if you'd never called me at all," she said. "I hope you don't regret it too much."

"Are you kidding? I'm just sorry about the circumstances." Nathan put a hand on her shoulder. "If you need anyone at all, even just to talk to, I'm here."

"Thank you, Nathan."

He kissed her on the cheek and then watched her go, down the steps and out through the gate. From what Nathan already knew about her, this whole thing paled in comparison to some of her previous traumas, but nothing ever entirely steeled one to death, no matter how much they'd experienced it before. For Nathan, there was no personal connection to these events. He'd never had a thing to do with "Bernadette" and barely laid eyes on her, but if there was one emotion he felt more than any other, that was anger. That son-of-a-bitch in the dark suit had walked right up to an innocent, unarmed woman in a public park, shot her point-blank, and apparently gotten away with it. This fury, this moral certitude, was the reason he'd chased after the assailants in the first place. Nathan Grant couldn't let something like this slide, no matter what kind of promise he'd just made. He went back inside and climbed the stairs to his apartment. At the very least, he could start looking around online a little as he'd said, just to see what came up.

Back at the kitchen table, Nathan logged onto the Wi-Fi with his laptop, routing his connection through a virtual private network as an added precaution, making it look like he was located in Zimbabwe, in case anybody was trying to track him. It always paid to be cautious. He started off searching for "Marble

Arch Murder" and quickly found a number of news articles about the killing. *London Woman Killed in Attempted Robbery*, read the most recent headline. Nathan clicked on the link and proceeded to read about how an armed vagrant on the edge of Hyde Park, near Marble Arch, had shot an unidentified woman to death while attempting to steal her purse. Nathan would not learn anything useful here. He went through what other articles he could find, but none of them gave any better information. Were the police trying to prevent a panic by keeping the truth under wraps? He couldn't see how an armed vagrant was any less frightening than the truth.

Closing his laptop, Nathan decided to check the kitchen cabinets. He found a box of tea bags, then filled an electric kettle with water and switched it on. When it had boiled, he dropped a bag into a mug and poured in some steaming hot water. Dunking it up and down as it steeped, he then tossed the used bag into a trash can and made his way into the living room to take in his million-pound view. It was mid-afternoon on a late summer day. A few of the leaves in the park across the road were just beginning to show some hints of color. The sky above was a deep, crisp blue that Londoners rarely got to see. In between the treeline and the heavens was that skyline. Nathan recognized a few of the buildings. He'd spent enough time in London to be familiar with "The Gherkin," shaped like a giant bullet, but which the locals somehow equated with a pickle. He also knew the "Walkie-Talkie," whose rectangular form resembled one of those hand-held devices, circa 1975. Further away, "The Shard" was a sharp and pointy glass structure that looked as though it were just waiting to tear into the next meandering dirigible.

As Nathan sipped at his tea, he tried to figure out how he was going to spend the bulk of his time here. His first goal, of course, was to spring himself and return to his cottage in southern

France, though that seemed to be entirely in the hands of the judge. What else could he do to make the most of this enforced downtime? Nathan only really knew one gear, and that was full speed ahead. He always was an adrenaline junkie, he understood, and as a trained intelligence operative and former special operations soldier, he didn't like sitting around. He put his mug down on a windowsill, licked his lips and crossed his arms, a man of action feeling the anxiety of forced indolence. He was gazing at that London skyline when the first bomb went off. One and then another, and then a third, blasting out the windows on the top floors of a building known as "The One Tower." Three fireballs burst into the sky and seconds later he heard the three consecutive blasts as the shockwave rattled his window and sent concentric circles vibrating in his mug. Black plumes of smoke rose into that deep blue sky. In his heart, Nathan knew there was some connection to the untimely demise of "Bernadette." Nathan was under court order to stay out of this entire affair. He'd made a promise to Natalia that he would. But come on. How could he be expected to just stand by and watch under these circumstances? Nathan felt that irresistible pull of curiosity and the familiar desire to take on a hopeless case. What could he possibly accomplish on his own? There was only one way to find out. Nathan moved to the kitchen table and picked up his apartment keys. Nobody told him he couldn't go out for a walk. Locking the door behind him, he hurried down the stairs. As he headed downtown along the sidewalk, he heard the first of the sirens, screaming toward the scene. Maybe this actually had nothing at all to do with "Bernadette." But then again, maybe it did.

Chapter Four

Hurrying toward the scene, Nathan was like the proverbial fish swimming upstream. Everyone else was fleeing in the opposite direction, including hordes of people on foot as well as cars, trucks, bikes and scooters. The only vehicles headed toward the explosions were police cars, fire trucks and ambulances, lights flashing as they weaved through the crowds and tried not to run anybody over on the way. It was only when he'd closed to within a few blocks that Nathan began to see the injured. People in torn and bloody business attire were being helped along. One man whose pants were shredded below the knees moved up the sidewalk with his arms around the shoulders of two colleagues. A woman walked past, seemingly in a daze, with hair askew and rivulets of blood running down her face. Nathan kept going until he came to a hastily arranged police checkpoint, where two patrol cars blocked a portion of the street, allowing only emergency responders and their vehicles to pass. Nathan looked up. From here he could see the flames, still engulfing the top three floors of the building, some four hundred or so feet above them. On the street directly ahead, broken glass covered the asphalt. Another blast above sent the few spectators cowering in terror and Nathan saw a shower of glass descending earthward half a block away, hitting the asphalt just past the police cruisers. It was too close for comfort. What was he even doing here? He hurried further backward.

Taking shelter in the doorway of a nearby building, Nathan was reminded of the September 11th attacks in New York, decades earlier. He'd been a teenager then, growing up on a ranch in Texas. None of it made much sense to him at the time, but he did understand that it represented a dramatic shift in what it meant to be an American. His own naivete was shattered. The world was a dangerous place, and that danger could find you anywhere. Nathan sometimes wondered, if it hadn't been for those attacks, would he have signed up for the Army and gone on to join the Rangers? Would he have shifted to a career with the Central Intelligence Agency? Those were questions he'd never been able to answer, but he had to wonder what changes this attack might presage. Who had carried it out, and why? No airplanes were involved in this one; he'd been watching when it happened. These bombs were planted on three different floors and timed to go off in quick succession. It might help if he knew what the target was, specifically. What businesses occupied those floors? Maybe it had nothing to do with politics. Maybe it was an elaborate workplace massacre. In the U.S. that sort of thing happened from time to time, only with guns not bombs. All the speculation in the world wouldn't get Nathan anywhere, though. Neither would standing in this doorway, eyeing the scene of disaster. What *would* get him somewhere? Talking to the right people would be a good start. At the moment, talking to anybody at all might help.

"Excuse me!" Nathan tried to flag down a man in a suit and tie who ran past carrying a brown leather briefcase. The man looked up long enough to take Nathan in and then hurried on without a word. Feeling the vibration of a ping on his phone, Nathan pulled the device from his pocket and saw two missed calls and a text from Natalia.

Where are you? she wanted to know.

Afternoon stroll, he texted back, then waited while the overloaded network tried to send it through. From Nathan's position on the street, he saw only a few other spectators watching the incident unfold from behind the police lines. Most of the civilians on the scene were attempting to flee. That included a steady stream of office workers, still exiting the tower and hurrying away, dodging the glass and debris as they went. Some were loaded into ambulances while others simply fled on foot. One behavioral pattern that Nathan had heard about years earlier crossed his mind. It was common knowledge, really, that when an arsonist set a building on fire, they could often be found among the onlookers, admiring their handiwork. Could the same be said for a bomber? Nathan didn't see why not. It made perfect sense that whoever set off these bombs would want to see how it turned out, up close. With that in mind, he began to watch the watchers. His interest was not in those fleeing the scene, but those who were drawn to it. Of course, just because a person was compelled to watch a spectacle like this one didn't mean he or she was behind it. But... whoever was behind it would likely be compelled to watch.

The first few people Nathan focused on appeared to be homeless. One man wore a filthy tweed coat with a tear in the sleeve. His unwashed hair was a mess. This man would never have been allowed inside the building, let alone had the ability to plant any bombs. He stood behind a hastily-erected barricade looking upward with what struck Nathan as an air of righteousness, as though those rich bastards on the fiftieth floor finally got what was coming to them, those men and women who passed his outstretched cup each day without bothering to drop a penny in it. Beside this man was a woman in equally diminished straits. She pushed a bicycle attached to a small cart that was loaded down with her worldly possessions. It all looked like so much garbage to Nathan, but he wasn't about to judge. What he did ascertain was that unlike the look of contentment in the eyes of the man beside her, this woman was all business. Nathan saw her scanning the other people around her, and the officers, and the fire trucks and ambulances that kept arriving. Surely there was something here she could add to her cart. Moving across an intersection, she approached a twisted piece of metal on the sidewalk, lifted it up for examination, then tossed it away and moved on.

None of the people Nathan saw in the area so far looked like the mad bomber type. A few other office workers from neighboring buildings stood watching, most of them trying to call home and report their status. A few filmed the action on their phones. It all begged the question, what type of person was Nathan even looking for? The answer, he supposed, was somebody much like himself. He was after a spectator with an eye on not only the fire fifty-stories up, but on the first responders. His target would be watching the firefighters, and the police, and the injured victims. This person might have an expression of self-satisfaction, much like the homeless fellow, though with enough social capital to gain entry to the building, at the very least. Maybe an office worker. Maybe a foreign terrorist. Nathan kept moving, working his way around the perimeter. The perpetrator, or perpetrators, could very well be watching it all play out on television from some distance away. All the same, what else did Nathan have to do?

Reaching other areas with a view of the action was not an easy task. The police were shutting down more of the approaches as each minute passed. Nathan had to go back one block, then over one. Finding this route inaccessible he went one further, then closed in until he could stand on one small corner with a cluster of onlookers, jostling for a tight view of the burning tower, seen between two other buildings.

"What building is that?" one man asked another.

"That's the One Tower."

"One Tower? What does that mean?"

"Beats the hell outta me. Does it matter?"

"I'll bet you the Arabs did it. Don't like our way of life, they don't."

"I'll bet you're right."

Whether the man was right or not, Nathan wouldn't speculate. What he did assume was that none of the people clustered on this small corner seemed like a bomber. Nathan moved on. The next street around was a broader avenue, blocked off by several officers manning barricades. Downwind here, acrid smoke filled Nathan's lungs. Besides the spectators, several television news crews were gathered, broadcasting live. Far overhead, he heard the whir of helicopter rotors. Nathan took a moment to check his phone again.

Afternoon stroll, where? Natalia had texted him back.

Downtown, he replied. *Strange weather. Glass showers with periods of fire and brimstone.*

What are you doing?! She fired back.

Just being me.

Nathan's phone began to ring. She wanted to talk some sense into him, but he wasn't in the mood. Instead, he rejected the call and went back to his surveillance. Sometimes it was the things you didn't expect that stood out. There was no telling if the Bernadette murder was connected to this attack, or if the perpetrators would be hanging around, but years of experience as an intelligence operative didn't just evaporate overnight. Nathan was an observer, taking in every detail and processing it all to make sense of anything out of the ordinary. What he saw in this current mix of curious spectators, emergency personnel, and walking wounded, was one commonality. Every single one of them had at least a measure of fear in their eyes. Some were more worried than others, but all of them were affected to one degree or another on a deeply emotional level. All of them, that was to say, but one. Maybe it was nothing, just a psychological peculiarity, but Nathan spotted one man standing by himself who seemed oddly unaffected by the drama playing out before them. The man was young, most likely in his early twenties, with what Nathan would describe as a blond pageboy haircut, like the Little Dutch Boy on the famous line of house paint. He was short in stature and thin, but with healthy, round cheeks. Something about his clothing was peculiar. It took Nathan a moment to understand why, but then it dawned on him that the young man's beige cotton jacket and blue pants appeared to be hand-made. All of the buttons were hand-sewn and not quite lined up. Even the man's blue canvas shoes, with their rope soles, looked hand-crafted. Nathan's first instinct was that this man, barely more than a boy really, must be part of a strict religious sect. Was he Amish, perhaps? In London? If so, how did he get here? Did the Amish fly on airplanes? They didn't even drive cars. They certainly didn't set off explosive devices inside the offices of multinational corporations. And yet, this young man was here, completely unperturbed by it all, watching as though he had some deeper understanding of how it related to his place in the world. Nathan knew only that this kid's reaction was peculiar, and under the circumstances that was reason enough to take a closer look at him.

The young man's position was some distance back from the bulk of the other spectators. He could still see the fire on the upper floors of the highrise, and he had a view up the street to where the fire trucks were gathered, with the ambulances loading victims as they came out and then whisking them away to the nearest hospital. If any other onlookers moved too close, the young man would take a few steps further away, as though he were afraid to catch some type of communicable disease.

Nathan made his way to the far side of the intersection and then a dozen or so yards up the block toward where the young man stood, stopping some distance away on the opposite side of the street. Despite Nathan's attempt to be inconspicuous, the young man picked up on him right away. Maybe he wasn't worried about this massive terrorist attack, but he did seem nervous about Nathan Grant. The kid stuffed his hands into the pockets of his homemade jacket and slouched, lowering his chin toward the sidewalk momentarily, then swiveled his head left and right before trudging away, quickly and with purpose. Nathan set out after him. Maybe this was all for naught. It was possible that Nathan was simply harassing some unfortunate young man on the spectrum, but until Nathan had some evidence one way or another, he couldn't let it go. At the very least, he wanted to have a few words with the young man, but first he had to catch up. The kid picked up his pace to the point that he was nearly running, and Nathan hurried after as the young man turned right at the next street. By the time Nathan reached the intersection, the kid was sprinting up the block at full speed. Nathan stopped where he was on the sidewalk and watched the young man go. He was an odd kid, with an unusual haircut and clothes and an unconventional reaction to a terrorist attack, but none of that meant he was involved. Nathan needed to control himself. He was supposed to be sitting in his apartment waiting for a call from the court, not chasing after phantom terrorists. Natalia was right, as usual. He powered his phone back on to check his texts.

I'm on my way to your place! You better be there when I arrive! Natalia had written.

Heading home, he wrote back. *Ten minutes. See you there.* Nathan tucked his phone back into his pocket and began the trek toward

Shoreditch. With everything that had gone down since his arrival here in London, Nathan felt a deep sense of dread. It was a feeling that he was getting sucked into something this time that was completely beyond him, an unknown force of evil that he couldn't comprehend. That Amish-looking kid might very well be involved, Nathan felt in his heart of hearts. But how? And what was coming next? He knew better than to expect that this attack would be the end of it. No matter what any judge said, or what the police said, or even Natalia, Nathan was in this one and he couldn't let up until he got some answers, or some justice, or preferably both. Natalia was either with him on this or in his way. The time to sort that out was now.

Chapter Five

Natalia was sitting on Nathan's front steps as he approached.

"I'm not allowed to take a walk?" he said as he unlatched the gate and let himself through.

"That depends where you walk."

Nathan didn't answer this one. Instead, he waited for her to stand. "What do you want, Natalia? Just checking up on me?"

"In part."

"I'm perfectly fine, as you can see. What's the other part?"

"I have some information," she admitted. In the near distance, they still heard the wail of sirens, and the roar of helicopters overhead. News choppers, police, fire-fighting helicopters; all sharing the crowded airspace.

"Cup of tea?" Nathan asked.

"No, but I'll come up."

"Sure." Nathan nodded, then moved past Natalia to open the front door and lead her up the stairs. Upon entering the apartment, they moved to the living room window to take in the skyline, with the smoldering One Tower building in the center. Unlike the Twin Towers on that fateful day, a few bombs were not enough to take this building down entirely. "What information?" Nathan asked.

"They ID'd Bernadette, I thought you'd like to know."

Nathan moved away from the window and took a seat on the small couch. Of course he wanted to know. "Please…" Nathan gestured toward a plush chair to one side. "You're sure I can't get you anything? Not that I have much to offer."

"Perfectly sure." Natalia lowered herself into the chair.

"Okay, then, who was Bernadette?"

"Her name was Megan Stirling, she graduated from the University of Manchester two years ago, and she came from a small village in the north."

"Named?"

"Cornholme."

"And?"

"That's all so far. The police haven't shared any more."

"You must have dug around."

"I haven't had much time yet, I came right over here. She studied finance, volunteered with some environmental organizations, that's about all I've come up with so far. Her final year in school she interned for an investment firm."

"Which one?"

"It's called Lange Capital."

"Never heard of it."

"Me neither, but it is a thread we can pull."

"We? I thought you wanted me to stay out of it?"

"*They...* It is a thread the police can pull."

"You don't want to let this go anymore than I do. Admit it, you're all in aren't you? You're telling me to stay out of it, but you're not willing to follow the same advice."

"My level of involvement is my own business. You, on the other hand, do need to stay out of it."

"Why are you here, then? Sharing this information with me?"

"As a courtesy. Even that goes against my best instincts."

"How can you say that? I thought we were a team!"

"No, Nathan, not a team! You are a loose cannon. What were you doing today, going for this *walk*?" she scoffed. "You were in the financial district. Weren't you?"

"What if I was?" Nathan was taken aback by her vitriol.

"What is the judge going to think about that?!"

"Nothing, if he doesn't find out. I thought you might be a little more appreciative that I'm on your side, here!"

"Appreciative of what? You didn't save Megan Stirling. You didn't catch her killers, or even slow them down. All you have done for me is create complications, in my professional life and my personal life."

"I see." A sense of shame seeped into Nathan's core as he saw things from Natalia's perspective. It was true that he was lucky no innocent pedestrians were injured during his ill-advised chase. It was also clear that his presence created a strain on her relationship with Ammon. The only thing that all three of them seemed to agree on was that everyone would be better off if Nathan was back in France.

"The court considers you to be Ammon's responsibility, at least in part," said Natalia. "If you don't follow the judge's orders, that will reflect quite poorly on him."

"I see." Rising to his feet, Nathan moved back to the window, eyeing the smoldering skyscraper in the distance as the afternoon turned to evening. "What was the target of the bombing?" he said. "If you're sharing. The top three floors of the building, one bomb on each. Who occupied those floors? Government? Business? A bank?"

"Those were the offices of Great Northern Petroleum."

"Huh," Nathan said, mostly to himself.

"What?"

"That seems a little bit odd, doesn't it?"

"What do you mean?"

"An oil company's offices get blown up the day after a young environmentalist is murdered just a few blocks away?"

"There is no evidence we know of to support a connection."

"Not yet."

"Did you hear a thing I just said, Nathan? You're going to stay out of this from here on, right?"

"The judge told me I couldn't leave the UK. He didn't say anything about a visit to Cornholme."

"Are you kidding me? You are not going to Cornholme! What do I need to do, handcuff you to a chair?"

"There's no better way to look into Megan Stirling's background than go directly to the source."

"You don't think the police are already there, interviewing every resident in the village?"

"We won't know for sure until we get there, will we?"

"Why on earth do you think I would come with you?"

"Somebody has to keep an eye on me, right? To protect Ammon's reputation?"

"Nathan, you're starting to make me angry, I mean it."

"I'm not planning to get in any trouble, just ask a few questions. Maybe we can find some people who knew her, who might share their insights."

"I don't even know what to say to you right now."

"You don't have to come, Natalia, but I'm willing to bet that you and I feel the same way about this. A young woman was murdered right in front of our eyes. I know you'll do everything you possibly can to bring her killers to justice. Who knows, maybe we'll talk to somebody up there that the police missed. Maybe we'll get that little nugget that leads to the truth. We owe it to ourselves to follow through. It's who we are, deep in our souls. You and I are two of a kind. That's why you came over here to share information in the first place. You knew I wouldn't give up on this until we reach a conclusion, until we get the justice Megan deserves. Admit it, Natalia, you still want my help. Don't you?"

Natalia sat in her chair, stewing. She couldn't bring herself to say it, but wouldn't deny it either. After letting the question swirl around in her head for a while, she took out her phone and checked an app. "Trains go from King's Cross twice per hour. I'd want to stop home on the way to pack a bag."

"Great." Nathan moved into the bedroom and shoved whatever he'd removed from his duffel back inside, then hoisted it over one shoulder. It felt good to be paired up with Natalia again, despite her resistance. Maybe it was partly true that she just wanted to keep an eye on him, but he preferred to think of it the other way around. The two of them made a great team. They'd proven it before and come out on top of a desperately dicey situation. No matter what they faced this time around, they'd have each other's backs. "Ready?" he said.

Natalia was deadly serious. "You're like an eager child, off on a big adventure."

"Is it that obvious?"

"Come on." Natalia stood and moved toward the door. "If we hurry we can catch the five thirty-three."

Chapter Six

They got off the train in Leeds and rented a car for the last leg of their journey. By the time they pulled out of the car park with Nathan behind the wheel, it was past 8:30 on a late summer evening, with the sun just dipping to the horizon. "Where to, Sherlock?" Natalia asked.

Nathan stepped on the brakes at the edge of the driveway. It always took some getting used to, driving on the left-hand side. He waited for a few cars to pass before easing onto the road.

"You want me to drive?" Natalia said.

"I got it!" Nathan snapped.

"I'm just saying…"

"I'm fine." They moved along through city traffic as Nathan tried to follow the directions from his navigation app. *West on Wellington St., left onto Wellington Rd., right at the roundabout to Highway A58.* Nathan kept driving out of the city until they merged onto Highway M62. They still had more than an hour to go before they reached the village, which meant an arrival time approaching 10 p.m., long after dark. Having investigated what they could while on the train, they'd learned the address of Megan's parents, but stopping by unannounced at this hour was not likely to go over well. There was also the question of explaining who they were and why they were here at all. No doubt the police had already questioned the Stirlings extensively. Besides that, the family would be grieving. The better bet would be to look for other avenues of inquiry, perhaps locate some of Megan's former classmates to see if they had anything useful to share. She must have kept in touch with at least a few of them. All the same, Nathan followed the navigation directions until they led to a small farmhouse on the edge of the picturesque little village. At the very least they could scope out where the young Megan grew up. The place reminded him a little bit of Aureille in the south of France, where his own small cottage awaited him. The biggest difference was that this place had a dampness about it, and the rolling hills here were less dramatic than the rugged peaks of Provence. None of that mattered, of course. What mattered was the police cruiser parked in the drive.

"It looks like the Stirlings have company." Nathan continued driving slowly past. He saw a light on in a large front window of the home, though the front curtains were drawn. Inside the police car was the silhouette of an officer behind the wheel, sitting alone in the dark. "That's a protection detail. They're worried that whoever came for the daughter might come for the parents next." Nathan made a left turn and headed toward the center of the village.

"Maybe we have this thing all wrong," said Natalia. "We shouldn't jump to conclusions. It could just have been a toxic relationship. Maybe Megan got involved romantically with the wrong guy. She met some sociopath online and then tried to break things off?"

"Sociopaths tend to work on their own. Megan's killer had a driver. Besides, that was a professional hit if I ever saw one."

"True," Natalia conceded. "I'm just trying to keep an open mind."

"We'd better find a place to stay." They entered the village proper, which was composed of narrow lanes with two-story stone buildings on either side of the road. Streetlights illuminated the scene, but very few people were out and about at this hour. Likewise, traffic was light. Nathan saw a farm supply store, a small grocery, some restaurants and a church. It didn't take long to spot their first pub, named the Saddle Inn, standing alone on a corner. Beside it was a small car park, half full. "What do you think?" he asked.

"Sure," Natalia answered. "A bed's a bed at this point."

"Let's find out if they have any." Nathan pulled into the car park and found a space before he shut off the ignition and they climbed out.

"You think the police might be keeping an eye on a place like this?" Natalia asked as they made their way to the front door. "To keep tabs on outsiders?"

"If they're smart," Nathan replied.

"You think they're smart?"

"I have no idea. We have nothing to worry about, right? It's not like we've done anything wrong."

"Not yet."

"What does that mean?"

"I've seen you in action, Nathan. I know where this might lead. Why do you think I'm here?"

Nathan stopped just outside the door. "I don't need a babysitter. If you'd like, I can drive you back to the train station."

"Don't get testy."

"I'm not getting testy. All I'm saying is that you don't have to be here."

"Neither do you. That was my whole point from the start, remember?"

"It's a little late to rehash this conversation. Are you with me on this, Natalia, or not? I'd like to know, once and for all."

Natalia had no words in response. He could tell she was angry, yet all the same, she pushed straight past him through the door. Inside, they found a cozy, traditional English pub, with wooden tables, a long bar, and a large fireplace on the far side. The place was quiet, with only a smattering of customers, including an older couple at a table near a front window and a pair of middle-aged men sharing pints at the bar. A round, gray-haired woman stood behind the bar, drying a glass with a rag. Everybody in the place looked over to the newcomers as they came in.

"Good evening," the bartender greeted them.

"Hello," Nathan replied. "We were wondering if you have any rooms for the night?"

"Rooms? No. One room? You'd be in luck."

Nathan looked at Natalia. She wouldn't be thrilled to share, he was quite sure. "Your call."

"One room is fine," Natalia answered.

"Follow me, then, and we'll get you checked in." The bartender put away the glass, wiped her hands on the rag, then came out from behind the bar and led them into a very small room to one side. It was more of a closet, really, with just enough space for a small desk. From one drawer, the woman pulled out a hotel register, flipped it open and slid a pen across. "Sign here. I'll need a copy of your passports as well, if you please."

Normally this was a situation where money might do the talking for him, but something about the innkeeper's demeanor suggested that might not go down well here. If she owned the place especially, she wouldn't want to take that sort of risk.

"My fiancé had his passport stolen just this morning," said Natalia. "But I can give you mine." She took her own passport from a pocket and slid it across the desk before lifting the pen and filling in their names in the ledger.

The innkeeper was skeptical. "Stolen, you say? Maybe you have another form of identification, then? Or did they steal that, too?"

"I can give you a driver's license. How's that?" He pulled his Texas license from his wallet and handed that across.

The innkeeper looked over Nathan's license and then Natalia's passport as she attempted to size up this couple in front of her. "Congratulations on your engagement."

"Thank you," said Natalia.

"I'll need to make a copy of these." The woman left the small office with the documents in hand. From another room behind, Nathan heard the whirring of a copy machine, and then the woman reappeared, handing the IDs back. From a box on the wall behind her, she took out a room key. "Just the one night?"

"Yes," said Nathan. "Just the one."

"First floor, room number four. The price is one hundred and twenty pounds, pay now or in the morning, it's all the same to me. Breakfast is included, eight to ten in the morning, check-out time is eleven."

Nathan took one hundred and twenty pounds from his wallet and put the bills on the desk before taking the key. "Any chance we could get some dinner?"

"Kitchen is closed. I could get you some soup if you'd like. Split pea or chicken noodle."

"Thank you, we'll be right back down."

After fetching their things from the rental car, Nathan and Natalia made their way up to the room, which was comfortable and cozy as well, with one large window facing the street and a single queen-sized bed. "I'll ask for a cot," Nathan said.

"Are you kidding?" Natalia replied. "We just told her we were engaged."

"So? Some people wait, you know."

"I don't think we look like that type."

"What type do we look like? Besides, what do you care what the innkeeper thinks?"

"She's already suspicious enough about your passport story. We don't need to be drawing any more attention. I know how these small villages work. People talk."

Nathan shook his head. She did have a point. He dropped his bag on a luggage rack and took a better look around. The wooden floor was covered by a rug in front of the bed. Nathan tapped at it with his foot. "I can sleep here."

"Why?" Natalia laughed. "Are you afraid of me?"

"Are you kidding? Of course I am. I've seen you in action."

"What does that mean?"

"We're not sharing the bed, end of discussion."

Natalia put her bag down. "Come on, let's get some soup before the innkeeper heads to bed."

Nathan followed Natalia back out of the room. The truth was not that he feared any impropriety, or even that she might feel uneasy with Nathan beside her. It had less to do with his moral compass and more to do with the emotions swirling inside of him. Just the thought of being in such close proximity to Natalia was unbearable. She was off limits, so why torture himself? No, the floor would do just fine.

Downstairs in the pub proper, the couple by the window were gone but the two gentlemen at the bar were still there, working on fresh pints. They barely glanced up this time before turning back to their beers.

"Here they are," said the innkeeper. "What's it going to be? Chicken or split pea?"

"Split pea for me," said Nathan. "Plus a pint of stout."

"I'll have the chicken soup," said Natalia. "And a pint of lager."

"You got it." The innkeeper reached for two glasses and started pouring the beers. "Have a seat where you'd like."

"Where do you think?" Natalia asked Nathan.

"How about here at the bar?" Nathan wanted to be near the two gentlemen, to strike up a conversation if possible and see what kernels of information he might glean. He'd hoped the pub would be busier, with some younger people included. He wanted to speak with some of Megan Stirling's contemporaries. In a village like this, nearly everyone in her age range was likely to have known her, but with none of them currently present, Nathan would have to do his best with what he had at hand.

"The bar works for me." Natalia took a stool two down from the men. "Mind if we join you?" she asked.

"Suit yourself," one answered, though neither man came off as welcoming. Nathan pulled up the stool next to Natalia as the innkeeper slid across her pint first, then his, before disappearing through a door in the back that led to a kitchen.

"How's the soup?" Nathan asked the men, as a means toward conversation.

"Can't say I've tried it," said the first man. He was a bulky type, wearing a threadbare sweater, with bushy red hair and mutton-chop sideburns. His companion was thin and gawky, in a worn wool sport coat. Nathan estimated that the men were in their late forties or early fifties. That meant they would have been roughly twenty years older than Megan Stirling. All the same, they might have known her. You never could tell what sort of information you might learn from a person until you tried. First it would help to win their trust, though in a village this small, trust of outsiders never came easily.

"I'm surprised," Nathan replied. "There can't be too many restaurant options around here."

"What makes you think we're from here?" said the second man.

"You're not?" Nathan asked.

"Passing through, just like you."

"I see, my mistake. Are you here on business or pleasure?"

"Just passing through," said the first man, as though that answered the question.

"It's lovely country, isn't it?" Natalia offered.

The men looked at Natalia as though she'd just offended their mother, but neither said another word. The first man lifted his pint glass and took a good long drink, nearly draining it.

"Nathan Grant." Nathan offered a hand, but neither man bothered to shake it. This was a tough crowd indeed.

The innkeeper emerged from the kitchen with two bowls of soup on a tray, along with a basket of sliced bread. She put the bowls and basket on the bar and then got some napkins and utensils. "Bon appetit."

"Thank you," said Natalia.

Nathan was considering another line of attack, but the two men abruptly finished their pints, tossed some pound notes on the bar, and got up to leave.

"Good night, then," the gawky one said to the innkeeper.

"To you as well," she replied.

The men headed for the staircase and made their way up. When they were gone, Nathan turned to the innkeeper. "Those two weren't so friendly, now, were they?"

"I'm never one to judge," she replied. "You never know another's burden until you've walked a mile in their shoes."

"All the same, a handshake might have been nice."

"Go ahead and finish your soup, now," said the innkeeper. "So's I can get off to bed myself."

"Sure." Nathan blew on a spoonful before taking a sip. It wasn't the proper dinner he'd have preferred, but the way things were going, he'd take what he could get.

"This is a very peaceful village," said Natalia.

"That's the way we like it. None of that big city madness up 'round here."

"You never told us your name," said Natalia.

"Harriet. That's my name."

"I'm surprised you only had one room left available," said Natalia. "Things seem awfully quiet around here."

"Well, we've only got the four rooms," said Harriet. "The retired couple you saw earlier are in one. Those two other gentlemen have a room each. That leaves the two of you in number four."

"What's the story with those two gentlemen?" said Nathan.

"I don't bother people about their business," said Harriet, implying that Nathan shouldn't either and upending his theory about small-town gossip.

"They don't strike me as the tourist type."

"I couldn't say. Sometimes my visitors like to talk, sometimes they don't. Those two don't."

"Tell me this, Harriet," Nathan decided to take a more direct approach. "Did you know a young woman around here named Megan Stirling?"

At this question, Harriet's entire body went rigid. She knew Megan Stirling all right, that was clear. "Why do you ask?"

"We heard some people talking, is all."

"That's definitely none of my business, what happened to that poor young girl."

"You heard about it, then?" said Natalia.

"Of course I heard about it! Everybody heard about it. I told her, don't go running off to the city, there's nothing there for you. Stay here where you belong. The young people these days, they don't want to listen, now do they?"

"No, they don't," said Nathan.

"Not that you big-city types would know anything about that."

"Natalia and I are both from small towns, not so different from this one."

"And you were off at the first chance, am I right?"

"Actually, I live in another small village now, in France."

"And how about your bride-to-be?" Harriet looked at Natalia. "She lives in this little village in France, too?"

"No, I live in London," Natalia answered.

Harriet had a hard time processing this information, that a couple could live in two completely different countries from one another.

"What do you think happened to Ms. Stirling? Do you have any idea?" said Nathan. "What's the word around town?"

"I've no idea, but that kind of thing doesn't happen 'round here, I'll tell you."

"I should hope not," said Natalia.

"I feel for the poor girl's family. Even more for William. She should have married him when she had the chance. She'd probably be alive today."

"Who's William?" said Nathan.

"William Davies. Awfully sweet on her, he was. Proposed to the girl, but she went and ran off."

"He's still around?"

"Oh, William's not going nowhere. Has his father's farm to run, now doesn't he?"

"Nearby?" said Nathan.

By this point, Harriet was exasperated, drawn into this conversation about Megan Stirling that she never intended. Now she shut the information off like turning a tap. "You two finish your soup, I'm off to bed. Leave the bowls in the sink behind the bar, I'll wash up in the morning."

"All right, Harriet, thanks for your hospitality," said Nathan.

"Have a good night." Harriet shut off a light in the kitchen and went to the front door where she turned the deadbolt before heading back to her private quarters behind the stairwell, leaving Nathan and Natalia to their own devices.

"Are we supposed to turn the lights off when we're finished?" said Natalia.

"I don't know." Nathan ate some more of his soup and then drank some beer. "I suppose we could help ourselves to another beer, if we wanted to."

"Go to town," said Natalia. "I think Harriet had the right idea. I'm ready for bed. Nothing, and I mean nothing, is going on in this village. I'm guessing this whole trip up here will prove to be a waste of time."

"Have some faith," said Nathan. "Let's see what tomorrow brings."

"I doubt we'll get anywhere near the family. Not if the police are camped out there all day."

"We definitely should call on William Davies. That could be a start."

Natalia finished the last of her soup and leaned back on her stool. "What did you think of those two gentlemen upstairs? Just unfriendly, or were they hiding something?"

"What do you think?"

"I think they're hiding something."

Nathan finished off his beer and considered helping himself to another, but decided against it. "What would two guys like that have to hide? They weren't the slick professional type, not like the two that went after Megan."

"Everybody has something to hide."

Nathan thought it over. "They could be law enforcement. Did they look like cops to you?"

"Not unless they were deep undercover."

Nathan concurred. "They did look pretty shabby. Just because people are private types doesn't mean they're part of a conspiracy, though, on either side."

"Maybe not, but at least we can try to keep an eye on them." They put their dishes in the sink behind the bar, shut off a few lights but left one on near the front door, and made their way back up to their room. Inside, Nathan found an extra comforter and some clean sheets in a wardrobe and made up a little bed for himself on the rug.

"You're sure you're going to be all right down there?" Natalia asked.

"Perfectly fine."

"Suit yourself." She went into the bathroom to brush her teeth and change into a pair of cotton pajamas. Nathan slept in a t-shirt and boxer shorts, and when he was settled into his floor space, Natalia climbed into the bed and shut off a bedside lamp, plunging the room into darkness. "Sleep well," she said.

"You, too, Natalia." The floor was a little hard, no doubt, but he'd had worse nights, on cement in full combat gear with the constant threat of incoming artillery. That was more than a decade earlier. Maybe he'd grown soft in the meantime, but one thing was for sure, there was absolutely no way he was going to share that bed with her. From an emotional standpoint, he felt a whole lot more comfortable down here.

Chapter Seven

The following morning, Nathan sat at a table downstairs with his full English breakfast while Natalia paced back and forth in the car park just outside, speaking to Ammon on her phone. Nathan tried not to pay attention, focusing instead on the headlines as he read the latest news on both the terrorist attack and the murder of a young woman on the edge of Hyde Park. As far as the former went, it was a deluge of information, much of it speculative. This was the biggest story to come out of London in nearly twenty years, since the train bombings in 2005 in which 52 people were killed and more than 700 injured. When it came to the attack the previous day, pundits questioned whether the perpetrators were members of some similar extremist group. The bombing of an iconic skyscraper did have some of the hallmarks of the 9/11 attack in New York City. The bottom line was that nobody knew anything concrete, or at the very least they weren't making it public.

Regarding the murder of Megan Stirling, the papers hardly covered that at all, perhaps because the bigger story got all the ink. Not one outlet suggested any connection between the two incidents, nor apparently did the police. Nathan put his phone down and ate some of his breakfast, then sipped at his coffee, which was black and a little bit burned. At another table nearby, the older couple were having their breakfasts in silence, hardly speaking a word to each other. It wasn't that they were angry or upset. Maybe after some fifty-odd years together, most of what there was to say had already been said.

By the time Natalia finished her call and came back inside, the two gentlemen from the night before were taking their places at the bar. Harriet took their breakfast order, and then came by for Natalia's.

"Just some porridge for me, thank you, Harriet. Can I get strawberries with that?"

"You sure can. And coffee?"

"Yes, please, coffee and orange juice."

"You got it." Harriet headed back to the kitchen.

"Any news on your end?" Nathan asked Natalia.

"There is," she answered. "Ammon spoke to the officer in charge of the Stirling case. They've got CCTV footage of the shooter in the park. It was enough to identify him."

"And? Who is he?"

"His name is Finbar Murphy."

"Irish. Let me guess, former IRA?"

"No, Mr. Murphy doesn't seem to be the political type. He's too young for all of that mess anyway." Natalia looked back to the bar where the two men were drinking coffee and minding their own business. "Maybe we ought to be having this conversation in private," she went on, lowering her voice. Harriet came over with the coffee and orange juice on a tray and placed them on the table. "Thank you, Harriet, you're a lifesaver," Natalia added.

"Enjoy." The proprietress moved away.

Nathan agreed with Natalia, they couldn't afford to be sloppy. "How's Ammon?" he changed the subject.

"Fine. Why?"

"I don't know. Small talk."

"You want to know how he feels about his girlfriend sharing a room with another man?"

"That's not what I said, is it?"

"I told him you slept on the floor."

"Did that make him feel any better?"

"Probably not."

Nathan laughed to himself. "And you're still making the poor guy represent me."

"Is that what you think, that I'm forcing him to?"

"Aren't you?"

"He was happy to do what he could for you, if you want to know the truth."

"I appreciate that." Nathan was chastened. He still had this sense that Natalia was out of Ammon's league, as they say, but by whose standards? Nobody's whose mattered. "I'm sorry to have doubted his motivations."

Natalia said nothing more, and they ate the rest of their breakfasts in silence, as did the two men at the bar. The only conversation in the room now came from the older couple, who were trying to plan their day.

"We're all the way up here, we might as well see it," said the woman.

"Why bother? A wall is a wall, as far as I'm concerned."

"You never want to do what I want!" the woman snapped. "You're selfish, that's what you are. All these years, I don't see why I put up with it."

"You've always known where the door was," the man replied.

"What is that, are you tempting me? Who's going to mend your socks if I'm not there? Who's going to fix your dinner? I know where the door is, ha! You wouldn't last a week without me."

"Maybe I ought to trade you in for a younger model, what do you think about that?"

"Oh, now you're really making me laugh! Who would put up with you? All I'm asking is to take a little side trip!"

"That's two extra hours driving, woman, each way! Little side trip…"

"Fine, but you don't need to be so rude about it."

The gentlemen by the bar paid their bill and headed out. Nathan watched them pick up their luggage by the front door and then walk out to a small yellow hatchback Ford and drive away. He made a mental note of the license plate, just in case. When he and Natalia were ready, they went upstairs to retrieve their things and brought them back down. "Tell me, Harriet, how would we get to the Davies' farm, if we were so inclined?" Nathan asked.

"Why would you want to do that?"

Nathan had no good answer to that question.

"I'm a lawyer," Natalia stepped in. "I was representing Megan Stirling. I'd appreciate it if you didn't share this information, since we don't want to cause a stir, but we'd like to ask William a few questions."

"You think young Willy had something to do with this? I'll tell you, surely not! That boy wouldn't hurt a soul!"

"I would never expect otherwise," Natalia said. "But it would still help if we could speak to him."

Harriet took a moment, making up her mind how much to share. No doubt the whole town would know exactly what she and Nathan were up to in very short order. Sometimes these things were unavoidable. Harriet took a piece of blank paper and used a pen to draw a map.

"We're here." Harriet pointed to an X she'd placed on their location. "The Davies' farm is here." She pointed again.

"Thank you." Nathan took the map.

"A girl like Megan, she never should have left for the big city. I told her…"

"It is a terrible tragedy," said Natalia.

"Terrible, terrible…"

Nathan put their remaining charges on his credit card. The older couple were still at their table, silent once again as Nathan and Natalia went past on their way out the door. It was a cool, damp morning, the asphalt wet from mist. "What else can you tell me about this Irishman?" Nathan said as they approached the rental car. "Finbar Murphy. What do we know about him?"

They put their bags in the back and then took their seats up front. "Ammon says he's a hired gun, suspected in numerous underworld hits, charged multiple times but never convicted."

"Underworld? He's with the mob?"

"A freelancer. He takes jobs from whoever is willing to pay, including the Sicilians in New York, Serbian rings in the Balkans, and the Boswell Crime Syndicate in London."

"Boswell?" Nathan put the car in reverse and pulled out of their parking space, then took a look at the map before taking a right turn onto the road.

"They call them firms here, family syndicates. Boswell is one of the largest and the nastiest, based in Hackney and headed by a man named Oscar Boswell."

"Any lead on Finbar Murphy's current whereabouts?"

"No," said Natalia. "He seems to have vanished."

"What about theories on a motive?"

"Nothing there, either."

This news wasn't helping much, so far, but if organized crime was involved, Nathan didn't like the implications. The mafia had resources. It wouldn't merely be a pair of gunmen they were up against, but a virtual army of criminals. It did make it seem less likely that the murder and the bombings were connected, as far as Nathan could see. The One Tower bombing had all the markings of an extremist group. An organization that pulled off that kind of attack would have an agenda based on their radical political views, whatever those happened to be. The mob didn't care about politics, not in the broader sense. They cared about two things, making money and protecting their territory. Whatever Megan had hoped to divulge, the information threatened some illicit dealings that apparently involved organized crime. Of course, Nathan didn't know who Finbar Murphy was working for in this case. If they were lucky, William Davies might have information that could lead them forward. It only took ten minutes before Nathan was pulling off the highway and down a long, narrow drive that led to the Davies' farm.

Nathan had grown up on a cattle ranch and Natalia on a farm, but every operation varied and while some aspects of this place felt familiar, like the smell of animals wafting across open fields, much about it was different, primarily the two long, narrow structures lined up one beside the other. Across from these buildings was a large pen, with just a handful of cows lazing inside. The rest of the herd would be inside, Nathan realized. This was a dairy farm, with a milking barn on one side and likely a bottling facility beside it. That made Nathan's job easier. Instead of tracking William Davies down across a wide-ranging property, they ought to be able to find him in one of these structures, or at least nearby. Nathan pulled their rental car up to park beside a few other vehicles, all of them covered in mud.

"Who's going to do the talking?" Nathan asked.

"I'll go first," Natalia answered. "If he's here."

"Let's hope."

They got out of the car and made their way across the wet earth into the milking barn, where long rows of stalls were lined up, each with a dairy cow inside. Following along beside the humming machinery, they came to a stall where a woman was busy adjusting a series of suction cups on bovine teats. She flipped a switch to tease out the precious milk. Unlike what

Natalia was used to from her childhood, none of the milking here was done by hand.

"Excuse me!" Natalia raised her voice.

The worker looked up in surprise. She wore a dirty pair of coveralls, with a blue bandanna on her head, and wasn't used to strangers interrupting her on the job. "Yes?" she said.

"Can you point us to William Davies?"

The woman stood straight and wiped her nose with the back of one hand. "Have you tried next door?"

"Not yet."

"You're here about the compressor?"

"That's right," Nathan butted in.

"It's about time. They're waiting for you." The woman went back to her task.

Nathan and Natalia made their way back outside, then on into the next building. This one was surprisingly quiet, given the fact that it was entirely filled with machinery. Empty milk bottles were lined up on conveyors, ready to be filled, but the whole contraption was shut down. Standing in front of it were three men, all in coveralls. One man's clothes were mostly splattered with mud, the other two mostly with grease. Nathan did a quick calculation as they approached, and it all seemed quite clear. "William Davies?" he said. The muddied man was in his early twenties, wearing glasses. His medium-length hair was tied back in a ponytail.

"Yes, I'm William," he looked over. "How can I help you?"

"We're from London," said Natalia. "My name is Natalia Nicolaeva. I'm a lawyer who was representing your former fiancée, Megan Stirling. Do you have time to answer a few questions for us?"

"Unfortunately, you've caught me at a bad time," William answered. "I've got two thousand gallons of milk I can't pasteurize until we get this fixed."

"We'll try to make it quick."

"Any other day would be better than this one."

"We're sorry, but this can't wait."

William turned to the two other men. "How long will it take to get that old compressor out?"

"An hour, maybe two."

"All right, let's get started." William and the men walked further into the building, leaving Nathan and Natalia behind. After coming all this way, neither one of them was about to give up that easily. They looked at each other and then followed after. At the far end of the building, they reached another series of tubes and pipes, storage tanks and equipment. A five-foot-square panel on one side had been removed, revealing the inner workings of the machine in question. Tools were spread out on the ground. "It started out making a horrible racket and then just up and quit," William explained to the men.

"Seen better days, no doubt about it," said one of the men in greasy coveralls. "Probably should have been replaced years ago. You got some good use out of it."

"As long as you have a replacement in stock, I'm happy."

"I'll take down the serial number and call it in."

"Be my guest."

"Maybe you have a few minutes while he takes care of that?" said Nathan.

"You two still here?" William was annoyed.

"Honest, we'll make it quick," said Natalia.

"I know nothing about who killed Megan or why. You're wasting your time, if that's what you're after."

"I was with her when she died." Natalia tried to pull at his heartstrings. "I know you loved her. I can see why, she was a special woman."

William's defenses bent, but didn't break. "Indeed. It's a shame she didn't love me back."

"I'm sure that she did, in her own way."

"Her own way wasn't enough, now, was it?"

"Don't you want to help bring the killers to justice?" said Nathan. "She'd want that, don't you think?"

"Like I said, I know nothing about it."

"We'd like to ask you some questions, in any case," said Natalia.

"And who are you, exactly?" William glared.

"I was her lawyer," said Natalia.

"We've got one that matches in our warehouse," said the man in the greasy overalls. "We can have it here by noon."

"Good enough," said William.

"We'll pull our tools from the truck and get to work hauling this out."

"Let me know if you need any help."

"We ought to have it covered."

"Great."

"All we need is ten minutes," said Natalia.

William scowled, considering whether to throw them out. "Ten minutes. In my office." He led them back through the building and out, past the vehicles parked in front and on to another, smaller structure nearby. Moving inside this one, he banged the mud off his boots on a metal grating in the floor. A receptionist behind a desk didn't say a word. The two guests took their turns banging the dirt off their shoes before William continued past the desk and led them down a hallway. Along the way, he leaned through the doorway to an office on one side.

"They say they can have a new compressor here by noon," he said to somebody inside.

"Could have been worse," came another male voice.

"If they need anything in the next little while, see if you can handle it. I'll be in a meeting." William walked into another office on the opposite side where he plopped himself down behind a desk. Nathan and Natalia took seats facing him. "Let's get this over with, shall we?" said William

"We don't mean to waste your time, Mr. Davies," said Natalia. "I will be as brief as possible. Can you tell me if Megan had any enemies that you knew of?"

"Megan? Enemies? You're kidding, right?"

"No, I am not kidding, Mr. Davies. Somebody shot her in cold blood. That's not something that friends do."

"It had to be a random act. Nobody would have killed Megan on purpose. No way. They'd have no reason."

"Have the police been by to speak with you at all?" said Nathan.

"The police? No. Why, you think I had something to do with it? With her killing?" William became further agitated. Natalia swept an annoyed glance at Nathan, as if to tell him to butt out, please.

"Nobody thinks you had anything to do with it," said Natalia. "We're all just trying to find out who might have had a motive. That's all. Had you heard anything from her recently?"

"No, not a thing since we split. After what she did to me, she knew better. Not that it gives me a motive, let me assure you! I may have been angry, but not that angry."

"What did she do to you, exactly, if you don't mind my asking?"

"I do mind."

"I'm sorry."

"She broke my heart, is what she did. I had no room left for her after that."

"Even so," said Nathan. "News of her demise must have been painful."

William's eyes began to glass over. The depth of his suffering was all still in there, struggling to find a way out.

"Maybe somebody else gave you updates?" said Natalia. "Do you know where she was working, or if she was seeing anybody else?"

"I'm the wrong one to ask."

"Who is the right one?"

William pressed his fingertips together and furrowed his brow in concentration. This question had sparked something within him. Perhaps if they gave it a few moments they might see a result. Eventually, William bounded from his chair. "Stay here," he commanded, then left the office and moved off down the hall. Nathan and Natalia remained seated, looking at each other but not saying a word. After a minute or two, William returned and this time he was not alone. Following behind was a solid woman in her mid-forties, wearing a dark green dress. "This is my mother, Glenda Davies," said William. "She knows more about it all than I do. You can ask her. I need to get back to work, if you don't mind."

"Thank you." Natalia rose from her seat to offer a hand.

William shook it, grudgingly. "You go easy on her."

"Of course," Nathan replied.

"Thank you, Mother," William said and then took off once more. His mom eased into the room cautiously.

"My son tells me this is about Megan?" said Mrs. Davies.

"That's right. I'm Natalia Nicolaeva. I was with the law firm representing Megan. This is my associate, Mr. Nathan Grant."

Nathan stood. "It's a pleasure to meet you."

"Representing her for what purpose?" said Mrs. Davies.

"Well, that's complicated," Natalia tried to explain. "She came to us as a whistleblower, but we never found out what information she wanted to share. Her killers took care of that before she got the chance."

"Whistleblower? What do you mean by that? Megan, a whistleblower?"

"That's correct, but we're still trying to figure out what it was about. We hoped that William might have heard something that might point us in the right direction. It seems that was not the case. Were you still in touch with Megan, Mrs. Davies? Had you heard anything from her?"

Glenda Davies wiped her hands on the front of her dress, her face taking on an air of distress. She was frightened, perhaps in part by her own troubled emotions. "You must understand, for quite a long time we believed Megan Stirling would be our daughter-in-law, that she and William would spend their lives together here on the farm. It was as much a shock to us when she left as it was to William. Maybe more so."

"I do understand," said Natalia.

"It is not so easy to turn that off. Not for me, in any case."

"You'd heard from her, then?" said Nathan.

"Yes." Mrs. Davies nodded. "We were in touch from time to time. Nothing earth-shattering, mind you. Pleasantries, that's all. I don't know a thing about any secrets she might have had."

"Do you know where she was working?" said Natalia. "Or if she was seeing anybody new?"

"She got a new job, yes, she told me that much. Megan was quite excited about it. Some financial firm."

"Lange Capital," said Nathan. "Was that the one?"

"Yes, yes, that was it."

"Had she mentioned anything in particular about the job, or maybe her co-workers? Anything that sounded unusual?"

"No, nothing unusual. That's not the kind of thing she would have told me, though. If there were any problems like that, she wouldn't have wanted to bother me with it. We tried to keep things light."

"What about relationships?" said Nathan. "Did she mention anything there?"

"She wouldn't have told me that, either." Mrs. Davies shook her head.

"Perhaps somebody else mentioned something?"

Nathan could tell they were very close to losing Mrs. Davies' cooperation. Just like her son before her, she'd had about enough. That didn't stop her from dropping one last bit of information. "They say she spoke quite a bit about a man named Dante."

"Who said?" Natalia pressed.

"Around the village, that was what I heard, whispered here and there," Mrs. Davies was embarrassed to be discussing such news. She looked over her shoulder, just to be sure she wasn't being overheard. "I never told William. I hope you won't, either. I don't know how he would take it."

"And you are saying they were involved?" said Natalia. "Megan and this man? Did they work together? Do you know how they met?"

"I'm saying she talked about him. That's all I know. If you don't mind, then, I'll walk you out."

"Of course," said Natalia. "Thank you for your help."

When they reached the car, Nathan wasn't feeling particularly inspired by their success so far, but at least it was something. "It's another lead," he offered. "For what it's worth."

"What kind of a name is Dante?"

"Thirteenth-century Italian."

"I know that much, but who names their kid that these days?"

"Nobody. I'll bet you twenty pounds he made it up."

"If so, it was an odd choice, don't you think? He must be an odd fellow."

"No doubt. Where to next? The parents' house?"

"We could try. What if the police are still there?"

"The Stirlings have every reason to speak with you. After all, you were the last one to see their daughter alive. Just explain to them that you're trying to get to the bottom of it, to finish what their daughter started, whatever it was."

"Sure, let's go." They climbed back into the rental car and drove away. Ten minutes later, they were pulling up in front of the Stirlings' house. The police car was still parked out front, but this time the front windshield was completely blown out. Round dimples that could only have come from buckshot peppered the hood, what the Brits called the bonnet. Slumped over in the driver's seat was an officer in uniform, with the left half of his face blasted off. Nathan quickly turned his attention to the house, where the front door was ajar. Megan's killers had come for her parents, and they might very well still be inside. Nathan and Natalia were unarmed, but that didn't stop the quick-thinking Natalia from jumping out of the car before it even came to a stop. By the time Nathan reached her side, she was already leaning into the police car to unholster a pistol from the dead officer's body.

"Sure, you get the weapon," Nathan said.

"Stay out here if you want."

"Fat chance." There was no way Nathan would let her go in alone, but given that she was the armed one between them, he did let her go first. When they reached the front door, he saw a man's inert leg on the other side of the threshold. Natalia kicked the door further open with one foot. On the floor of the front entryway was the rest of the body, a middle-aged man, flat on his back. He wore brown pants and a cardigan sweater. A shotgun blast had cratered the center of his chest. Natalia moved quickly into the house with Nathan just behind and they searched from room to room. Nobody else was in evidence, inside anyway. On the far side of the kitchen, another door opened into a garden. That was where they found Mrs. Stirling, face down in the grass and shot in the back.

"I'll tell you what I don't understand," said Nathan. "What kind of mobster carries out a hit with a shotgun?"

"What kind of mobster kills a middle-aged couple in Cornholme?"

"Something tells me the local police will be in over their heads."

"Can you blame them?"

"You want my suggestion? We wipe down that gun you're carrying and return it to its rightful owner before calling this in. Otherwise, we'll have a lot more explaining to do."

They headed back through the house. So far all they had were a lot of disparate parts to this story, none of which seemed to fit together in any discernible way. Nathan thought back to the two gentlemen from the pub the night before. They'd have had the time, while Nathan and Natalia were off at the dairy farm. But did they have the motive or the inclination? Without much else to go on, this was certainly a thread Nathan felt compelled to pull. One thing seemed clear by now, he and Natalia were in this thing until the end.

Chapter Eight

By the time Nathan and Natalia were cut loose from the local police station, it was already late afternoon. They'd had an exhausting day of questions, first from a local detective, DCI Gareth Hollings, and then by investigators from both the National Crime Agency and MI5, two of whom were flown straight from London. Everyone wanted to make sense of this thing, but nobody understood what the connections meant. A young woman was murdered, followed a few days later by her parents, 500 miles away. In between, the biggest terrorist attack in the UK in a generation. The investigators were not ready to draw any conclusions, but for his part, Nathan was pretty sure they all had something to do with each other. What he did know was that this latest killing meant one more trial he'd need to be a witness for, if this killer was ever apprehended.

Standing in front of the local police headquarters as the sun neared the horizon, Nathan and Natalia had a decision to make. First off, they needed something to eat, but after that they could either head back to London, or they could spend one more night at the inn. "You think Harriet would put us up for another night?" Nathan asked.

"As long as she's got the room."

"I would understand if you were eager to head south."

"By the time we drop off the car and take a train to London, it's going to be awfully late. Besides, I wouldn't mind seeing how things shake out here tomorrow. We could check in with Hollings in the morning, to find out where things stand."

"That works for me."

"I'll need to check in with Ammon, of course." Natalia said the words, but they lacked enthusiasm. It was the first hint of potential rough spots in their relationship, but that just made it a normal relationship.

"Sure," Nathan avoided that topic. "Let's see what Harriet has on the menu besides soup."

They wound their way back to the Saddle Inn, but when they entered this time, an older man was sitting behind the bar. Neither Harriet nor any guests were in sight. "Good evening," said Nathan. "We're wondering if you have any rooms for tonight?"

"Good evening to you. I believe so." The man came out from behind the bar and shouted past the front desk and down the hallway. "Harriet! We've got a nice couple looking for a room!"

A few seconds later, Harriet ambled up the hallway. "Look who we have here, back again," she said.

"Anything available?" said Natalia.

"Same one, if you want it."

"That would be fine," said Nathan. "Same guests in the other rooms?"

"No, fresh lot." Harriet took out her ledger and swung it around for Nathan and Natalia to sign in. "I heard about the Stirlings," she said. "The whole town is talking."

"I'd imagine," said Nathan. He noted a hint of fear in her eyes. Nobody trusted anybody after something like that went down in their town, especially outsiders.

"I still have your IDs on file." She made a note in the ledger, then took out the room key and slid it across the desk. "Tell me, though," she worked up the courage to ask. "What is it that you two are doing in our lovely village, again? Poking around about Megan Stirling, questioning poor William?"

"Just enjoying the scenery, Harriet. Beautiful countryside you have up here," said Natalia.

"We'd like to have some dinner tonight, if you don't mind," said Nathan. "Are we in time for a regular meal?"

"Claude will help you with that. He's the chef tonight."

"Terrific."

After dropping off their bags, Nathan and Natalia returned downstairs to take a table by the window. "I'll just step outside," said Natalia.

"Be my guest."

"It shouldn't take long." She excused herself and went back out to make the call as Claude dropped off two menus. Nathan perused his choices, looking up from time to time to watch Natalia pace back and forth in the parking area. This conversation was heated. He couldn't hear what was being said, but saw Natalia's face turn red as she argued her point. As for Nathan himself, he would sleep on the floor and stay out of it as best he could.

When Natalia came back in, her face was flush with emotion, though she tried to downplay it. "Anything good on the menu?"

"The usual pub food. Everything okay with Ammon?"

"Super." Natalia picked up her menu and attempted to focus on it. "What are you having?"

"The French dip sounded all right. I figure a guy named Claude ought to know his French dip."

Natalia slammed her menu back onto the table and looked up toward the bar. "Hey Claude! Two French dips, a Guinness and a Strongbow!"

"That'd be pints?"

"Yes, pints," said Nathan. "Thank you, Claude."

While they waited for their drinks, Natalia was lost in her thoughts and stewing in anxiety. The conversation with Ammon had gotten to her, for one reason or another. This was about more than one extra day away. Couples didn't argue like this without simmering grievances underneath. Sometimes they learned to work these things out, sometimes they didn't. Nathan was beginning to wonder whether, in this case, maybe they wouldn't. Natalia was an exceptionally independent woman. You didn't tell her what to do or how to do it. Not if you wanted to maintain her respect. Perhaps Ammon hadn't learned that lesson yet.

When the pints came out, they drank in silence. What could Nathan say that wouldn't risk inflaming the situation? He finally opted for something entirely innocuous. "How did you know I wanted a Guinness?"

"You don't seem like the type who enjoys cider."

"I don't mind a good cider now and then. A pale ale might have been nice, too."

Natalia put down her glass and glared at him. "Are you going to give me crap about this?"

"No!" Nathan raised his hands in the air, tempted to laugh, but he knew better than that. "Absolutely not!"

"Just drink your beer and keep your mouth shut."

"Come on, Natalia, what did *I* do?"

"Nothing. Not a damn thing."

Nathan was in exactly the place he'd hoped to avoid, which was to say, between Natalia and her boyfriend in some inexplicable way. The only strategy he saw before him was to switch back to the business at hand. Maybe that would distract her. "I was thinking I might take a look through Harriet's books later tonight," he said quietly so that Claude couldn't overhear.

"I'd bet my last dollar those two men from last night were involved in all of this. I didn't like their vibe."

"You think they're murderers because you didn't like their vibe? Half of the human race disgusts me, but that doesn't mean they're all criminals."

"Hey, you were the one who said she didn't trust them, remember? You thought they were hiding something."

"And you thought they were a couple of slobs who couldn't have had a thing to do with it."

"I didn't say that, exactly."

"Close enough."

"Anyway, which half?"

"Which half of what?"

"The human race. Which half disgusts you?"

"Not only men, if that's what you're implying. Plenty of women draw my ire."

"That's good to know. I'd still like to find out a little more about those two guys from last night. Is that all right?"

"Do what you want."

"Don't be like that, Natalia. Are we a team? I thought we'd settled that."

Natalia didn't answer. Instead, she took a good long drink of her cider as Claude brought their sandwiches to the table, au jus on the side along with salad and fries.

"There you are," said Claude. "Do you need anything else?"

"No, thanks, this looks terrific." Nathan picked up a shaker of salt from the table and sprinkled some on his fries.

"Enjoy."

"Actually, Claude, do you have any ketchup?"

"I forgot about you Americans and your ketchup. I'll see what I can do."

Nathan ate a fry and then lifted half of his sandwich, diagonally cut in the middle, and lowered it briefly into the bowl of dip before taking a bite. After an eventful day, he was starving and the sandwich tasted great, but that didn't quell his concern over Natalia's shifting attitude. She seemed ready to give the whole thing up. After their episode at the Stirling home, he couldn't entirely blame her. If she dropped out at this stage, though, would he? It was hard to imagine pursuing this thing further on his own. He and Natalia would head back to London where Nathan would try to advocate for release from his confinement. Whether Ammon helped him any further or not, Nathan had to convince the court to let him go back to France. How could he possibly be expected to wait for the trial of a man who had not even been apprehended? It was absurd and Nathan knew that on appeal to any other judge, it would not stand. That would be his focus from this point on, getting the hell out of England as soon as possible.

Claude stopped by the table and dropped off a bottle of a suspect-looking British version of ketchup.

"Thank you, sir," said Nathan.

"Anything to keep the guests coming back." Claude returned behind the bar and Nathan tentatively squeezed a little of the watery tomato sauce onto his fries.

"I'll tell you one thing," said Natalia. "I've endured my share of life's challenges, but sometimes it feels like nothing is as hard as relationships. Those always seem to trip me up."

"I'm sorry."

"Oh, it's not your fault."

"You can talk about it if you want. I'm not much of a shrink, but I can listen."

"I'd rather not."

"Fair enough."

Natalia took some time out to eat her dinner and drink her cider, their silence broken only when Claude came by the table to clear their dishes. "Can I get you two anything else?" he said. "Coffee? A nice dessert, perhaps? We've got a beautiful cheesecake."

"Scotch," Natalia replied. "Or maybe an Irish whiskey. What have you got, Claude? Bushmills?"

"Just for you. Should I make it two?"

"Sure," Nathan agreed. He could use something stronger than the stout, and Bushmills would do just fine. "Neat with a splash," he added.

"Of course." Claude took the dishes and moved off. In the meantime, another man and a woman arrived, with luggage. Nathan and Natalia both recognized them from that afternoon. She was tall and thin, the man short and round, both wearing business attire. She'd represented MI5 during their witness interview. He was from the National Crime Agency, both of them having flown up from London to help investigate the case. Their eyes took in Nathan and Natalia, but nobody said a word. Claude checked the pair in, gave them their keys, and then dropped off the two glasses of whiskey to the table.

Nathan lifted his glass. "What are we drinking to?"

"The mysteries of the human heart," Natalia answered.

"You're sure about that?" Nathan managed a laugh.

"You come up with something, then."

"To good friends," he said.

She tapped her glass to his and they both took a healthy drink. "You can't imagine what my life was like growing up, on a small family farm in the poorest region of the poorest country in Europe. It was a hard life, Nathan."

"I don't doubt it."

"I could barely afford to dream, even. I never imagined that I would end up in London, studying law and making a life for myself in the world. I was going to be a farmer's wife, working the fields with dirt beneath my fingernails until the day I died. I was even engaged to be married. Did I ever tell you that?"

"No, I don't think you did."

"It's true, to a farmer's son."

"What happened?"

"It didn't work out," was all she would say.

"I'm sorry about that."

"It was for the best."

"And look at you now."

"Yeah. Look at me." Natalia wasn't pleased.

"What?" said Nathan. "You're where you wanted to be, right? On the verge of great success?"

"What is it you Americans say? Ammon, he's starting to piss me."

"The phrase you're looking for is *piss you off.*"

"Fine. He's pissing me *off.*"

"I can sleep in the car if it makes the two of you feel any better."

"Never. I make my own decisions."

"And what if he can't abide that? Is that what this is all about?"

Natalia lifted her whiskey in the air and a sly smile crossed her lips. "Na zdorovye."

"Cheers," Nathan replied. They tapped their glasses and downed them.

"Anything else I can get you two?" Claude stopped back by the table. "Decaf cappuccino? Cuppa tea?"

"Let's have vodka," Natalia answered. "Give us a bottle." She got up and moved to one of the bar stools before looking back at Nathan, still in his chair. "You coming?" she asked.

"What are you getting me into?" Nathan didn't know where this was headed, but maybe it wouldn't hurt to forget all of their problems for one night. "Heaven help me, Claude. Something tells me I'm in for a rough go." Nathan joined Natalia at the bar.

"Join us for one, won't you Claude?" said Natalia.

"If you insist, I won't refuse." Claude took out a fresh bottle of vodka from a small freezer, untwisted the cap and filled three shot glasses before holding one of them in the air. "To England."

"I'll drink to that," said Nathan. "God save the King."

They tapped their rims, and then down the hatch, no turning back.

Chapter Nine

For the rest of the evening, they didn't talk about Ammon, nor the Megan Stirling murder. They didn't mention Megan's parents, or the terrorist attack in the heart of London. Natalia needed a break from all of that, focusing instead on getting entirely shit-faced. Her mood shifted back and forth between glee and frustration, joy and anger. Typically she was more of the stoic type, keeping her feelings close to the vest. Nathan was taken aback by this unexpected flow of emotion, but she clearly needed the release. Bottled up inside of her, the pressures of law school, her internship, the murder, and maybe most of all, relationship issues, brought Natalia near the breaking point. By the time the vodka bottle was half empty, Nathan's vision was blurred, the room slightly swaying. One thing that did not surprise him was this Moldovan woman's ability to drink him under the table. Natalia lifted the bottle and filled their glasses once more.

"You sure you don't want to slow down?" said Nathan.

"What are you going to do, make a woman drink alone?" she challenged him.

Nathan picked up his glass. "It's a good thing we don't have to get up early."

"There is no future, there is no past. Only the present."

"All right, Yoda. What are we drinking to this time?"

"The present!"

"You're the boss."

"Yes. I am the boss." Natalia made eye contact, tapped her glass to his, and downed her shot in one go. Nathan followed suit. As soon as he put his glass back on the bar, she refilled it again. In Nathan's peripheral vision, he saw the two investigators from London enter the room and take a table not far away.

"What can I get you two?" Claude called over to them.

"Two half-pints of ale, if you please," said the man.

"Half pints," Natalia chortled. "Having a big night?"

The investigators looked at Natalia with some derision but declined to respond.

"Come on, Natalia, be civil," said Nathan. He should have known better than to take sides. Even Claude was beginning to look at Natalia with concern.

"Civil? Who says I'm not civil?" Natalia turned back to the investigators. "Did I offend you?"

"No," said the woman. "Of course not."

"If they can't handle the grog, that's their business," Natalia said to Nathan.

"Some of us prefer not to make spectacles of ourselves," the male investigator took the bait.

"Oh, a spectacle? Is that what I am?" Natalia rose to her feet and took a few steps toward the table.

"Whoa, come on, Natalia. Come back to the bar and leave the detectives alone." Nathan hopped up and moved after her, putting a hand on her shoulder, but Natalia brushed it away.

"Don't touch me, I'm only being civil! We wouldn't want to make a spectacle of ourselves, now would we?"

"Most certainly not."

"These two have a couple of murders to solve! Isn't that right?"

"I think your friend has had enough," the woman said to Nathan.

Natalia offered a smile. "Nobody is responsible for me, but me."

"If you want my advice, you're not doing a very good job of it," said the man.

"Why are you even here?" said the woman. "You're not a lawyer. Megan Stirling was not your client. You have no role whatsoever in this investigation, and yet the pair of you came all the way up from London. How do we know you didn't kill the Stirlings yourselves?"

"It would make perfect sense, wouldn't it?" the man concurred. "Who else was known to be at the scene of both crimes, first the daughter and then her parents?"

"Genius!" Natalia lifted a finger in the air and pointed from the man to the woman and back. "Why did I ever doubt you two?"

"Let's go, Natalia. I think we've had enough." Nathan gently took her arm again, hoping for a better outcome this time, but Natalia shook his hand off once more.

"I told you not to touch me."

"Look, it's been a long day. Maybe we ought to get some sleep."

Natalia stood where she was. This could go either way, Nathan knew. It would either get really ugly, or she'd back down. Nathan was relieved when she turned toward the bar, and then picked up the half-empty bottle and the two glasses. "Put this on our tab, Claude," she said.

"You two have a good evening," Claude replied.

Natalia gave the investigators one last look of disdain and then moved toward the stairs, swaying gently as she went. Nathan followed behind. Upstairs, they entered their room and Nathan shut the door behind them. Natalia set the glasses on a desk and filled them again.

"No, no, I'm done." The alcohol clouded Nathan's mind. How many was it, a pint of stout, some whiskey, nearly half a bottle of vodka...

"Oh, come on!" Natalia pestered him.

"We've both had enough, Natalia. It's time to sleep."

"Sleep," she scoffed. "What do they say? I'll sleep when I'm dead."

"I'd like to sleep now, too." Nathan took the extra comforter and a blanket and began to arrange his bed on the floor. Natalia watched him as he took a pillow and placed it at one end.

"No, no," she said, her antagonism fading. "I will take the floor. It is my turn."

"I don't mind. You take the bed."

"No!" she countered. "Fair is fair."

Nathan stood where he was for a moment, but he didn't want to argue anymore. "Fine. I'll take the bed."

"Good."

In the bathroom, Nathan brushed his teeth, splashed some water on his face in a fruitless attempt to sober up, and then put on a clean t-shirt and boxers to sleep in. By the time he came out, Natalia was already curled up under the comforter on the floor with her clothing piled on a nearby chair. Nathan switched off the light and climbed under the covers on the bed where he lay motionless, listening to Natalia's soft breathing. Even from here, her floral aroma danced in his nostrils. He tried to think about anything else.

It was some hours later, in the middle of the night, when Nathan woke up, bathed in the light of a full moon shining through the window. Curled up beside him under the covers, he felt Natalia's warm body, one arm draped across him. Nathan froze in place. This was trouble, there was no denying it. The right thing to do would be to disentangle himself and move to the floor. Even better, move to the car. But Nathan wasn't sure he had it in him. He was lonely, too, just like Natalia seemed to be at this particular moment. How long had it been since he'd felt a woman's touch? And yet, what would happen when she woke up in the morning and realized this wasn't Ammon by her side? Nathan understood that it would have to be the car for him, there was no other reasonable option. Very carefully, he lifted the comforter and then gently grasped her wrist, attempting to move her arm away. Natalia groaned and shifted her body until she was half on top of him, remaining that way briefly before her eyes opened. Nathan saw her looking straight at him.

"Why did you take away the covers?" she asked.

"I'm going to sleep in the car," he replied.

"The car?" She was half awake now, but perplexed. Natalia grabbed the covers with one hand and pulled them back over them both. "You're not going to the car."

"I think it's for the best."

"You're not attracted to me?"

"I never said that."

"So?" Natalia rolled over further so that she was completely on top of Nathan, his back pressed into the mattress. She sat up, straddling him under the bed covers, one knee on either side of his torso. A playful smile crossed her lips. She might still be drunk, but she was enjoying this nonetheless. Natalia reached down and grabbed the bottom of his t-shirt with both hands, sliding it up and then over his head. Nathan let her, raising his arms in the air until she'd pulled it off completely. For him, this was not about joy so much as desire and his complete inability to resist. When she lowered her body onto his, he felt her bare breasts against his chest. Her hair hung in his face, and when she swept it to one side, Natalia's soft lips caressed his own. Nathan's adrenaline surged, heart pounding as she shifted her body and then reached down to place one hand between his legs, rubbing him through his boxers.

"One of us still has clothes on, so unfair," she said.

"It's not too late to back out," he answered.

Natalia's face was alive with delight as she scooted back on her knees. She slid his underwear off before spinning it around with one finger and flinging it across the room. "No regrets."

Nathan might have come up with something pithy to say, or said anything at all, but none of it would have made any difference in the end. This was happening. No matter the consequences, neither one of them had the power to stop it.

Some hours later, the clock on the nightstand read 4:17 a.m., but Nathan was wide awake, these events still playing in his head. Beside him, Natalia was sound asleep, having drifted off in a state of bliss once their desires were spent. When he attempted to slip out of bed this time, Natalia continued gently slumbering. After climbing to his feet, Nathan found his scattered clothing and put it all back on, adding socks, shoes and a sweatshirt. He made sure that Natalia was fully covered, adjusting the comforter over an exposed thigh before he took his phone and left the room, filled with a mixture of his own post-coital bliss and a lingering concern for the consequences.

Downstairs, Nathan switched on the lights in the deserted pub. He wanted a cup of coffee, but couldn't figure out how to make one without waking the entire house while grinding beans and running the espresso machine. Instead, he found a box of teabags and a kettle. He heated the water, then filled a mug, dropped in a bag, and took a seat at one of the tables. He'd mostly sobered up by this point, though it felt as though somebody had hit him between the eyes with an ax. A few aspirin would have been nice, but Nathan wasn't so lucky. While he waited for the tea to cool, he used his phone to pull up their route back to London, some 230 miles away. If they went by car instead of the train, it would take them four and a half hours, give or take. If he was able to get Natalia up and out by 8:30, they'd be back in the city by early afternoon. He pulled up his car reservation, cringed when he saw the fee for a London dropoff, but made the change anyway. Once they'd returned, his next step would be to get a judge to vacate that order holding him in the country. If he could somehow manage it in the next week or so, he'd head back to France and put this whole thing behind him as best he could. And what of things with Natalia? That was up to her. She was the one with entanglements. All the same, the whole thing felt sordid as a new day dawned. It wasn't his fault, he shouldn't have felt guilty, but on some level he did anyway. As for the latest Stirling murders, his curiosity had not abated. Nathan had a few hours to kill before the sun came up, so he checked the news. Most of it was still about the attack in London. No suspects had yet emerged, only a few unnamed "persons of interest." Somehow this coordinated attack had been carried out with three separate bombs planted on the top three floors of the building. In addition, the perpetrators had added an accelerant to make sure there was not only an explosion, but that the resulting fire burned hot and spread quickly. In the end, the top four floors were completely destroyed, twelve people were killed and twenty-five injured. The rest of the building suffered extensive fire, smoke and water damage. All of it pointed to some sort of inside job, but there was no indication that the attack was related in any way to the Stirlings.

Nathan made himself a second cup of tea. Outside the windows, the sky in the east showed the first signs of light. It wouldn't be too long before Harriet was up and preparing for the day. Maybe then Nathan could have an actual coffee, and breakfast. In the back of his mind, he felt a nagging sense of urgency. If he wanted to look through Harriet's files, he didn't have much time. He didn't have to do anything with the information, right? He could gather it. Preserve it. Have it ready in case it was needed at some point in the future. In the end, he couldn't resist. There weren't many inns here in Cornholme. If the investigators stayed here at the Saddle Inn, why not the killers, too? Nathan couldn't discount those two surly men from the previous night. Natalia was right, something about them rang his alarm bells, too. He put down his tea and moved from the dining room to Harriet's front desk, switched on a light and then made his way around to the other side. The drawers were all locked. If he busted them open, she'd realize it rather quickly. Instead, he set about searching for a key, running his hands through a series of small cubbyholes at the top with no luck. Turning around he saw several shelves behind him with a few stacks of papers, mostly just tourist brochures. On the end of one shelf was a small houseplant. He lifted the pot in the air. Beneath it was a small brass key. Too easy.

Inside the desk, Nathan quickly found the guest register. He ran his finger down the list until he came to the two men from the previous night. The first was named Reginald Barth and the second Graham Adams. They'd each stayed one night. Listed with their names were their English driver's license numbers and addresses, along with the number plate, make and model of their car. If they were here on an assassination mission, it was probably all fake information, but you never knew. Criminals often weren't the sharpest tools in the shed, and that included low-level mobsters. Nathan laid the register flat on the desk and took a photo of the page, then flipped back and took the previous pages as well, just in case. He put the register back in the drawer and opened another one below. A set of file folders contained photocopies of the guests' passports and IDs. He pulled out the pages for Barth and Adams and snapped photos of each, then went through and took photos of everybody else who'd stayed there for the previous week. His and Natalia's pages, he folded up and slipped into his pocket, just from force of habit. He was putting the last of the files back in the folder when he heard some stirring in a back room. Quickly, Nathan locked the desk back up, put the key where he'd found it, and returned to the dining room which was now bathed in the light of a new day. He took a seat and a few minutes later, Harriet appeared, surprised to find one of her guests awake before her.

"Well, good morning to you!" Harriet said. "You're up early."

"Eager to get going, I suppose."

"Cornholme has a way of doing that to a person," she replied.

"I think it's a lovely village."

"But it's not London, now is it?"

"No, that's true."

"All the same, it suits me fine. Let me fix you some breakfast, then. Eggs and ham do you?"

"Yes, that would do just fine. Over easy if you please, and I'm dying for some coffee."

"That lovely lass planning to join you, or is she sleeping it off?"

"Just me for breakfast, I'm afraid."

Harriet's disapproval showed. "You look after that one, you hear?"

"I try. She's the independent type."

"I don't care what type she is."

"Yes, ma'am. You got that coffee coming?"

Harriet laughed. "She's not the only one can't hold her liquor, then?"

"She can hold it just fine. I'm the one who's feeling it."

When he'd finished his breakfast, Nathan took a small pot of coffee and a mug upstairs for Natalia but she was still sound asleep. He took the opportunity to have a shower, then packed his things before settling into a chair by the window. After another hour, he moved to the bedside and gave her a nudge. He wasn't going to sit here all day. "Come on, Natalia, time to get up."

Natalia groaned and rolled to one side before opening her eyes. It took a moment to remember where she was, and what had happened, but then it hit her like a shockwave and she clutched the comforter up around her neck, eyeing Nathan with alarm.

"It's a little bit late to be modest," he said. "Come on, we need to hit the road. I'll be downstairs when you're ready. There's lukewarm coffee in the pot there if you're desperate." He hoisted his bag and left the room.

Forty minutes later, they were driving south with Nathan behind the wheel. They hardly said a word to each other for the next two hours, but the tension was palpable. From what he could tell, Natalia seemed to blame him, if not for the alcohol then certainly for the result. In the back of his mind, he'd known it would go down like this. He'd tried to fight it in the moment, but what could he say at this point? They were both only human, bound by the same swirling emotions of longing and desire, loneliness and sorrow. He'd have preferred to simply pretend the whole thing hadn't happened, but her demeanor told him it was time to pay the price, whether he deserved it or not. So far, it was her silence that spoke the loudest. Eventually, after his mostly sleepless night, Nathan's exhaustion began to catch up with him. His vision grew bleary as he struggled to maintain consciousness. "You want to take a turn at the wheel?" he asked.

"Sure, I can drive."

They pulled over at a rest stop, filled the tank with petrol and used the facilities. When they got back onto the highway, Nathan did his best to get comfortable in the passenger seat. Five minutes later he was out cold. He didn't wake up until they'd entered the outskirts of London. Natalia drove through the city to her apartment, or maybe Ammon's, Nathan wasn't sure. When Natalia finally parked, she didn't get out of the car right away. Instead, she stayed put, hands on the wheel, staring straight ahead.

"Nothing happened last night, right?" she said.

"Okay."

"I mean, I know it happened. What I'm saying is, it didn't happen."

"I know what you're saying. I think that's for the best."

Natalia still didn't get out of the car. She wasn't finished yet, but she struggled to express whatever else was on her mind. "The thing about Ammon is that when it comes to relationships, he has very traditional views on gender roles," she finally said.

"I see," Nathan replied, though in fact he had no idea what she was getting at.

"He had a conservative upbringing. His father was the breadwinner. His mother ran the home."

"And he expects the same of you?"

"Not exactly the same, but not so far off. His career comes first. His life comes first."

"And you're supposed to be secondary? I hope you can forgive me for saying so, but all-in-all, the two of you don't seem like such a great match to me. You're a proud, independent woman, Natalia. You need somebody who can respect that."

"I know." She still didn't get out of the car. In part, it seemed to Nathan that she wanted to explain her relationship with Ammon, but she also wanted to understand it herself. "We make an unusual pair in some ways, but you should see him when he turns on the charm. He can light up a room. I guess you could say that he's a bit of a clown at times, always ready with a funny word. I was a little surprised when he first asked me out. I hadn't seen it coming, and I nearly turned him down, but he won me over."

"Maybe it's not too late to salvage the whole thing. You just need to lay down some ground rules. Your career matters. Your needs matter. Natalia Nicolaeva is secondary to no one. He just has to come to terms with that."

"I think he's cheating on me."

Nathan sank deeper into his seat, his body heavy as lead. There it was. For Natalia, what had happened between them the night before was all about revenge. It was a misguided attempt to regain agency in her faltering relationship with Ammon. This hadn't been about Nathan at all, really. It probably shouldn't have mattered on his end. He'd had plenty of drunken, meaningless sex in his life. It didn't have to mean anything in this case either, but the truth was that it did. He'd hoped for more. It would have been an inauspicious start, but it might have been a start. Instead, it felt more like an end. "I'm sorry," he said.

"Yeah. Me, too. I've suspected for a while. You know how it is, women have a sense for these things." Natalia looked up, her eyes meeting Nathan's in a valiant attempt to hide her pain. "Last night, when I called to tell him we were staying one more night, he was happy!"

"Is that so bad? Maybe it shows that he trusts you?"

"Another night sharing a hotel room with a man that wasn't him. You'd think he'd be concerned, at least."

"I think you're making too much of this. Just because you caught him in a good mood, it doesn't necessarily mean a thing. He might have just wanted a pub night with the boys."

"Ammon doesn't do pub nights with the boys. He's not the type. Look, forget it. I thought you deserved an explanation, that's all. I should have kept my mouth shut." Natalia finally got out of the car and retrieved her bag from the back seat. Nathan climbed out of the passenger seat, then watched Natalia walk through a front gate and up a small set of stairs before letting herself into the building. As the door swung closed behind her, Nathan was hit with a deep sense of loss, mourning all that might have been. Something told him he might not be seeing her again, maybe not for a long time. Maybe not ever.

After climbing in behind the wheel, Nathan started up the car and drove on. He should go straight to the rental agency offices to drop it off. Then he could take public transport back to the apartment in Shoreditch and shift his focus back to where it belonged; getting the hell out of England. Instead, he couldn't seem to help himself. Maybe he merely needed the distraction, but unanswered questions pestered him like the tap, tap, tapping of a tiny hammer on his brain. He had the car already and this would give him something less personal to occupy his mind. After pulling over to the side of the road, he took out his phone and searched his photos from the Saddle Inn for the address of one Reginald Barth. According to the man's driver's license, he lived in Brixton. Nathan entered the address into his navigation app. Pursuing this any further was a bad idea all around, but if the previous night proved anything, it was that a bad idea didn't always stop him.

Chapter Ten

The four-story brick building didn't look like much from the outside. It was what locals referred to as a "council house," or what was called public housing back in America. Apparently, crime didn't pay, or at least not that well, assuming Reginald Barth was a criminal after all. To be honest, Nathan had no idea. He also wasn't exactly sure what he was planning to do here. Ideally, if Barth wasn't home, he'd find a way into the apartment and have a look around. Perhaps he'd find some incriminating information, or anything at all tying Barth to Megan Stirling or her parents. If he got really lucky, he might even find a shotgun, recently fired. On the other hand, he might learn that Reginald Barth was just your ordinary Joe, traveling around the country for some completely justifiable reason. If Barth *was* home, a few questions could potentially shed some light on that.

A pair of teenage boys was coming out of the building when Nathan approached and he caught the front door and let himself inside. Barth's apartment was number 302, so Nathan took the elevator to the third floor and made his way down a dusky corridor. By this time it was mid-afternoon and he inhaled a mixture of aromas, from cigarette smoke and beer, to garlic and onions cooking on a hot stove. The door to 302 was in need of a paint job, with the numbers tacked just a little bit crooked above a fish-eye peephole. Nathan rang the bell and then knocked for good measure. A few seconds later, he heard a woman's voice.

"Who is it?" the woman hollered through the door.

"I'm looking for Reginald Barth," Nathan answered.

"What's it about?"

"I've got a few questions for him."

The woman took a moment, perhaps checking with Reginald himself before her voice called out again. "He ain't home!"

"I'd love to talk to you, then." Nathan wracked his brain for a way to get her to open the door, to get a conversation going at least. He stood and waited. Finally, he heard the bolt turn in the lock and the door swung open. On the other side was an incredulous-looking Reginald Barth.

"What the fuck do you want?!" said Barth.

"I wanted to ask you some questions."

"You was up in Cornholme, you an' your lady... Why the fuck you followin' me?" Barth puffed up his chest, doing his best to look intimidating. It was unsuccessful. Nathan knew right away that this man was no mobster. Despite the bluster, he was frightened. A mobster would not have been frightened, he'd have been armed. Nathan was tempted to turn around and simply walk away, but he'd come this far. He might as well see if there was anything to be learned.

"I'm here about the Stirlings," said Nathan.

"Who the bloody hell are the Stirlings?" The man was dumbfounded. If he'd just killed two people by the name of Stirling, he'd have tensed up at the very least.

"Can you tell me what you were doing up in Cornholme?"

"None of your fucking business, is what!" He tried to slam the door shut, but Nathan put his foot in the way, stopping it from closing.

"Look, I don't want to be a nuisance, Mr. Barth. I'll leave you alone, I promise, if you'll just answer the question, please."

Barth peered through the crack in the door, trying to decide on his next move. "Me mate's mother passed away," he conceded. "We was up there makin' arrangements."

"Oh. I'm sorry to hear that. What was the cause of death?"

"The cause of death was bein' ninety-eight years old. Now if you please."

"My condolences." Nathan pulled back his foot and the man slammed the door. So much for that. Nathan headed back down the hall. He was back at the car, just climbing in, when a text from Natalia came through. It seemed that she hadn't written him off entirely. There was no message, just a link to an article from a Manchester news outlet. Nathan clicked on it and read the story about the brutal murder of a married couple in the small village of Cornholme, a Mr. and Mrs. Stan and Geraldine Stirling. It also mentioned the killing of their daughter a few days earlier. Neighbors commented on what a wonderful family they'd been. Others speculated on a drug gang connection. The common wisdom seemed to be that Megan Stirling brought it on them all somehow, through a descent into big-city drug culture. If she'd just stayed closer to home instead of running off the way she did, none of it would have happened. It sounded to Nathan like the same refrain he'd heard from Harriet, more or less. The police were not willing to speculate. The only added piece of evidence Nathan hadn't heard yet was that the perpetrator of the Cornholme attack had purportedly taken off in the Stirlings' automobile after committing the murders. The car was recovered, abandoned and wiped clean, some 100 miles to the north in the town of Carlisle.

Thanks for the update, Nathan texted back. Natalia didn't respond further, so he started the car and began pulling out of the parking space. Then he decided he should look up this northern city, Carlisle. The killer would be long gone by now, but Nathan was tenacious. He couldn't help but follow every lead to its conclusion. He eased the car back into the space and opened his phone once more. Carlisle was a city of 75,000 people in the Cumberland District, 261 miles north of London. Built at the confluence of three rivers, it was known for Carlisle Castle, a fortress first built under the reign of William II in 1092. The town was also home to Carlisle Cathedral, built in 1133. None of this was particularly enlightening to Nathan, at least not for his current purposes. Going further back, the area was home to a Roman settlement, built to service several forts along the northern boundary of Roman Britain, marked by the stone fortification known as Hadrian's Wall, which stretched 73 miles from one edge of the island to the other in an effort to deter the barbarian hordes to the north, later known as the Scots. From a historical standpoint, it was all interesting, but it didn't help Nathan much. What connection, if any, did the killer have to this place? A very small private airport was located five miles north of the city. No doubt the police were already scouring the records of all flights in and out over the past few days.

For Nathan, this seemed like another dead end. As he drove back toward the rental car office, however, something else was bothering him. He wasn't sure what, exactly. It was like trying to remember a name flitting around in your brain, just out of reach. You know it's there, and you can almost remember, but not quite. That was how he felt as he continued along the road, entirely unsatisfied. He wanted to call Natalia, to run it all past her, but he wasn't ready for that. Twenty-five minutes later, after stopping to fill the fuel tank on the way, Nathan was pulling into the rental car agency lot. An attendant asked if he was dropping off, then directed him to the correct lane where Nathan eased the car to a stop and got out.

"I'll just need to check 'er over, if you don't mind. You know, for scratches and what not," said the attendant.

"Knock yourself out." Nathan stood to one side as the man went over the car, inside and out, checking items off a list on his tablet.

"You're good to go. I'll just need to get your approval and you're on your way." The man tapped a few more things on his device before handing it across.

Nathan took the tablet in his hand, but his mind was distracted. That little nugget of information, flitting about in his brain, was beginning to make itself known. It was the wall. Hadrian's Wall. That elderly couple at the Saddle Inn, they'd spoken of visiting a wall, two-hours drive away. She'd wanted to go. What had she said? They were already this far, they might as well go see it? It was hard to believe a quaint couple like that could be responsible for such brutal killings as the Stirlings'. And then go on along with their holiday? In the victims' stolen car? It all sounded preposterous, but maybe that was what gave them an advantage. The police would never in a million years suspect them either.

"Excuse me? Sir?" said the attendant.

"I'm sorry," Nathan replied, handing the device back. "I'm going to hold onto the car a little bit longer. Can you add another day to my reservation?"

A surprised expression crossed the attendant's face but just as quickly receded. "Of course, sir. One more day." He tapped away at his tablet.

"I'll see you tomorrow, then." Nathan got back in the car and drove away. When he'd gone a few blocks, he found another place to pull over, in the parking lot of a fast-food outlet. He went inside for a bite to eat, placing his order and then settling into a booth where he looked through the documents he'd photographed at the Saddle Inn. According to the register, the retired couple's names were Rupert and Elizabeth McGown.

They lived in Watford, an hour and a half away from where Nathan sat at the moment, though it was just going on rush hour. He looked at the address on Rupert's driver's license and plugged it into his mapping app, zooming in on street view to take a look at the place. What came up was a modest single-family home with a manicured garden in front. An online search told him that Rupert had previously worked as a teacher at a local high school. Elizabeth was a retired bus driver. They seemed to be living out their golden years with the occasional getaway to explore the country of their birth, hardly the murderous types. The whole thing about the wall could be a coincidence but Nathan didn't like coincidences, not unless he'd checked them out. Was that why Natalia sent him the link, so that he'd check into it? More likely, she was just trying to keep him informed, to satisfy his curiosity. Well, if he found anything out, he'd return the favor. For now, he dug into his fast-food burger, washing it down with some soda. Even with traffic, he ought to arrive in Watford before the sun went down. With some luck, he'd learn more this time than he had from Reginald Barth. For Nathan it had been a long day on the road already, but what else was he going to do? Sit around his Shoreditch apartment watching television, ruminating on his romantic failures? He might as well put the time to good use. Ten minutes later he was back on the road, heading north yet again. It was a strange hobby he seemed to have picked up, unraveling international terrorist plots. He hoped that this next visit would be more productive than the last. Just one and a half hours from now, he'd find out one way or the other.

Chapter Eleven

The house looked just as it had online, but with the garden out front in full bloom. As Nathan pulled up, he saw Elizabeth McGown on her knees in one of the flower beds, doing some late afternoon planting. In one hand she held a small shovel. Beside her was a box filled with nasturtiums in small cups. Nathan watched as she dug a hole and then lifted one of the cups in both hands. Holding the flowers at the base, she shook the plastic cup loose and then lowered the plant into the hole before shifting dirt over the roots and tapping it down. When she'd finished with that one, she looked over to see Nathan's eyes on her. Elizabeth put her shovel down and rose to her feet, brushing the dirt from her fingers on her pants.

"Good afternoon." Nathan got out of the car and took a few steps forward.

"I know you. Don't I?" said Elizabeth. "From the inn, isn't that right? Up in Cornholme?"

"Yes, ma'am, that's correct."

The woman took a quick look over her shoulder, as though searching for her husband. She was confused, and a little worried, but that didn't stop her from putting an insincere smile on her face. "You've come a long way to see us then, haven't you?"

"I have, yes. I am sorry to disturb you. My name is Nathan Grant, I'm working as a private detective. I have some questions I'd like to ask you."

"Private detective? What is this about?"

"I'm working with the lawyer who was representing Megan Stirling. Maybe you heard about her case?"

"Megan Stirling," Elizabeth repeated the name.

"Is your husband home? Perhaps I can talk to you both at the same time. It would save me asking my questions twice."

"Yes, yes, Rupert is inside. We've already had our dinner, I'm afraid, but I can offer you a cup of tea."

"That would be great, thank you. I'd love a cup of tea."

Elizabeth took a last look at her flowers before leaving them behind. "Come inside, then." Nathan followed her through the front door, where she carefully wiped her feet on a mat and then called out to her husband. "Rupert! We've got some company!"

From somewhere in the house, Nathan heard the sound of a BBC anchor reading the headlines. "Who is it?" Rupert called out.

"Come and see, dear!"

The sound of the television shut off.

"This way," Elizabeth guided Nathan through an entrance hall and on back to the kitchen. Cooking vessels rested on a drying rack by the sink. A wooden table was arranged against a window with chairs on three sides. Elizabeth lifted an electric kettle and began to fill it with water. "There's cake if you'd like."

"What's this now?" Rupert appeared in the doorway, looking Nathan over. "You're that fellow from up north," he said.

"Mr. Grant is a private detective," said Elizabeth. "He has some questions for us."

"Questions? For us? You don't say." Rupert motioned toward the kitchen table. "Please, have a seat."

"Thank you." Nathan pulled out a chair and lowered himself into it. He was joined by Rupert on the other side of the table.

"What questions, then? This is exciting. We don't often have private detectives calling on us."

"When have we ever?" said Elizabeth.

"Never," said Rupert.

"It's about that Megan Stirling girl, he says," Elizabeth answered.

"Is that so?" said Rupert. "Terrible tragedy, a young woman's life cut short like that. I wish we could help you. All we know about that is what we read in the papers. And the telly, of course, the BBC."

"You did hear about it, then?" said Nathan. "And her parents as well?"

"Yes, yes, of course. Quite the coincidence that we were in Cornholme when that happened, but I hope you don't think we had anything to do with it!"

"No, of course not. I'd have no reason to suspect you."

"Then why come all this way?" Elizabeth came straight to the point. "There is such thing as a phone, last I checked. You could have called."

"Let the man ask his questions," said Rupert. "And then he can be on his way."

Elizabeth was not appeased. Her comment was the first sign that Nathan wasn't entirely welcome, but she lifted the glass dome from a cake platter and cut three slices.

"I thought you might have some ties to the area there, in Cornholme. Perhaps you'd met the Stirlings before?"

"No, sir, never met them. No ties to Cornholme," said Rupert. "Just a little getaway, what the kids these days call a city break."

"I see. Why Cornholme? It seems a little bit off the tourist radar."

"What better reason then, to give it a look?" said Elizabeth.

"To be honest, we only stopped there on the way to the Lakes District. That was our primary destination," said Rupert. "We don't know a soul up around there. Never heard of the Stirling family until we heard it on the news."

"We are sorry if we've wasted your time." Elizabeth put three small plates of cake on the table, along with forks. "At least we can offer some hospitality before you go."

"That's very kind of you," said Nathan. He watched Elizabeth pour the hot water into a teapot and add some tea in a metal clasp. She placed three teacups on the table, along with a container of cream and a bowl of sugar, before joining them in the third seat. "Thank you, Elizabeth."

"Please, call me Betty."

"Thank you, Betty." Nathan lifted his fork and took a bite of cake. What he needed to do was put them ill at ease, to knock them off guard. Most likely they were telling him the truth. How could this friendly, middle-class couple have anything to do with a brutal murder like Nathan had witnessed at the Stirling's home? It was hard to imagine a motive, but then nobody knew why the couple had been killed. If he wanted an indication of the McGowns' culpability, he'd need to push them out of their comfort zone and gauge the reaction. "How was the Lakes District, then?" he asked.

"We enjoyed it very much, thank you," said Rupert. "Have you been?"

"Never."

"You really should see it sometime," said Betty.

"I'd like to. Maybe you can give me some tips? Did you spend any nights in the national park?"

Rupert and Betty looked at each other, as though they wanted to make sure they had their story straight before answering. Maybe Nathan was onto something after all.

"One night, yes," said Rupert. "A nice little inn. What was the name of the place, dear? Ambleside?"

"That's right," she answered. "The Ambleside Inn."

"We would have stayed longer, but responsibilities, you know," said Rupert.

"What sorts of responsibilities? It looks like you lead a quiet life here."

"It's quiet now, but we have a granddaughter, you see. Our son's child," said Betty. "We care for her three days a week."

"A little terror, she is," said Rupert.

"But lovely all the same," said Betty.

"I'm sure."

"Do you have any children yourself, Mr. Grant?" Betty filled the three cups with tea.

"I do not. Maybe someday."

"The pitter patter of little feet is what makes life worth living, I always say."

"Thanks for the advice," Nathan offered a smile. "One more question about your trip, though. Did you end up going further north at all, or was Ambleside the limit of your journey?"

"Just the Lakes District," said Rupert. "We had no time to go further."

"I see." Nathan had another bite of cake, white with vanilla frosting and a little sweet for his taste. "I heard you talking about a wall when we were in Cornholme. I thought maybe you meant Hadrian's Wall." He threw this out there and let it hang in the air. Betty's anxiety level noticeably spiked. Her face flushed red and she turned away, unable to look Nathan in the eye. Rupert was more measured. He warmed his hands on either side of his teacup.

"No walls on our trip. You must have been mistaken," said Rupert.

"I could have sworn you said something about a wall, two hours away."

"You were mistaken!" Betty snapped. "We never said a thing about any wall."

"My apologies, then." Nathan knew that he was being lied to. What he didn't know was why, exactly. He sized up Rupert, trying to picture the man wielding a double-barrel shotgun and unloading it on another husband and wife of similar age and social station. Perhaps it was some grudge going back a generation? Such were the vagaries of this case that anything was possible. "Tell me, Rupert, what is there to do in a place like Watford for a retired man? I see Elizabeth enjoys her time in the garden, but I think it might get a little dull. Am I wrong?"

"There's always plenty to keep a man busy, if he's got an active mind."

"I suppose so. What keeps you busy in this part of the world, though? Golf, maybe?"

"No, I've never been a golfer."

"No, me neither. Back home, we like to go hunting, but there's not a whole lot else to do in the Texas hill country. Horses, dirt bikes and hunting. That's about it. You do any hunting over here?"

"Nope. Not my style, either. My father-in-law, he was a hunter."

"Is that so?" Nathan turned to Betty. "Your father? What sort of game was he after?"

"Deer, mostly. You should have seen the buck mounted over our fireplace growing up. Twelve points."

"I can imagine. He must have been proud of that one." Nathan blew across the top of his tea and took a sip, washing down the sugary sweetness of the cake.

"My father passed many years ago," said Betty. "That passion died with him."

"I'm sorry to hear that."

"Yes, well, I'll tell you what, Mr. Grant. It's been lovely visiting with you, but I've got a bit of gardening left to do and the daylight is fading."

"Of course. I'm sorry to have taken your time."

"I wish we could have been more help," said Rupert.

"I appreciate it," said Nathan. "You never know what might lead somewhere, and what might just be a dead end. You've got to follow every angle."

"And why exactly did you consider us an angle? You can't be interviewing every soul who's come and gone from Cornholme?"

"I'm just talking to as many people as I can. Speaking of which, I have one last question for you." Nathan decided to throw it out there in a last-ditch effort. "I've heard that somebody named Dante might be involved. Do you have any idea who that might be?"

"Dante?" Betty shook her head, though her cheeks flushed redder than ever. "I can't say it rings a bell."

"Didn't he write some book back in the day?" said Rupert.

"Presumably, that was a different Dante. Again, I'm sorry to have taken your time." Nathan took one last sip of tea and rose to his feet. Instinct told him there was a shotgun hidden somewhere in this house, a hand-me-down from Betty's father, and ballistics tests would be able to tie it to a double murder. Unless, of course, they'd had the foresight to chuck it in a lake somewhere near Ambleside. He couldn't very well search the house on his own to find out, not when the McGowns were here in any case. Maybe he'd come back at a more opportune time. For now, he'd make a tactical retreat. "Thanks again."

"Good luck with your detecting. I hope you're able to come up with something. Such a tragedy," Rupert repeated.

"I'm not one to let you go empty-handed," said Betty. "Let me get you some cake to take along."

"No, that's fine, I don't want to impose," Nathan replied.

"You're not imposing!" Betty continued.

"It's in her nature," said Rupert. "She's always been hospitable."

Nathan breathed a sigh. At this point, he simply wanted to get going, but taking along some of Betty's cake wouldn't kill him. He'd be a good guest, even if he tossed it in the bin at his first opportunity. "Thank you, Betty."

She went to the cake platter and this time cut off a bigger hunk than before, a double serving. "Just let me find something to put it in." She scurried out of the room.

Rupert rose from his seat. Nathan didn't like the pair separating like this. He'd rather have kept an eye on both of them. If they'd killed the Stirlings, they were potentially armed and dangerous. "I'll just wait out front," he said.

"Sure." Rupert held one arm out.

Nathan took a few steps forward. As soon as he set foot in the entrance hall, Betty McGown came swinging around a doorway with fire in her eyes, pointing a double-barreled shotgun straight at Nathan's face.

"Don't you move or I'll blow your fucking head off," she said.

Nathan stood where he was, slowly raising his hands in the air before she'd even asked. This was an interesting development. He'd known that any guns would have likely come from her side of the family, but he'd still been more focused on Rupert. Natalia would not have made that mistake. One thing working on Nathan's side was the fact that a woman like Betty McGown would prefer not to shoot a man in her own home. That would create a mess she'd never fully be able to clean. Blood stains on the rug beneath his feet and seeping into the floorboards below, brains splattered on the walls... No, not here. If he was right, that would buy him some time at least. "Does this mean I don't get to take the cake?" he said.

"You think this is funny," said Betty. "Ask the Stirlings how funny it was."

"I would, but I saw what you did to them, Betty, and it wasn't pretty."

"You make any sudden moves and you'll be next."

"Something tells me I'll be next regardless."

So far Rupert hadn't said a word, but he hurried past Nathan to his wife's side, behind the shotgun barrel and not in front of it. "What should we do with him?" Rupert asked.

"Let's put him in the basement," said Betty. "Then we'll call Dante and see what he wants us to do."

"Good idea."

"Dante," said Nathan. "I guess I struck a nerve when I asked about him, now didn't I?"

"Go out to the shed and get some rope," Betty said to her husband. "We'll tie him up."

"Right." Rupert hurried out the front door.

"Don't think I can't use this thing," said Betty. "I can, and if I must, I will."

"Oh, I have no doubt about that," Nathan replied. "Like I said, I've seen your handiwork."

"Who sent you here, asking all of these questions?"

"Nobody sent me."

"You told us you were a private detective. Who hired you?"

"Nobody. I lied about that part."

"How do I know you're not lying now?"

"You don't," Nathan conceded.

"You're not making things any easier on yourself."

"No, I don't suppose I am." What Nathan understood as he stared down the barrel of Betty's shotgun was that this was a major breakthrough in the case. Not only had he identified the perpetrator of the Cornholme murders, but he had the murder weapon in sight as well. It also tied the whole thing to Dante, which led right back to Megan again. The downside, of course, was that he might be next. Betty had already proven her facility at using the weapon, twice. In the case of the Stirlings however, neither of them was a former Army Ranger with years of combat training under their belt. Nathan had faced a whole lot worse in his years than a belligerent grandmother, though a shotgun was a shotgun in anyone's hands. The trick would be in disarming her. He felt somewhat confident that an opportunity would present itself, but Nathan had to be ready when it did. What he wanted right now was as much information as he could get out of Betty and Rupert McGown. "Who is Dante, then, and what has he got to do with all of this?" he tried. "Was he Megan Stirling's boyfriend? Was this all about some lover's quarrel?"

"Megan Stirling's boyfriend?" Betty's face screwed up in disbelief. "Ha! She wished."

"Who is he, then?"

"Dante is the man you wish you could be. He's who every other man on earth wishes he could be."

"Wow. That's quite the endorsement, Betty."

"Shut up! Keep your trap closed."

Nathan complied while they waited for Rupert to return. Betty's finger hovered just at the edge of the trigger. She shifted the sights from Nathan's head to the center of his chest. He could try dodging left or right, she might miss, but this was buckshot at close range. She probably wouldn't. Instead of making any sudden moves, he bid his time until Rupert finally reappeared through the front door, holding a tangled mess of rope.

"I'm afraid this was all I could find," Rupert said. "It's a bit wound up."

Betty gave her husband a glance, annoyed. "Tie his wrists as best you can. You better make it good and tight."

"It's not too late to take a big step back," said Nathan. "If you continue on this path, things will not end well for you."

"You are not the one to talk," Betty sneered.

"What happens if you shoot me, Betty? You think I'll be the last one coming around to ask questions? It will only get worse from here."

"I told you to zip it!" She glanced back to Rupert. "Go on, then!"

"Oh, all right." Rupert loped toward Nathan like a schoolboy following orders. He'd closed half the distance when the bulk of his body passed between Nathan and the barrel of the gun. It was only for a second or two, but this was the moment Nathan had waited for. He lunged forward, grabbing the older man around the middle and driving him backward like it was football practice on the dusty fields of Texas. He pushed the stumbling Rupert one step, then two, straight toward Betty and then, BOOM! A shot went off and all three of them toppled to the floor in a pile. Nathan reached for the gun and grasped it by the barrel, yanking it out of Betty's hands before quickly climbing to his feet. The retired couple stayed where they were on the floor, with Betty struggling to right herself. From Rupert, Nathan only heard a groan, but when he rolled the man over with his foot he saw one more example of the damage that this shotgun could inflict. Rupert's entire midsection was torn apart, with a bloody foam leaking from his mouth. After one last attempt at breathing, the man was dead at Nathan's feet.

"Now look what you've gone and done, Betty. You've killed your husband," said Nathan.

"What?!" Betty got to her knees and leaned over the man, shaking him by his lapels. "Rupert! Get up! Come on, get up!"

It was almost enough for Nathan to take pity on the woman, though not quite. "Why did you do it, Betty?" He was a lot more comfortable asking questions with the gun in his hands. Betty had fired off one chamber, but Nathan cocked the second hammer. One shot remaining. "What's this all about?"

"YOU!!!" Betty turned to Nathan with fury in her eyes. "You did this! It's your fault!"

"Excuse me, Betty, but it's not my gun and I didn't pull the trigger."

"You will pay for this, I swear you will!"

"Maybe so, but why don't you tell me what it's all about? Who is Dante?"

Betty turned her focus back to her husband, leaning over Rupert's dead body and sobbing. "Oh my dear, my dear, what have they done to you? My beautiful man!" Losing one's loving spouse was a brutally painful experience, even under the circumstances. Maybe even more so knowing she'd shot the man herself, but Nathan was not about to go soft on her. Betty McGown was a ruthless killer, and she had answers about this whole conspiracy that Nathan still needed to pry out of her somehow. The problem was, a neighbor might have heard the shot. The police could be on their way. Nathan hadn't killed anybody, she'd done that on her own, but he didn't want to get tied up in any additional complications. Things were complicated enough already. Should he wait around and try to explain the situation? Or should he high-tail it out of there while the going was good? He was leaning toward the latter when Betty let out a piercing scream. She turned back to Nathan for a split second, the look of the devil in her eyes, and then flew across the entryway straight at him. Nathan just had time to pull the trigger.

The second round of buckshot exploded into Betty's chest, knocking her backward where she dropped on top of her husband, eyes wide with panic. A few seconds later and she was gone, joining her husband on the other side. Maybe it was just as well, except that all of Betty's secrets died with her. Besides, now there were two corpses to leave behind and even if it was self-defense, Nathan was responsible for one of them. The best he could do was to remove any sign that he'd ever been here and hit the road.

Nathan didn't bother moving the bodies. The blood stains would alert whoever entered the house to what had gone on here. Instead, he took the gun into the kitchen and used a towel to very carefully wipe it down. Next, he washed any dish he might have touched, and all other surfaces he'd been anywhere near. A crack forensic team might sweep the whole house for stray strands of hair, searching for a DNA match. Would they bring in a crack forensic team? Maybe. In a kitchen closet, he found a small hand vacuum. Holding the handle with the rag, he went through the kitchen and then the entryway, vacuuming any area where he might have walked. Careful not to step in any of the blood in the hallway, he vacuumed as much as he could of the dead couple's clothing. How long had this all taken him? Less than five minutes, but that was too long. It was time to go. He took a last look around and let himself out the front door, bringing the vacuum with him to dispose of on the way. He thought about taking their electronic devices as well, to search for clues later if he could crack them, but Nathan didn't want to have anything in his possession that connected him to these people. He'd learned a few things and eliminated those responsible for the murder of Megan Stirling's parents. That would have to do, for the time being. Back out front, he walked through the garden, past Betty's implements, and out to his rental car. No signs of police, yet, or anybody else around for that matter. No witnesses that he could see, just a quiet summer evening in the burbs north of London. He started the car and headed back toward Shoreditch, to give the whole episode some thought. The last thing he felt as he pulled away was a small bit of sympathy for the couple's grown children, one of whom would no doubt discover their parents in this sorrowful state. There was nothing much for Nathan to do about that. The McGowns had gotten themselves into this mess, somehow and for some reason. All Nathan knew for sure was that it all had something to do with a man named Dante.

Chapter Twelve

Nathan needed to talk this over with somebody, to try to make sense of it all. He'd ditched the McGowns' hand vacuum in a dumpster halfway back into the city, dropped off the rental car, and was back in his apartment for the first time in three days. He realized, of course, that the only person he could discuss any of this with was Natalia Nicolaeva, and she no longer wanted anything to do with him. That was the risk of sex between friends, if that was even what they were. Mostly, she'd used him in some ill-conceived attempt to get back at her boyfriend, desperately seeking relief from the psychological torment in which she'd found herself trapped. She was hurt and lashing out, and Nathan just happened to be in the wrong place at the wrong time. He'd wanted it, sure, but not like that. Not when it came with the massive regrets that she harbored. The bottom line, though, was that Nathan still needed a partner and ally. They would have to find a way to move beyond the personal stuff, to put what happened at the Saddle Inn behind them for the greater good. When he pulled up her name in his contacts, pushed aside any anxiety and tapped on her name. Natalia picked up on the second ring.

"What?" She sounded annoyed, as though he should have known better than to bother her.

"It's not about what you think."

"How do you know what I think?"

"Good point." He couldn't afford to be explicit over the phone. One never knew who might be listening in.

Natalia breathed a heavy sigh. "What did you do this time?"

"I've learned a few things that I think you should know. Can we meet?"

Natalia laughed but didn't say a word.

"What's so funny?" said Nathan.

"And I thought I might never see you again. It ends up, that didn't even last a day."

"There isn't anybody else I can talk this stuff through with." Nathan knew she could easily reject this overture and go on her way. He half expected her to. In the end, however, her curiosity and determination were as strong as his.

"Where are you?" she said.

"My apartment."

Natalia took some time before she answered, weighing her decision. "I'll be there in an hour."

"Thank you, Natalia." Nathan hung up the phone.

When she arrived fifty minutes later, they took a walk around the neighborhood. The police presence was strong in central London after the bombing, with cruisers parked at major intersections and foot patrols roaming the streets in pairs.

"Which way?" said Natalia.

"I need to stretch my legs. Not downtown. Somewhere quieter."

"Shoreditch Park isn't far."

"Sounds good." The sun had set by this time, but the late summer evening was still comfortable as they set off, walking north along a residential street.

"What's the big news you were so desperate to share?"

"I know who killed Megan's mom and dad."

"Good for you, but why tell me? I thought we were going to let the police handle this from now on."

"The perpetrators are dead. Without going into the details, it is possible that I could be deemed partially responsible."

"Oh, Nathan! Come on, what is it with you?"

"Look, Natalia, there's no time for any bullshit or recriminations. I think we're onto something even bigger than anybody realizes. Put what happened between us aside and help me sort through it. I need a confidant here."

"Why is it that we have to figure all of this out ourselves?"

"Because if I go waltzing into the police station talking about some dead pensioners in Watford, the very first thing they'll do is lock me up. Besides, I don't think the authorities are seeing the big picture."

"And what is the big picture?"

"This guy Dante wasn't Megan Stirling's boyfriend. He's not a mobster either."

"What makes you so sure?"

"Because a mobster doesn't seduce an educated young activist to his cause. He doesn't enlist a pair of happy-go-lucky British pensioners as eager assassins."

"What pensioners? You can't mean that couple from the inn?"

"Forget that for now. What I'm trying to tell you is that I think I know what type of a man this Dante person actually is."

"And what type of a man is that?"

"What if it's some sort of cult, and he's the leader? The perpetrators were all members, the couple from the Saddle Inn, yes, and whoever planted the bombs in the One Tower. Megan Stirling, too, even. Maybe she was trapped in it, looking for a way out. She was trying to stop them."

Natalia took in what Nathan was telling her. "That doesn't make any sense to me. We already know that Finbar Murphy is a mafia assassin. Don't tell me a guy like that would join some sort of a cult. People join cults because they're desperate for answers. Mafia assassins are in it for the money, and that's it."

"Yeah. I know." Nathan rubbed his chin as they walked. "That part of it I don't understand."

"What you're telling me sounds like a whole lot of speculation. That's all it is."

"It's a theory. You have to start somewhere."

"Even if you are right about that part, where do we go from here?"

"We need to track down this Dante person. He's behind it all, whoever he is. That much I know. The McKowns basically admitted as much."

"Okay, I get it. You can't take this to the police, but maybe I can."

"And tell them what? There's nothing you can say to them that won't get me into trouble, eventually. I don't want to spend the rest of my life in jail for killing somebody in self-defense."

"Forget about it, then. You were careful, I assume?"

"Of course, as careful as could be, but you never know. I'm already on their radar, we both are. Sharing what I've discovered is not an option, but I can tell you that the One Tower bombings won't be the last of it. You and I are the only ones who can act on this information." Nathan could tell he was on the verge of losing Natalia. She didn't want to be involved any longer, and she wanted nothing to do with Nathan, either. She wanted to go home and forget about it all as much as possible. The one thing that Nathan had in his favor was Natalia's deep desire for justice. She'd always fought for the underprivileged and the powerless. Natalia had a history of putting her life on the line for a cause. That was the reason she'd gone to law school, to continue that fight in another venue. Nathan was confident he could win her back to his side if only he could push the right buttons. "I think you're in danger," he tried, "of losing sight of who you really are."

"Is that so?"

"Yes, it is."

"And who am I, then? *Really*?"

"You're a woman who doesn't give up on her values. Someone who never shies away from a fight. At least that's what I used to think."

"Sometimes you need to let other people do the fighting. Why do I always have to be the one?"

"You know what they say, if you want something done right, you've got to do it yourself."

"That's the oldest cliché in the book."

"But it tends to be true."

"What about you? Why are you even bothering? I don't understand. Let it go, Nathan!"

"I don't need to remind you that a young woman was murdered right before our eyes. Her parents were next. Who knows how far these people will go? Whoever Dante is, he needs to be stopped. I believe that you and I, as a team, have the best chance at stopping him. What do you say, Natalia? Are you with me?"

"Aaarrrgh!!!" she cried out, putting her face in her hands. "Why did I even come down here?"

"Because you know it, too. You owe it to Megan, and her parents. If these people get away with murder, you'll never be able to live with yourself. They are ruthless and they won't stop until somebody stops them."

Natalia halted in her tracks on a quiet city street, lit from above by a single streetlamp. She looked Nathan straight in the eye. "I suppose you have a plan?"

"Not exactly," he admitted. "I was hoping we might brainstorm a little bit, you know, knock our heads together and come up with something."

"To track down some enigmatic cult leader?"

"That's the idea."

Natalia had a secret of her own that she was carrying close to the vest. From the look in her eyes, Nathan sensed that she wasn't being entirely forthcoming with him. She was carrying some additional piece of information. Sharing it would plunge her forward, further into this thing, no turning back. Or she could bury whatever it was and get on with her life. In the end, Nathan was right about her. Natalia couldn't ignore such an egregious miscarriage of justice. She had the blood of a vigilante in her veins, just like he did. Only one true path existed for either of them, and that path was full steam ahead. Natalia reached into her pocket and slid out a crumpled piece of paper, folded into a square with Natalia's name written in ink. "This was in my mailbox when I got home today." She handed the paper to Nathan, who unfolded it to reveal a handwritten note. By the light of the overhead streetlamp, he started to read.

Ms. Nicolaeva, I'm writing to you because I don't know where else to turn. I'm afraid for my life and I don't know who to trust. Megan Stirling was my flatmate. Before she was killed, she told me about you and how hopeful she was that you could save her from her horrible predicament. Megan was mixed up with some very bad people, and now I am afraid that those people are after me, too. I have spoken to the police already, but I don't think that they can protect me. I don't know what to do. I was hoping you might offer some advice. I am afraid to go home, afraid to use my phone or talk to any of my friends or family. Can we meet? If so, text me at this new phone number, +44 7975… Signed, Suzanne.

Nathan folded the note. "Were you planning on telling me?"

"I wasn't sure."

"Will you contact her?"

"I already have." Natalia checked the time. "We're meeting in an hour."

"It could be a set-up."

"I know."

Nathan tried not to take it personally that she'd organized this meeting without telling him. "Where this time? Please tell me it's not at Marble Arch."

"No, not a public place. She told me where she's staying."

Nathan rubbed his chin. "This whole thing sounds suspect. Why would she trust you, after what happened to Megan?"

"Because Megan trusted me."

"Yeah, and look how that turned out."

"It wasn't my fault."

"But does *Suzanne* know that? I don't like it, Natalia."

"What do you want from me? You just said you're looking for leads, and here's a lead. You said more people would die if we didn't get involved. Here's someone we might be able to save."

"One thing I've learned so far, if you can't trust an amiable retired couple, you can't trust anybody. Especially somebody we know nothing at all about."

"Go home, then, Nathan. I can take care of it myself. Maybe it's better if I do."

Nathan handed the note back. It was true, he'd wanted a lead, but this could have been written by anybody at all, even Dante himself. "Heaven help us. At least tell me we're not going into this thing unarmed."

"No weapons. If you insist on tagging along, you're welcome to wait outside."

"Where is it?"

"A pub in the docklands, The Horse and Hound."

"Tell her you want the meeting place on your terms, not hers."

"She's terrified as it is. If I start making demands, we're going to lose her."

Natalia did have a point. If Suzanne was on the up-and-up they'd need to coddle her, to gain her trust. If she wasn't who she said, that was when the problems would get real, but this was an opportunity they couldn't afford to miss. They might get some information that led to the elusive Mr. Dante himself. "Fine, we'll do things your way," Nathan conceded. He'd have felt a whole lot better going in with a weapon, but sometimes you just had to improvise.

Chapter Thirteen

The pub was a seedy dive on a dingy street a few blocks from the river. They'd arrived on public transport and then walked the last quarter mile, but now they stood across the street, taking the measure of the place. It was a two-story brick building, with light pouring out of the ground-floor windows. Upstairs, the rooms were dark. Offices, Nathan surmised, or maybe vacant accommodations. Inside, they saw a smattering of guests seated at bar stools or standing with pints in hand. Nothing extraordinary here, just your typical London pub scene. "You coming inside, or would you prefer to keep an eye on things from out here?" Natalia asked.

"I'll come in."

"Afraid I can't handle it?"

"Are you kidding? I just want to take the measure of this woman for myself."

"Let's do it, then." Natalia went first as they entered the bar. Everybody in the place looked over at them, six patrons and not a single female. Neither were any under forty. It was that kind of a place. The man behind the bar had a large gut, a paunchy face, and a round, bald head. "The bartender is our contact," Natalia said to Nathan as she walked forward.

"Can I get you something?" said the man.

"I'll have a greyhound," Natalia replied.

The bartender looked from Natalia to Nathan and back. "Two?" he asked.

"Yes, two."

"I see."

"I'm looking for your special guest," said Natalia.

The bartender mixed two greyhounds and placed them on the bar as the rest of the men in the place went back to their conversations. "Who's your friend?" the bartender asked.

"A little extra security."

Wiping his hands on a rag, the man looked Nathan up and down. "You two wait here." He moved from behind the bar, then on to the back of the room and out a rear door. Nathan lifted his greyhound and took a sip. It wasn't bad.

"You're sure you trust that?" Natalia asked.

Nathan put the drink back down. "They were expecting you to come alone?"

"Let's hope it's not a problem."

A minute later, the bartender came back into the room, cocking his head to one side toward the rear. "Come on, then, she'll see you."

Again Natalia led the way as they moved past the bartender, through the rear door and into a walled courtyard lit by a single lamp. On the far side, a set of stairs went down into a cellar. A set of heavy wooden doors was swung wide on either side. Nathan didn't like this, at all. When they reached the top of the stairs, he stopped. "Maybe I ought to keep an eye on things from here," he said to Natalia. It wouldn't do for the both of them to end up locked inside there.

"Sure," she answered.

"Suit yourself," said the bartender. He led Natalia down the stairs. The man knocked twice on another door at the bottom, said a few words, and then he and Natalia went on through. Nathan stood where he was for a few minutes before the bartender came back out. The man said nothing more as he returned across the courtyard and went into the pub. Nathan looked up at the star-filled sky as he waited for word from his partner below. When a few more minutes had passed, he began to feel anxious. What was up? He descended the steps himself, picturing worst-case scenarios. He swung the lower door open to reveal a small cellar with crates of beer and steel kegs along one wall. Natalia sat at a wooden table in the middle with a young woman roughly Megan Stirling's age. Both women looked up when Nathan came in.

"This is Suzanne," said Natalia. "Suzanne, meet Nathan Grant. He's a friend."

Suzanne eyed Nathan without saying a word, but she was anxious. She didn't trust him. He saw it in the way her eyes narrowed as she took him in. The way things had gone down with her flatmate, he didn't blame her in the least. Suzanne wore a pair of brown cotton pants, with a white cotton shirt and jacket. On her feet were a pair of espadrilles with rope soles. Her long brown hair was tied back in a ponytail.

"Everything all right?" said Nathan.

"Sure. Fine," Natalia replied.

Nathan continued into the room. He still didn't like the setup. It might be better to wait in the pub, where at least he could keep an eye on things. That would be the prudent option, but Nathan had questions of his own for Suzanne, and he wanted to ask them. He took an empty seat at the table. "Do you mind if I join you?"

"I don't think so," Natalia replied. "Do you mind, Suzanne?"

Suzanne shook her head and then turned her gaze to the floor.

"I'm sorry that you're having to go through this," Nathan began. "It must be terribly hard on you."

"Suzanne was just telling me of her experience with the police," said Natalia.

"I told them how afraid I was, but they wouldn't listen. They said the killers weren't after me, but how do they know that? Nobody knows anything! They could be looking for me right now. I might be next."

"Why do you think you'd be next?" said Natalia. "Do you have any idea why Megan was killed? Can you give us any clues at all?"

"I don't know, but it wasn't some random act. It was planned, anybody can see that."

"Maybe you can tell us what sort of things Megan was involved in," said Nathan. "Were the two of you close? Perhaps you had common friends?"

"She was just an ordinary girl. I don't know why anybody would ever want to hurt Megan. She cared so deeply about the world, about this planet."

"I've heard that before. She was an environmentalist."

Suzanne nodded. "That's how we became friends, volunteering for the same organizations at uni."

"What organizations were those?" said Natalia.

"The usual, you know, Greenpeace, World Wildlife Fund, nothing dramatic. We helped raise money, that's it."

"What about her employer?" said Nathan. "Can you tell us anything about that?"

Suzanne's eyes blinked open a little wider. This question seemed to get her heart rate going. "Finance. She worked in finance."

"We know the company was called Lange Capital," said Natalia. "Megan was planning to blow the whistle on something. Do you think it might have been work-related?"

"No, I don't think so." Suzanne shook her head.

"Why not?" said Nathan.

"She liked her job. She thought her boss was ace."

"Who was her boss? Do you remember the name?"

"It was Mr. Lange," she said. "He owned the company. I don't know his first name, she never used it."

"They got along all right, Megan and Mr. Lange?" said Natalia.

"Sure. They got along fine. She was just an entry-level associate. She thought he was handsome, though. And rich, he was very rich."

"You don't think Megan was going to blow the whistle on Lange, then?" said Natalia.

"She never said anything about it."

"Tell me this, Suzanne," Nathan steered the conversation back to his more immediate concerns. "How did you end up here, hiding out in this pub cellar?"

"It seemed like the safest place."

"Certainly, but *how* did you end up here? Did anybody help you?"

"I know the owner. He's a friend of my uncle. He said I could stay in here as long as I want."

"It doesn't seem particularly livable," said Natalia. "No bed, no toilet. Are you sleeping down here?"

"No, of course not," Suzanne shook her head. "I'm staying upstairs. My uncle has a spare room."

"Why didn't you meet with us upstairs, then?" Nathan had questioned enough people in his intelligence career to know when somebody wasn't telling the truth. Suzanne was obfuscating. Maybe it was just because she was scared, but he saw her eyes shift toward the door, as though expecting somebody else to come in at any moment. But was she expecting a friend, or a foe? Nathan looked her up and down once more. Something about this young woman wasn't sitting right with him. Partly it was the fact that she didn't seem entirely forthcoming, but there was more to it. Was it the way her hair was pulled back? The lack of any makeup on her face? Neither of those things seemed particularly concerning. Was it her clothing? He eyed her cotton jacket. It was of a very simple construction, likely handmade. He noticed that the buttons on the front were not quite lined up correctly. The same could be said of her pants, and all the way down to her shoes. He'd seen shoes like those before, on the young man at the scene of the bombing. That person wore the same style of clothing as Suzanne, all hand-sewn. In his mind's eye, he pictured the men upstairs in the bar. Something about them had stuck out to Nathan as soon as he'd seen them, but until this moment he hadn't been able to put a finger on it. Now he realized. It was the same with these men, and the bartender, too. Every single one of them appeared to be wearing handmade clothing. "Natalia, I think we ought to be going," he said.

"Why?"

"Now," Nathan added. "We ought to go right now." He stood from his chair and pushed it back.

"What about me?" said Suzanne.

"You've found a good place to hide out here. Go back up to your room and stay there, you'll be fine."

"Don't you have any further questions for Suzanne?" Natalia was confused. "I know I do. We can't just abandon her like this."

"Can we talk about this later?" Nathan moved to the lower door and pulled it open. Immediately, he saw that the storm doors at the top had been closed, trapping them inside, just as he'd feared all along. "I think we're in trouble."

Natalia immediately joined his side. "Maybe it's just for security." She passed Nathan and moved up the stairs, pushing on the storm doors that lay flat across the top. They wouldn't budge. Natalia tried knocking and then gave a shout. "Hello! Open up!"

"It's no use," said Suzanne with a flat affect in her voice, her face completely blank. "They'll open the door when they're ready."

"Who will open the door? Ready for what?" said Natalia.

"I think we found our cult," said Nathan. "And they're gathering in the courtyard."

"Stand back!" came a shout through the storm doors.

"Let us out!" Natalia yelled back.

"You better do as they say," said Suzanne. "If you don't want to get shot."

"Was Megan part of your group?" said Natalia. "Was she with you, or against you?"

"You better do as they say," Suzanne repeated.

Nathan and Natalia stepped back, retreating into the cellar.

"You can open them now!" Suzanne hollered through.

The cellar doors swung clear and a shout echoed down the stairway. "Come out, nice and slow!"

Nathan took a liquor bottle from a crate, twisted off a metal cap, and emptied the liquid on the floor. "I hate to see good whiskey go to waste," he said before smashing the end of the bottle against the stone wall. He clutched the intact neck and examined the jagged edge that remained. This could do some damage, if given the chance.

Natalia lifted one of the wooden chairs and smashed it onto the floor. It took three tries, *bang, bang, bang,* before she held a splintered leg in hand.

"It's no use fighting, there are far too many of them," said Suzanne. "Besides, I already told you they have guns."

"I'll go first," Nathan said. He wasn't going to simply give up. In the tight confines of a crowded courtyard, they might still stand a chance.

"Why you?" said Natalia.

"No time to argue." Nathan moved to the stairs and raced up three at a time clutching the bottle in his right hand. When he got to the top, he saw the courtyard filled with men, about a dozen in all. They stood facing him, spread out and carrying bats, crowbars and wooden sticks. He saw no guns. This was a promising start. The nearest man swung his bat at Nathan, who parried the blow and sliced him across the chest with the jagged glass. In a flash, they all came at him at once, but Nathan spun around, crushing one man's windpipe with the back of his elbow and slicing another in the arm. A crowbar glanced off his forearm and the bottle flew from his grasp, but Nathan still had his fists. To his right, Natalia made quick work of some of the others with martial arts skills and her table leg. Blows rained down on Nathan's back and arms, but he felt no pain, the adrenaline took care of that. He managed to get one of the men into a headlock and was choking the breath out of him when out of the corner of his eye, he saw a two-by-four in the hands of another aggressor swinging high in the air. Nathan didn't have time to move. Instead, the board came down with full force on the side of his head. This one did indeed hurt, but only for a second because after that Nathan slumped to the ground, out cold as the world around him went black.

Chapter Fourteen

Nathan came to sitting up, with his arms and his legs duct-taped to a chair. His vision was blurred and nerve endings throughout his body lit up the pain receptors in his brain. The blows had rained down all over, but what stood out most notably was the throbbing welt on his head. Despite that, he managed to examine his surroundings as best he could. It appeared to be a back room at the Horse and Hound, with dart boards on one wall and a pool table at the far end. Surrounding him were most of the men from the courtyard fight, at least those who hadn't been rushed off for medical attention. That meant eight of them, plus one more he hadn't yet seen standing directly in front of him. Toward the back and trying to keep a low profile was the young man Nathan had seen downtown, hanging around in the aftermath of the One Tower bombing. Watching over the proceedings impassively from a seat at the bar was Suzanne. Directly beside Nathan and taped to another chair was Natalia, awake but pissed and straining at her restraints, eager to tear into them all over again.

"Wakey, wakey," the new man said to Nathan. He was tall and solidly built, wearing green pants and a blue coat. On his head was a faded felt hat with a brim that drooped on one side. The man's fingernails were each painted a different color, red, blue, green, yellow... In his left hand was a shiny .38 caliber revolver. Nathan was still a little groggy, but he could see right away that this man had an electric charisma. It was evident in the man's glee, the way he carried himself, and the spark in his eyes.

This was a man profoundly confident in himself and his unique place in the world. Nathan had seen the type. They drew various reactions. For many people, an iconoclastic rule-breaker like this made them mildly uncomfortable. Sometimes majorly so. For another subset of the population, a man like this offered freedom from traditional thinking and the possibility to follow a different, previously unthinkable path. To that subset, a man like this one could be extremely persuasive, especially if he was telling them what they already wanted to hear, giving permission to follow their hidden instincts. The perfect cult leader.

"Dante," Nathan said.

"Bravo!" The man seemed impressed, turning to share this sentiment with the others in the room. "My reputation precedes me!"

Nathan shifted his attention to Natalia. "Are you all right?" he asked her.

"She's fine," Dante answered. "It's you we were more concerned about. That gash on your head, tsk, tsk, very painful, no doubt. We weren't entirely sure you'd wake up at all."

"One more murder to the list, eh?"

"Now, that's not fair! Not fair at all! You two are the ones who attacked us, isn't that right?" He looked around at his men once more and received nods in return.

"That's right," one of them confirmed. "We's just mindin' our business when this bloke comes out swingin'!"

"We'd like to know why you killed Megan Stirling," said Nathan. "If you don't mind sharing."

"Megan Stirling?!" Dante recoiled. "We most certainly did not kill Megan Stirling! She was one of our own, why on earth would we do that?"

"Because she was about to betray you," Natalia shot back.

Dante tilted his head to one side as he considered this response. "She was, yes, that is true. Quite disappointing."

"She was trying to prevent the One Tower bombing. Isn't that right?" said Nathan. "Your doomsday environmental cult was set to blow up the offices of a major oil company, and for Megan that was a step too far."

"You think you have it all figured out, don't you? The motivations of Megan Stirling are lost to us now, I'm afraid," Dante replied. "We will likely never know the answer to that."

"If you won't admit to having her killed, then who else might have done it?" said Nathan.

"Who indeed? What I would like to know is, why are the two of you poking around in my business? Hmmm? Answer me that!"

"The death of Megan Stirling is my business," Natalia seethed.

Dante smiled on the right side of his mouth as he rubbed his chin. He leaned forward and tapped Nathan on the side of the head with the barrel of his gun. "The pair of you have caused me an awful lot of trouble."

"We were invited," said Nathan. "Isn't that right, Suzanne?"

Suzanne shrugged but didn't answer.

"I must admit, I find this all perplexing," said Dante. "Quite perplexing, indeed."

"Join the club," said Nathan.

"Two members of my flock are murdered in their home, and then you two show up here causing trouble. I'd like to know why."

"Your flock, you say?" Natalia pounced on the term. "Does that make you some sort of minister?"

"A minister in the church of Mother Earth. Yes, I like the sound of that." Dante tilted his head back. "Not a church, Mr.

Grant. We are an organization. The ELF, also known as the Environmental Liberation Front."

"And these here…" Nathan looked to the others in the room. "You count them as your followers?"

"I would never be so presumptuous. These good souls are believers in the cause."

"You did blow up the One Tower, didn't you?" said Nathan. "You think you're going to single-handedly save the planet?"

"Not single-handed, of course not. There's an army of us!" Dante was becoming more animated as he went along. Nathan sensed that the man liked nothing more than a fresh audience, and a captive one was all the better.

"What about respect for innocent life?" said Natalia.

"Yes, but how many of us are truly innocent, hmm? Answer me that. I'd say not a one."

"What was Megan Stirling guilty of, exactly? Tell us that. You murdered a young woman in the prime of her life."

"No!" Dante held a finger in the air, taking issue with the accusation. "I was not responsible for her unfortunate demise. I have already told you."

"Because she was talking to me, ready to tell her secrets," said Natalia.

"That was problematic, yes."

"She was about to betray you," said Nathan.

"Perhaps."

"She was going to blow the whistle on your whole plan," Nathan went on, "and you couldn't let that happen."

Dante made a fist as the veins in his temples began to throb. "You make our project sound like a bad thing! We *are* saving the planet, don't you understand? The human race has squandered the one true resource we have, our home. We don't deserve it, not a one of us! I did not have Ms. Stirling killed, no I did not, but I would murder every soul on earth if I could manage it. Wipe out every single one."

"And how do the rest of your followers feel about that?" said Nathan.

"Ask them," said Dante.

"Well?" Nathan looked from one to the other of all the people in the room.

"We are ready to die for the cause if need be, all of us," said one man.

"How about you, Suzanne?" said Natalia.

From the back of the room, Suzanne was discomfited by the question. She looked to the floor as she nodded her head. "Yes," she said, but there was no conviction in it.

"It doesn't have to be this way," said Natalia. "We can solve the world's problems without resorting to mass murder. Don't you think?"

"No, no, no," Dante shook his head. "Such a naive view, Ms. Nicolaeva. We are a selfish species. A plague on the earth. The only cure is drastic treatment. Change will only come with action. We intend to provide the necessary motivation."

"So, you plan to blow up the offices of every oil company on earth?" said Nathan. "Is that it?"

"You make it sound like it can't be done. Anything can be accomplished with enough people working toward a common goal."

Nathan had already realized that the One Tower bombing was only the start, and that it had to have been an inside job. Whoever planted those bombs had access to the building. They would have been everyday workers, maybe janitors, or financial analysts, or college interns. These were not the types of people who would show up on a law enforcement database. They were ordinary people converted to the cult of the Environmental

Liberation Front. Nathan looked again at the men in the room. They could be anybody, working anywhere, ready to wreak the same kind of destruction in furtherance of their cause. Nathan eyed the gun still in Dante's hand. Would he and Natalia survive long enough to blow this thing wide open? There had to be a way out, but as he, too, struggled against his restraints, Nathan couldn't figure out what it was.

Dante placed the barrel of his gun against Nathan's temple. "Just because we didn't kill Megan Stirling doesn't mean we won't kill you two. Nothing will deter us from our goals, you see. No laws, no false morality. You think that our methods are unsound? We are fighting for the survival of this beautiful blue ball floating in space. Wiping out this infection that is the human species, well, there is nothing immoral in that."

Dante took a step back and handed the gun to the man at his side. "Kill them both," he said. "Just wait until I'm gone, will you?"

"Yes, sir, Dante," said the man.

"Come, Suzanne, you've done well. Martin, you can join us, too."

Dante moved toward the door with Suzanne and the young man who'd been at the One Tower bombing. The rest of the men stayed put. Before they left the room, Dante took one look back. "Goodbye Ms. Nicolaeva, Mr. Grant."

"At least you can tell us who you think had Megan killed," said Natalia. "You must have your suspicions."

"Sometimes life's mysteries remain unsolved. If I were you, I'd focus your remaining moments on communing with whatever God you pray to. You'll be joining him soon enough." With that, Dante disappeared from view.

"You don't have to do this," Nathan said to the man who held the gun. He was greeted with a smile in return.

"We'd better wait a few minutes," said another man, "to let Dante get some distance."

"He's gone. That's all he asked for," said the man with the gun. "I say we do it right now."

"Which one first?" said another man.

"Ladies first." The man with the gun was enjoying every moment of it.

"Maybe we should have some fun with her," said another man. "Seems a pity lettin' this nice piece go to waste."

"Dante said nothin' 'bout havin' fun," said another. "He said shoot them, that's all."

"I'm not sayin' we ain't gonna shoot them."

Natalia continued to struggle fiercely, a fire burning inside her as she stared the men down. Nathan knew one thing, they couldn't rape her while she was tied to a chair, and if they untied her they would regret it, big time.

"She's a feisty one," said the man with the gun. "All spit and vinegar."

"Just shoot them both and get it over with," said another man.

Nathan continued to wrack his brain for a way out. He couldn't concede that his end would come down to this, murdered by a pack of bumbling idiots. He searched the room for anything that might give him an advantage, or a way to free himself. A sharp object, perhaps. He saw nothing. Could reason work on the idiots? That might be the only option. "Look, I'm all for saving the planet," he tried. "Killing the two of us isn't going to help in that endeavor. You'll only end up facing murder charges."

"Shut up!" shouted the gunman. "Unless you want to go first?"

"That would be the chivalrous thing to do."

"Let's do 'em in the courtyard. Easier to hose down after," said one man.

"Good point," said another.

Nathan and Natalia turned their attention to each other, both equally stunned by their predicament. "I'm sorry I got you involved in this," Natalia said.

"Come on. I got myself involved."

"You said it might be a set-up. I should have listened."

"Would somebody shut these two up?!" said one of the men.

"This one first," the gunman motioned to Nathan. "Let's get some hands on his chair."

Four of the men converged, grabbing Nathan's chair and hoisting it into the air. They carried him through the room and out into the courtyard. They tossed the chair onto the ground where it crashed to its side on the bricks. The men gathered around in a circle, watching as the gunman approached. He took his time to savor the experience, reveling in the power that he held in his hand. "What's it gonna be?" he said to Nathan. "Any last words? You better make it quick, I ain't got much patience."

"I'll make it short, then. Go fuck yourself." Craning his neck to look up, Nathan saw the man's face burn with hatred.

"I'll make sure they carve that on your tombstone." The man placed the cool barrel of the pistol against the side of Nathan's head once more. Nathan Grant closed his eyes. This was where it ended, the last few precious seconds of his life. He wanted to take everything in, to absorb the sensations of living while he still could. He felt that ring of steel against his temple, smelled the chalky odor of the bricks beneath his cheek, heard the shuffle of feet as the men jostled for the best view of his brains being splattered across the courtyard. Nathan flashed back to the local church he'd attended with his family, hearing the voice of the preacher in his head, promising salvation. Nathan had never paid much attention, but suddenly that question loomed large. Would he receive it? He'd sent a lot of other men to meet their maker, and at least one woman. They'd all deserved it, he was quite sure, but now he had to wonder. Who was he to judge? And how much would that count against him in the end? He'd find out soon enough.

"Move out of the way," the gunman said to one of his co-conspirators. "You're in the line of fire, jackass."

"Hang on!" The other man scooted to one side.

Nathan opened his eyes and took a deep breath of that fresh, glorious air. His only regret was that he'd failed Natalia. He didn't mind leaving this world himself. He'd seen enough, done enough... lived enough. But Natalia? That was another story. She was a better person than Nathan would ever be, with such a promising life ahead of her, and he'd let her down. He'd gone and gotten them killed.

"You gonna do it or what?" said one of the men.

"Shut yer trap!" said the gunman.

"Pull the trigger already! Why don't you just shoot him!"

"I ain't never killed a man before. It ain't so easy."

"Let me do it, then!" said another voice.

"I said shut it!" the gunman continued. "I'm gonna do it. Just give me a minute."

"You got ten seconds, then I'm gonna wrestle that gun from your hands."

"What's that noise?" said another.

"What noise?" said the gunman. Nathan felt the gun pull away. What struck him most was the irony, that he'd gone up against seasoned insurgents in Afghanistan, and Russian assassins in Estonia. He'd tracked a German arms dealer across the war zone in Ukraine, but these amateur idiots were the ones who would finally get him in the end. Such was life sometimes. He closed his eyes once more, but then he heard it, too. *Bang! Bang! Bang!* It wasn't gunfire. It sounded like somebody kicking in the front door to the pub, or maybe using a battering ram, he wasn't sure which. That could only mean one thing. The police had arrived. They weren't entirely the incompetents Nathan had assumed them to be. The men in the courtyard rushed inside the pub to face their adversaries, leaving Nathan behind. With a splintering sound, his saviors gained entry. Nathan expected the usual commands, along the lines of, "This is the police, put your hands in the air!" Instead, he heard a lot of shouting and commotion, and this time gunshots did ring out, one after another, along with the crashing of furniture. He twisted his head in an attempt to see anything at all. This was not police. Nathan heard terror in the men's voices, and desperation, as if the devil himself had swept into the room. When he did finally see something, it was one of his tormentors fleeing past through the courtyard, but the man didn't get far. Another man, dressed in a black suit, walked into the space with a gun in his hand, pointed it at the fleeing stooge and pulled the trigger, once, twice, three times. Only after that did the man look down at Nathan, taped to his chair on the courtyard floor.

"Who have we here?" The man leaned close for a better look.

Nathan recognized him right away. "Finbar Murphy."

"Who are you and where the fuck is our money?" The Irishman pointed his pistol at Nathan's head.

"This thing with the guns at my head is getting to be a little repetitive," Nathan replied.

"WHERE IS THE MONEY!"

"Which money is that, Finbar? You'll need to be a little more specific."

From inside the pub, Nathan heard a voice call out. "There's a woman in here! Tied to a chair!" Behind the Irishman, Nathan spotted another man entering the courtyard. He recognized this one as the driver from the getaway car, armed as well this time. "What we got here?" he asked in a similar Irish brogue.

"He knows my name," said Finbar. "I don't like it."

"So, shoot him."

"Not until he tells me about the money."

"Well, that's some motivation right there," said Nathan.

"Shut it!" said Finbar.

"All right." Nathan had somehow traded one group of imbeciles for another. "I hate to sound cliché, but what money, exactly?"

"Let's get 'im up," Finbar said to his partner. The pair of them stuck their guns into their waistbands, then reached for the chair and lifted it upright.

From his new vantage point, Nathan saw into the pub's main room, littered with dead bodies, with blood sprayed across the walls and running along the floorboards. "That's quite a mess you left in there." Nathan had to admit, despite his pithy demeanor, he was a little horrified.

Finbar Murphy took his gun back out and brandished it at Nathan. "I'm happy to add to it if I don't get what I want."

Nathan was hit with a dilemma. He had no idea what money they were talking about, but what could he say to buy some time? "Why don't you explain the situation to me," he tried.

"Why'd they tie you up, you and the girl?" The getaway driver motioned toward the pub's back room.

"Hey, Natalia, you all right?!" Nathan shouted.

"What the hell is going on?!" she shouted back.

"The girl is fine," said Finbar. "You want to keep it that way? Start talkin'."

"Maybe we can help each other," said Nathan. "Dante has your money, is that right? I'd say we're both after the same man."

Finbar leaned forward, examining Nathan's face. "You a cop?"

"No. Not a cop."

"Who, then?" said the driver. "What the 'ell you doin' here?"

"My partner in there is a lawyer. We're tracking Dante, that's it."

"What for?" said Finbar.

"For a client. To tell you more would violate attorney-client confidentiality."

"Did you get a load 'o that shit?" the driver said to Finbar in disbelief. "Attorney-client what the 'ell."

"Who is your client?" said Finbar.

"Why don't you let me and my partner go and maybe we can help you find Dante. He's the one with your money, right?"

Finbar took a few seconds to think this over. He was frustrated, disappointed, upset that after all this killing, he still wasn't any closer to his goal. While he mulled his options, Nathan heard the faint whine of police sirens in the distance.

"Shit," said the driver. "You 'ear that?"

"We ain't done here yet," Finbar replied.

"We could shoot him, and the girl, too."

"What for?" said Nathan. "We have nothing to do with your money."

Finbar had very little time to ponder such questions. Instead of using his gun, he passed it to his left hand, then wound up his right and followed through, belting Nathan in the face and knocking the whole chair over onto the floor once more. For Nathan, it was enough to switch out the lights as his consciousness drained away to black yet again.

Chapter Fifteen

Upon regaining consciousness once more, Nathan's chair was upright, but this time he was surrounded by heavily armed police in black tactical gear, one of them holding a finger to Nathan's carotid artery.

"He's alive." The officer removed the finger and stepped back.

"What the hell happened here?" said a police sergeant beside him.

Nathan was still too woozy to answer, but from among the officers, out came a knife, and the tape binding his wrists and ankles was sliced away. "Natalia!" Nathan managed to croak. He tried to rise but was gently pushed back into the chair.

"Nobody said you could go anywhere," the sergeant added.

Nathan heard more sirens arriving, and made out the bustle of new bodies entering the pub. From the doorway, he saw Natalia emerge unscathed, escorted by another officer and rubbing her wrists.

"Nathan!" Her face lit up.

"Aren't you a sight for sore eyes?" He was more relieved for her sake than his own.

Interrupting their reunion, a man and woman in navy business suits with slick ID badges arrived and began giving orders. Nathan recognized them both. It was the same pair who had questioned them in Cornholme before staying at the inn. Nathan and Natalia were taken through the pub on the way out to the street, and he got a better look at the scene on the way. It was even worse than he'd originally thought, if that was possible. Ten dead bodies littered the establishment, along with shattered glass, whiskey, blood and brains. It was an orgy of violence. Nathan had to admit, on some level he was impressed that those two Irishmen had managed it all on their own, and with nothing more than pistols. He spotted Dante's gunman, flat on his back with a bullet hole between the eyes, his revolver still in hand. He hadn't even gotten a shot off.

After an examination by paramedics outside, Nathan was bandaged up, given some painkillers, and asked a few brief questions before he and Natalia were driven off in separate cars. That would keep them from colluding on any of the facts in the meantime. They weren't trusted, but what else was new? Once again, they'd have a lot of explaining to do.

The process by this point was tiresome and predictable. First, Nathan was locked up. Then he was questioned. Then locked up again, separated from Natalia the entire time. They couldn't keep him forever without charges, and he wasn't a suspect as far as he could tell, but Nathan would say little without a lawyer present. Who could he call, though? Ammon was most definitely out, and Nathan didn't know any other lawyers in London.

"All we want is to get to the bottom of this," said the woman in the navy suit. "You two have a habit of showing up at all of the murder scenes. We would greatly appreciate it if you could explain why."

"It doesn't help that you keep treating me like a criminal," said Nathan, chained to a table in an interview room. "How can you expect my full cooperation when my wrists and ankles are shackled?" He raised his arms to accentuate his point.

"We found you in a pub with ten dead bodies," said the man. "Of course we have to be careful."

"I was tightly bound to a chair. Explain how I was responsible for any of it under the circumstances?"

"Who was responsible, then?"

"Finbar Murphy. Same as the murder of Megan Stirling."

"And how do you know that? Was he the one who tied you up?"

"No. The dead men tied me up."

"Why did they do that?"

Nathan inhaled as his patience was pressed. Why was it that he always seemed to know more than the authorities who were supposed to be investigating these things? It wasn't that all of them were inept, but an awful lot of them sure seemed to be. Perhaps it was the same in any profession. There were the competent ones and the incompetent ones, and you never knew which you were going to get until you were headlong into the job. Maybe this pair knew more than he assumed, though they hadn't shown many signs of that so far.

"Look," said the male official, a bulldog of a man, with a large round head. "We ain't got time to muck around with formalities. What we want to know is, why'd you get tied up, why are there ten dead bodies in the pub, and what has this got to do with London Unity?"

"What's that?"

"If I weren't an officer of the law, I'd smack you across the mouth right about now, I would."

"You don't go for the whole police brutality thing?"

"London Unity is an international climate conference starting in our fair city in two days' time," said the woman.

"Well, that's interesting," said Nathan.

"What about it is interesting, in particular?" said the man.

"Those ten dead men at the pub, they were climate activists of a sort."

"What sort?" said the woman.

"The sort who would blow up the top three floors of the One Tower building to make a point."

The officers looked at each other as if to concur that they were finally getting somewhere. "How do you know that?" said the woman.

"Because their leader admitted it right to my face. Bragged about it, actually."

"Is he among the deceased?"

"Nope. He left before all that carnage went down."

"And what is this person's name, if you don't mind saying?"

"I have no idea what his real name is, but he goes by Dante."

The bulldog of an officer wrote this down in a notebook. "Can you tell us where to find him?"

"That seems to be the million-dollar question. Or maybe million-pound question in your case."

"Why do you say that?"

"Because Finbar Murphy was asking the exact same thing."

"What do you mean?"

"He was after some money. For Murphy, that's what it was all about."

"What money?" said the woman.

"I have no idea. He said that Dante owed him. That's all I know."

"Thank you, Mr. Grant. You can expect to hear more from us soon," said the man. "Don't think you're off the hook. We'll have our eye on you. One false move and next time we'll come up with some charges." The officials left and Nathan was put back into a cell, but only for a short period before he was unceremoniously released.

When two guards dumped Nathan off in a waiting area, Natalia was already there. By her side was Ammon, whose presence caught Nathan entirely by surprise. For his part, Nathan had no idea what to make of that. Did Ammon know what had happened in Cornholme? Nathan assumed Natalia had kept her mouth shut on that front. "How do you feel?" she asked him now, as though there was nothing unusual in this arrangement at all.

"Besides the fact that I nearly had my head bashed in?" said Nathan. "Could be worse, I suppose."

"There are some papers for you to sign," said Ammon. He had the demeanor of a man chastened by guilt, called out, and trying to make up for it. "The prior restrictions still apply. You are to be available for further questioning by the authorities at any time, and no leaving the country until the current issues are resolved to the satisfaction of the court."

"Why are you still representing me?" Nathan was dumbfounded. Even if Natalia hadn't told him what happened, Ammon must have suspected.

"I'm your lawyer," Ammon replied. "Isn't that what I'm supposed to do?"

"Yeah, but..." Nathan did his best to snap out of it. "I know you're a busy man. I appreciate your help."

"Of course." Ammon led him to a desk where Nathan put his signature on three documents without reading them and was free to go.

"Please tell me that you're finished with this madness going forward," said Ammon. "I do have my other work to consider. I'd prefer not to keep coming down to the court to bail you out."

Nathan struggled to keep his mouth shut. He hadn't asked for Ammon's help, not this time or ever. This whole episode between the three of them left him feeling seedy. Nathan wasn't the cheating type. Neither was Natalia, and yet here they were. This was one charge that apparently all three of them were guilty of. When they reached the street, Ammon didn't rush off back to his office this time. It seemed that he didn't want to let Natalia out of his sight. "How about the three of us get some coffee?" Ammon said.

"I could definitely use some coffee," Nathan replied, though it felt like he was being released from one prison and thrown into another. The temptation was strong to simply walk away, to leave them to sort out their miseries without him. Instead, the three of them walked two blocks in silence until they came to an American-style diner, open late, and went inside to find a table in a red vinyl booth. A waitress took their order. On the plus side, this place served breakfast at all hours and he was able to order scrambled eggs with potatoes and bacon. Getting pummeled always seemed to make him hungry.

"I think the three of us need to have a frank discussion," Ammon launched right into it. "I deserve to know what's going on with the two of you."

"Ask your girlfriend," said Nathan, "only leave me out of it."

"But you are right in the thick of it, don't you see?"

"No, I don't. If the two of you are trying to work out some issues, work them out between yourselves." Nathan looked at Natalia, whose expression had gone completely pale. Had she not seen this coming?

"What happened up north?" Ammon demanded.

"In Cornholme? Well, let's see, first Natalia and I witnessed the scene of an innocent couple's brutal murder, then she somehow began to realize that you were cheating on her, she got rip-roaring drunk, and I'll leave the rest to your imagination." Nathan couldn't help himself after being ambushed like this. Natalia had brought it on herself by throwing the three of them together.

Ammon's pudgy face burned red hot. "Me? Never!" he stammered, realizing that whatever comeuppance he'd expected to extract would not be forthcoming.

"Don't lie to me, Ammon, it's unbecoming," Natalia finally spoke.

"Do we really need to do this?" said Nathan.

Ammon scrambled to his feet, standing his ground as he endeavored to come up with some final statement. In the end, whatever wit he may have possessed failed him, and he stormed out of the diner without a word.

"Why did you say that?" Natalia gaped at Nathan.

"I'm sorry, I just… I don't know."

Natalia didn't wait around long enough to continue the conversation. Instead, she rushed out and hurried up the block after Ammon. Nathan was left to shake his head in disbelief. The server placed a mug of coffee on the table in front of him. "You still want those eggs?" she asked.

"Absolutely," Nathan replied. Things might be entirely messed up on every level, but he wasn't going to let a good breakfast go to waste.

Chapter Sixteen

For the next two days, Nathan was at an impasse. He'd always been a take-charge kind of guy, but at this point, there seemed to be nothing to take charge of. The court said he couldn't leave the country, he no longer had a lawyer, and he had nothing left to say to Natalia. As the big climate conference got underway at the ExCel Centre, Nathan watched some reports about it on the news in his flat. He wasn't about to go down there, or get anywhere near it. If Dante and his minions expected to attack that event, they would have their work cut out for them. With heads of state from around the world in attendance, security would be impeccably tight. For Nathan, it was best to put it out of his mind as much as possible. On his second night out, he ordered Indian takeout, streamed a few movies in the apartment, and waited, for what, he didn't know. In the back of his mind, Nathan couldn't entirely escape the conviction that Dante and his twisted crew were still up to something. They would certainly strike again, and it wasn't likely to be long.

The following day, Nathan watched reports of the American president arriving for the conference. From time to time, he got up and went to the window, looking out in the direction of the docklands and expecting to see another plume of smoke. None appeared. When he couldn't take sitting around any longer, Nathan locked the apartment and headed out for a stroll. His body was still bruised and sore from the beating he'd taken, though in recovery mode. Maybe this downtime was not such a bad thing in the grand picture. He walked around the neighborhood to stretch his legs and ended up in yet another pub, where he ordered fish and chips along with a pint. Settling in at a booth, he had a clear view of a football match on the telly, Aston Villa at Fulham. Nathan never was a huge fan of this particular brand of football, he preferred the good old American gridiron, but at least it was a distraction. Besides, he needed to eat. When his food arrived, he doused the fish in salt and vinegar and dug in. By the time he'd finished, Aston Villa was running away with it 3-1 with time winding down. Nathan nearly ordered another pint, but he preferred to stay sharp, so he had a black tea instead. While he waited, his thoughts drifted back to Natalia. He'd tried to put her out of his mind, to forget about her as much as he could, but in the end that wasn't possible. Nathan was still pissed at her, and frustrated, and disappointed. All Ammon had done was make her life miserable, from what Nathan could see, but it hadn't stopped her from running straight back to him. She deserved better. Nathan couldn't deny that despite everything, in his heart of hearts he wished that she'd chosen him. Maybe that was it in a nutshell. He was jealous, and all he had left to do was work through it and move on. When his tea arrived, Nathan sipped at it while a sports reporter interviewed the victorious Aston Villa manager after the match.

"Can I get you something else?" his server asked.

"No. Thanks. I'm good, just the check."

Walking back to his apartment, Nathan pondered his next move. Primarily, that would mean calling around for a new lawyer first thing the following day. He might tap some of his old government contacts. A little bit of pressure from the CIA could help, and he still knew a few mid-level bureaucrats with the British Foreign Service. He needed his passport and permission to travel, that was it. If the Brits wanted him to avoid getting any further involved in this whole mess, they'd let him go already. It would be best all around to get him out of the country and out of their hair. No doubt, Natalia would be relieved to have him gone as well. Her life would be a lot less complicated without him around to muck things up. That was why he was so surprised when he came around the corner to see her sitting on his front steps. She watched him advancing along the sidewalk but didn't say a word as he approached. Likewise, Nathan kept his mouth shut. He considered a few pithy remarks to break the tension, but decided they would only undermine the dignity of the moment. Instead, he paused at the front gate, then let himself through and walked the short distance up the path. Natalia didn't get up.

"Hello," Nathan broke the silence.

"Good afternoon."

He stood in front of her, waiting for Natalia to give him some indication of what her intention was. "Would you like to come up?" he offered.

"No. I'd rather not."

"You have something to tell me, then?"

"Care to take a seat?" Natalia gestured toward the step beside her.

Nathan sat. The traffic on the road in front of them was light, with just a few cars meandering past. In the park directly opposite, a pair of mothers walked with strollers toward a playground. Nearby, a man played fetch with his dog. Above the leafy green trees, Nathan saw the very top of the skyline, with the charred remains of the One Tower partially in view.

"I thought about ghosting you," said Natalia. "That's what people do in these situations normally, isn't it?"

"What situations?"

"You know, drunken revenge sex... Do I have to spell it all out?"

"No."

"I decided that's not how friends treat each other."

"That's very respectful of you."

"I wanted to apologize."

"For which part?"

"All of it."

"Okay. Apology accepted." Nathan was terse. As far as he saw it, what happened between them in Cornholme was ancient history and not worth dwelling over. What bothered him more was that after all of the angst on display that night, she'd gone right back to Ammon in the end. Of course, it wasn't Nathan's place to comment, that was entirely her business.

"Why is it that this feels like the least satisfying apology I've ever made?" said Natalia.

"I don't know, are you in the habit of making apologies?"

"I said I was sorry, what more do you want?"

"I don't even know what you're sorry for!"

"Then why are you so moody?"

Nathan laughed. "Am I?"

"Yes."

"That's on me, then. Something about being trapped in a place, I guess. It makes me antsy."

"We're good, then? You're sure?"

"I'm sure."

"OK." Natalia rose to her feet and headed up the walkway. When she reached the gate, she stopped and looked back. "Not that you probably care one way or another, but just to keep you up to speed, Ammon and I are finished. It's over."

"I'm sorry. I know that's always hard, even if it's for the best." Nathan felt an undeniable wave of relief.

"Thank you. If you need any help finding another lawyer, I can ask around."

"No, thanks, I can find one on my own." Nathan appreciated that she'd shared this news, but was she done with Nathan now as well? When she walked off up the road, the very real possibility existed that he might never see Natalia Nicolaeva again, for real this time. This could be the end of it. "We never did figure out what the London mob has to do with a cult of environmental terrorists," he said.

"No, we didn't did we?"

"I'm still curious what money Finbar Murphy was after."

"Yes, I do hate loose ends."

"All the same, it's best to let it go."

"I think that's good advice all around. Take care, Nathan. Good luck with your passport."

"Thank you." Nathan watched Natalia let herself out the front gate. She stood on the sidewalk for one last moment before walking out of his life.

"You know who I would talk to, though, if I was still in this thing? The one man who is bound to have some answers?" she said.

"Don't tempt me, Natalia."

"Fair enough. Goodbye, Nathan." She headed off up the sidewalk.

"All right, I'll bite!" he called after her. "Who should we have talked to?"

Natalia looked back. "Oscar Boswell, of course."

This name shouldn't have caught Nathan by surprise. The mobster who hired Finbar Murphy would know a thing or two, but that didn't mean he would open up to them or anyone. Quite the contrary. Asking those questions of a known mob boss would likely get one killed. "You can't just waltz in and talk to a guy like that."

"I know."

Nathan admired Natalia's chutzpah, merely to entertain such an idea. "Even if you could get to a guy like Boswell, he's not going to say anything."

"Yeah, never mind. Forget I mentioned it. Take care of yourself." She started to walk away once more.

"You, too," he replied.

Natalia was halfway up the block when Nathan saw something in the distance beyond the treeline. She spotted it at the same time and slowed her stride. A column of smoke was rising into the sky, somewhere to the southeast. The docklands? He couldn't tell from here, but it was the right direction. Then he noticed another column, straight south, and then a third to the west. Fires seemed to be breaking out simultaneously, all over the city. Natalia came to a halt, unsure whether to continue on home or not. The pedestrians in the park hardly seemed to notice until they heard the muffled pop, bang and rumble of explosions. At this, concern spread quickly and people began to grab their children, or their pets, and hurry home with fear in their eyes. For her part, Natalia came back to stand in front of Nathan's gate once more. No matter how hard they tried to stay out of it, and apart from each other, they just couldn't seem to manage.

"Boswell, you say?" Nathan asked.

"I do believe he'd have some answers."

"How do we find him?"

"Hackney. If we start poking around there, I suspect he'll find us."

"And then what?"

"I don't know."

"And here I thought you were giving me the boot. What happened to that?"

"I guess the ghosting will have to wait."

"Just try not to shoot anybody until we get some information, all right?"

"Shoot them with what? We're unarmed!"

"For a woman of your talents, that's a mere formality." Despite their long odds, Nathan couldn't help but feel a sense of contentment in his soul. He and Natalia were back at it, out to save the world, together. Somehow, there was nowhere else he'd rather be.

Chapter Seventeen

Getting from Shoreditch to Hackney was the first problem. It was only a few miles, but neither of them was in the mood to walk it. After a string of simultaneous terrorist bombings, the entire public transport system was shut down as a precaution, and getting a taxi was all but impossible. Not that they didn't try. Standing on the nearest avenue, they tried to flag one down but the few cabs that did come by whizzed past without slowing. Natalia's ride-sharing app fared no better. "We can take scooters."

"What, those electric things?" said Nathan.

"Yeah, why not? You have the app, right?"

"No, I don't have the app. Those scooters are a plague on humanity, come on!"

"Sure they are, until you need one." Natalia opened her app and zoomed in on a map of the local area. "I see some parked nearby. Come on!" She started off up the street with Nathan close behind. When they reached a cluster of electric scooters, she paused. "We could double up if you want."

"What, you mean share one? No thanks!" Nathan quickly downloaded the app himself and added his payment. They each unlocked a scooter and away they went, zipping along on the electric charge. For the most part, the streets were eerily quiet and deserted. The residents of London were huddled in their homes, it seemed, glued to their televisions and afraid to venture out. Things changed when they reached Haggerston. Nathan spotted a group of youths hanging out in front of a bottle shop, more than a dozen in all with a gleeful air, as though it were one big party. Bottles of liquor were passing between them, and Nathan noticed a shattered window in front, with young men hustling in and out as they looted the place.

"Oy, where you goin?!" one of the boys called out before side-checking Natalia as she went past, knocking her to the pavement. Nathan skidded to a stop just ahead.

"What have we here?" Another of the boys approached, whiskey bottle in hand. "Out for a ride, are we?"

Nathan made his way over to Natalia and helped her up as she checked for scrapes and bruises. "You all right?" he asked.

"I'll be fine," she said as the group of youths began closing ranks around them, forming a tight circle.

"I will give you the courtesy of one polite warning. We don't have time for this," said Nathan.

"Oh, ho ho, the courtesy, eh?" said the whiskey boy. "You sound pretty posh for a Yank! Where's your wallet? Show us some bees and honey, China plate!"

"What the fuck are you even talking about?"

"I'm talkin' quid, squid, pound sterling, come on, chop chop!"

"Back the fuck off." Nathan held up one hand as Natalia lifted her scooter from the ground and propped it on the kickstand. From somewhere deep inside the shop, Nathan heard the sound of breaking glass, then laughter, and finally he saw three more youths scurry out through the shattered window as flames erupted behind them.

"Which one of you ingrates knocked me over?" Natalia demanded.

"Why, you planning to do something about it?" The guilty party stepped forward, quite pleased with himself.

"I might be."

Nathan had a pretty good idea what was coming next. He watched as Natalia took a stance some four feet away from the offender, sized him up briefly, and then flung her body 360 degrees, spinning her right foot into the air in a roundhouse kick that connected to the side of his head, knocking the young man to the pavement, out cold. Without giving whiskey boy a chance to respond, Nathan punched him hard in the face and it was two down. He was going for number three when it dawned on the rest of them that they were in over their heads. The lot took off running, leaving their unconscious compatriots behind. Nathan and Natalia went back to their respective scooters. "You're sure you're all right?" he asked again.

"Only my pride is injured."

"I think you took care of that." Nathan looked back to see the bottle shop engulfed in flames, lighting the evening with a flickering orange glow.

"Any excuse to cause mayhem. The human race is so predictable." Natalia zipped off up the road and Nathan followed behind. The rest of the way to Hackney was mostly uneventful but for a few police cars roaring toward central London. In all, it took just over twenty minutes to reach the Hackney town hall, but that was where their plan terminated. The streets here were also largely deserted, with all of the businesses shuttered. They pulled to a stop in a small square. "What now?" said Natalia.

"I don't know, this whole thing was your idea." Nathan took a look around. On the far side of the square, he saw light in the windows of what looked like a small restaurant. "What's that?" he said.

"Let's take a look, shall we?"

They closed out their scooters and walked across the square toward the building in question. An electric sign above the front door read *The Empire Bar*.   Inside they found just a few customers, gathered at one end and drinking beer as they watched an overhead television. The bartender's eyes were also fixed on the screen, which showed a live news broadcast. A reporter stood with a cloth covering her nose and mouth while an oil refinery burned out of control in the frame behind her, smoke and flames twisting and dancing into the sky like a scene out of *The Inferno*. Nobody looked up when Nathan and Natalia came in. These people did not look like gangsters. They were middle class, a small knot of three men and two women, all well-dressed and respectable.

"Who among you fair ladies and gentlemen can help me to locate a man named Oscar Boswell?" Nathan cut straight to the point. He didn't have the patience for small talk. In response, he was met with blank stares all around.

"Have you seen the news?" one of the women asked him.

"Boswell," Nathan ignored her question, just like she'd ignored his. "Oscar Boswell. I've heard he's from around here."

"Never heard of him," said one of the men.

"You're from the area?" said Natalia.

The man pointed toward the ceiling. "Right upstairs."

"What's your interest in Mr. Boswell?" said the bartender. The name seemed to mean something to this one.

"We'd like to speak with the man," said Nathan. "Can you tell us where to find him?"

This query left the bartender visibly uncomfortable. "No," he answered. "Can't say as I'd be any help in that regard."

"But you know him?" said Natalia.

"I've heard the name. I've heard lots of names."

On the television screen, the shot switched to a different reporter, this one near the ExCel Centre. Nathan saw that the facility was intact. Dante's minions had been unable to breach that security, but with so many world leaders in attendance, the place was in full lockdown and guarded by armed troops.

"Perhaps you could point us in the right direction," said Natalia. "Who else around here might know Mr. Boswell?"

"If you want to find Boswell, you're in the wrong bar," said the other woman.

"What's the right bar?" Nathan asked.

The woman looked to the man beside her, hoping for affirmation, but this gentleman kept his eyes on his pint. Nobody, it seemed, wanted anything to do with Oscar Boswell.

"The Old Guard Tavern," said the woman. "You might try over there."

"Thank you, kindly," Nathan replied.

Back outside, Natalia looked the place up on her phone. It was only three blocks away. After a brisk walk, they found it easily enough in an old brick building on a smaller square. Entering this tavern, they saw that it had a larger crowd, with several dozen people enjoying beers and cocktails with nary a television screen in sight. Whatever was happening in greater London, it was just another night at the pub in here. Nathan did make out a few gazes following them as soon as they entered. Nathan felt another twinge of regret at being unarmed. The local crew here had more of an edge than in the last place. He saw plenty of tattoos, shaved heads, bulging muscles under tight t-shirts, and men with gold necklaces hanging on hairy chests. It was a working-class establishment.

"Maybe we ought to start out with a drink," Natalia said, scoping out the room herself.

"Sure." The pair of them walked straight to the bar. "What'll it be?" Nathan asked.

"Irish whiskey would be fine," said Natalia.

"Let's try Jameson this time," said Nathan before putting in an order with the lone bartender. The man took down two whiskey glasses, placing them on the bar.

"Neat with a splash," Nathan added.

"Right." When he'd poured the whiskey, the bartender added a splash of water. "Anything else?"

"No, thanks."

"Ten quid."

Nathan took out a ten-pound note from his wallet, but as he paid the man, he noticed that the bartender's attention was elsewhere. Nathan turned to look and quickly saw why. Four thugs were approaching. They merged on either side of Nathan and Natalia, standing with chests puffed up. "You the pair been makin' noise 'bout Mr. Boswell?" said one of the men.

Nathan lifted his whiskey. No use letting it go to waste. He took a drink before he answered. "That's right."

"Maybe you ought to be mindin' your own business," said another.

"I believe that Mr. Boswell might like to speak with us," said Nathan. "To discuss our mutual interests."

"Which interests are those?"

"A certain man who owes Mr. Boswell some money."

"What do you know about it?" the first man growled.

"That information is for Boswell."

"You two coppers? You got a lot of nerve comin' in here."

"We're not police," said Natalia. "I'm a lawyer. Mr. Grant is a private citizen."

"Private citizen..." the man repeated, not at all sure what to make of it. He crossed his arms and tilted his chin in the air as he considered his next move. "Keep an eye on them," he said to his colleagues before walking off and moving through a door in the back. That suited Nathan just fine, it gave him time to savor the rest of his whiskey. As for Natalia, she left hers untouched. After a few minutes, the thug returned. "Follow me," he said. Nathan and Natalia were escorted by all four thugs, through the door in the back and into an antechamber, where they were made to stand with their hands on a wall while they were frisked, one at a time. It was just as well that they'd come unarmed after all. When the search was finished, they were led into yet another room, with wood paneling and plush green couches on either side of a large fireplace.

"Sit," said one of the men. Nathan and Natalia took their places side-by-side on a couch. Two of the thugs stood near the door, hands crossed in front of them, while the other two went through yet another door. Just a few minutes later, a rotund man with a round, fleshy face entered the room.

"What's this all about?" the man said.

"Oscar Boswell?" said Nathan.

"I'm Boswell. This better be good."

"We hear you're looking for a man named Dante. We think we might be able to help each other."

"Who says I need help?"

"You've located him, then?" said Natalia. This comment struck a nerve, as Boswell's face glowed red in response.

"That's my business. Innit?"

"It is, certainly," said Nathan. "But it's ours as well, you see."

"How so?"

"Revenge. Nothing more, nothing less. Whatever money can be pried out of him is all yours."

"Who'd he kill, your granny?"

Nathan turned to Natalia. They couldn't very well mention Megan Stirling. Boswell himself was responsible for that one.

"That's our business," said Natalia. "What we can tell you is that we want to wipe him from the face of the earth, or at the very least have him arrested."

"Whoa, whoa, whoa!" Boswell held up a hand. "There ain't no room for coppers in this. It's a private matter!"

"Of course. All we want is to eliminate the man," said Nathan.

Boswell put a hand to his chin. "You think you're gonna waltz right in here and get me talkin'? Just like that? I don't know who you are, but you've got a lot of nerve. Don't press your luck or you might not walk out."

"How did Finbar Murphy track Dante to the Horse and Hound?" said Natalia, pressing her luck all the same.

This time it looked like Boswell's head might explode as he struggled to maintain his composure, hands forming into fists. "Show our friends the door," he said to his lieutenants.

"What about Megan Stirling?" Natalia crossed the line. "What did she have to do with it?"

"Better yet," Boswell said to his men, "dump their cold, dead corpses in the river."

The four men surrounded Nathan and Natalia, still seated on the couch. Two of the men drew their guns.

"Tell me when it's done," Boswell added.

"Yes, sir, Mr. Boswell."

"Let's go, on your feet, let me see your hands," said another of the thugs as Boswell left the room.

Nathan looked to Natalia. "I guess this wasn't such a good idea."

"It's my fault," she admitted. "Next time, I'll defer to your judgment."

"There ain't gonna be no next time, Missy," said one of the thugs.

"All we want is some information," Nathan replied. "Is that worth risking your life over?"

"*My* life? I didn't know we were in the presence of a comedian."

"I may be multi-talented, that's true, but I'm not joking at the moment. Tell us what we want to know and we'll leave you alone, on my honor."

"On your fucking feet! Now!"

"I'll take the two on the left," said Natalia.

"Sure," Nathan replied. The pair of them rose from the couch with an easy manner, as though it were just any old day. Two of the thugs held their pistols while the other pair was content to rely on their fists, if need be. That was a mistake. Nathan and Natalia took a few steps toward the door with a relaxed gait and then, *boom*! Nathan ducked to one side as his left hand swung at one of the pistols, knocking it away. His right fist punched the man in the face. It only took one blow and the man dropped to the ground, just like the kid at the bodega. Almost too easy. The second man was more of a challenge. He got a blow in to Nathan's midsection, then another before barreling forward and sending them both to the floor. The man had Nathan in a chokehold from behind, cutting off his air. Nathan was struggling to breathe, trying not to pass out cold, when he heard Natalia's voice.

"Let him go!" she said.

Looking up, Nathan saw Natalia standing above them, holding one of the guns.

"Hands where I can see them!" she added.

The chokehold released and Nathan scrambled to his feet. Three of the men were passed out on the floor, with only this fourth still conscious. Nathan took a step back, wound up, and kicked him in the head, knocking him out cold. "Thanks," he said to Natalia.

"Any time."

Nathan put a hand to his neck. That was likely to bruise. He reached down and lifted the other pistol, a 9mm Luger. "Maybe these will help convince Boswell to talk," he said.

"They ought to be persuasive."

Nathan went first, through the door Boswell had just left by. It opened onto a hallway, with two more doors on the right side and another at the far end. From somewhere deeper inside, Nathan heard music and the sound of laughter. He moved forward. The first door to the right opened into a bathroom. The next one led to a stairway. It was the last door that the noises came from. It sounded like a family dinner, with children's voices calling back and forth and the pitter-patter of little feet running across the floor. Nathan was hit with an unexpected jolt from his conscience. Barging into a room full of children with a Luger might scar them for life. He turned back to look at Natalia. "It sounds like kids," he said.

"So?"

"I can't go waving a pistol at a bunch of kids, come on!"

Natalia was perturbed, but acceded to his concern. Before Nathan had a chance to discuss it any further, she'd tucked her gun into the waistband behind her back, turned the doorknob and headed on through. Nathan slid his gun into a similar position and hurried after. Inside the room, they were greeted by the scene of a birthday party in full swing, with a dozen children gathered around a large table, squirming and bouncing and bopping in their seats, most of them with festive paper party hats on their heads. At the far end of the table was the birthday girl, sitting tall in her chair while a woman bent low, lighting the candles on a birthday cake. A few other grownups were snapping photos but none of them paid Nathan and Natalia much attention, except for Oscar Boswell, who sat in a large easy chair nearby. When Boswell spotted them, his eyes grew as large as saucers. Nathan could just about read the man's mind. How did these two get away from his henchmen, and who was left to protect him? His eyes moved to a second door that led to a kitchen, but before he could bolt, Nathan and Natalia were on him, one standing on either side of the chair.

"All right, all right, quiet, children!" said the woman with the matches. "It's time to sing happy birthday to Lizzy! Are you ready?"

"Yessss!" the children called out.

"On the count of three, then! One, two..."

"Happy birthday, to you!" everyone in the room began to sing. Everyone besides Nathan, Natalia, and Oscar Boswell. Nathan kept an eye on Boswell's hands, visible on the armrests of his chair. They waited until the song concluded, cheers erupted, and young Lizzie blew out her candles.

"We need to talk," said Nathan. "We tried the polite approach. We'd hate to ruin your celebrations."

"You're going to pay for this."

"It's too late for threats, Mr. Boswell," said Natalia.

"Let's go, on your feet, nice and slow," said Nathan. They'd have to find a quiet place to question the man, but not on the premises. His thugs were likely to wake up at any moment, and they'd be pissed. "Through there," Nathan nodded toward the kitchen door.

Boswell thought about it for a brief moment before looking to one of the women in the room. "I've got some business to take care of, dear," he said. "I won't be long."

"You'd better not. We're about to open presents!" she replied.

"Don't wait for me. You go ahead."

The woman wasn't happy at all. "Hurry back, then."

Boswell gave her a quick nod and they proceeded through the door into the kitchen, where two servers were busy preparing plates of ice cream to go with the cake. "Keep going," Nathan said to Boswell. On past the kitchen, they came to an entryway at the back. "Where's your car?" When Boswell didn't answer, Nathan pushed him against a wall and quickly checked his pockets, pulling out a wallet, a phone, and a Range Rover key fob.

"Nobody treats me like this!" said Boswell.

"Yeah, yeah, blah de blah." Nathan took out the Luger and pointed it at the side of Boswell's head. "Where the fuck is your car?"

The gangster was used to dishing out this type of treatment, not taking it. Nathan was afraid the fear might incapacitate him, but Boswell tilted his head sideways. "Out the back."

"Come on." Nathan gave him a light shove in that direction. Outside, they found themselves in an alley. At the end of it were six parking spaces, all of them taken but only one by a Range Rover. Nathan pressed a button on the fob and the door locks flipped open. "You drive, but no funny stuff if you want to get through this, got it?"

Boswell didn't answer. He climbed in on the driver's side as Nathan took the rear passenger seat just behind him and Natalia sat shotgun, pistol in hand.

"Pull out onto the street, nice and easy," Nathan continued.

"Where are we taking him?" said Natalia.

"Somewhere quiet. I'm open to ideas."

Natalia thought about it for a split second and then said, "Turn right." She directed him, left, left, right, until they entered a park called London Fields. "You can pull over here."

Boswell parked the car on the side of a quiet road under leafy green trees, lit by streetlamps. Nobody else was around. "This will do," said Nathan. "Start talking, Boswell. If you want to get out of this alive and see your lovely Lizzie again, you'll tell us everything we want to know, starting with your association with Dante. What do you two have to do with each other?"

Boswell still wasn't sure he was ready to cooperate. It went against the mobster code to open his mouth about any of his business. He kept his mouth shut.

Nathan leaned forward and placed the barrel of the Luger against the man's temple. "It would be a shame to blast your brains all over this nice leather upholstery," he said.

Boswell tensed up further. "The bastard owed me money," he said. "That's it."

"What for?"

"Goods delivered. We had an arrangement. I held up my end, Mr. Dante stiffed me on his. Half up front and half on delivery, only he stiffed me on the back end."

"You'll have to be more specific," said Natalia. "What goods?"

"Explosive materials."

"I see," said Nathan. "The kind of explosive materials that might have been used in a bombing like the One Tower?"

"It didn't interest me what he wanted the stuff for."

"How much are we talking about?" said Natalia. "Enough for today's attacks?"

Boswell managed a laugh at this question. "Times ten."

"That's a lot of explosives," said Nathan.

"It was a lot of money, too."

"Why did you have Megan Stirling murdered?" said Natalia. Boswell balked at this question, unwilling to answer it, so she pointed her gun at his left thigh. "You want to walk again, Mr.

Boswell? Because I have no qualms about leaving you in a
wheelchair for the rest of your life. Why Megan Stirling?"

"To send a message!" Boswell admitted. "We had to show
the man we meant business!"

"So you murdered an innocent young woman?"

"Who's innocent? That woman was one of them. Look at
what they did today, blew up half the fuckin' city!"

"With explosives that you provided," Nathan pointed out.

"Megan Stirling was trying to come clean," said Natalia. "She
was meeting me that day to expose the whole thing. You had
Finbar Murphy kill her before she had the chance."

"Well, excuse me. Your innocent young woman was the go-
between. She's the one who arranged the whole deal!"

"What about her parents?" said Nathan.

"I had nothin' to do with that!" Boswell insisted. "Nothin' at
all, on my honor!"

"Gangster's honor, huh?" said Nathan.

"I swear to God!"

"All right, all right." Nathan ran it through his mind, putting
the pieces together. Boswell put a hit on Megan Stirling to send a
message, in an attempt to pressure Dante over the money owed.
Dante sent the McGowens to murder her parents because if
Megan was willing to expose his plans, she might have already
told her mother and father all about it. This all made some
perverted sense, but it didn't help them get any closer to locating
Dante. "How did you track Dante and his people to the Horse
and Hound?"

"I can't tell you that."

Natalia took her pistol from Boswell's thigh and pointed it at
his temple as he tried to lean away.

"You don't have the guts," he said.

"Oh, she certainly has the guts, Boswell. I've seen her at work. You'd be impressed. How did you track Dante?"

Boswell grimaced. "I have a contact."

"Go on."

"On the inside. The NCE. That's all I can tell you, no names. You're gonna have to shoot me."

"What did this contact tell you?"

"A time and a place."

"Ask for another time and place," said Natalia.

"It don't work like that. I get a call, maybe twenty minutes out. This Dante, he's not in London anymore, I can guarantee you that. What he pulled off today? That was only the beginning."

"Why do you say that?"

"The amount of material I provided, you joking? He ain't done, I'll tell you that."

"You know you're complicit in all of it, right?" said Natalia.

"I didn't blow up nothin' and nobody. That was Mr. Dante and his lunatics."

"We don't have time to litigate this here," said Nathan. "What else can you tell us that might help locate the man?"

"I can tell you that Dante ain't his real name. Once upon a time, the man went by Collin Bruce."

"Scottish?" said Natalia.

"Smart girl. Mr. Bruce came of age in the city of Glasgow. Got his start working oil platforms in the North Sea. What do you call that, irony is it? Went on to serve as a helicopter pilot in the Royal Navy."

"How do you know all this?" said Nathan.

"I already told you, I got my contact. Want to know the funny part?"

"Sure. What's the funny part?"

"Dante, Bruce, whatever you want to call the man, he don't give a shit about the climate. He's only in this for the money. All those people followin' the man around, doin' his bidding, they're a bunch of suckers!"

"What do you mean Dante is in it for the money? Whose money? His followers'?"

"No, I'm talkin' real money! He told me himself. Said when this thing was done he'd be filthy rich. I told him that was all well and good but I don't wait for my cut. They say a man is as good as his word, but that man is a son-of-a-bitch."

"How exactly was it going to make him rich?" said Natalia.

"Fuck if I know. I do business the old-fashioned way."

"But you have no idea where the man might be right now?" said Nathan.

"I got feelers out. In my business, a debt owed is never forgiven. Mr. Bruce, he'll pay in the end, with his money or with his life. One way or another, I'll be made whole."

"Assuming that you can find him."

"Oh, I'll find him. Maybe you two ought to help me. You took out four of my best men. Don't think I'm not impressed."

"Thanks, but no thanks," said Natalia.

"Who are you to cast a stone? What, you think you got some moral high ground? Don't make me laugh."

"How about this?" Nathan suggested. "If you find the man, let us know and we can take him out for you."

"Fat fucking chance. How the hell do I get my money, then? Tell me that."

"You just said you'd settle for revenge."

"No," Boswell shook his head. "Revenge on my terms. I want that bastard to know where it's coming from."

When Nathan thought about it, there was something strangely comic regarding the prospect of teaming up with Boswell. In the plus column, the man could provide a small army, and most likely the weapons to go with it. He also had connections that might actually locate Dante. On the other hand, it was Boswell's men who killed Megan Stirling. Natalia would never in a million years be able to ride shotgun with a man like Finbar Murphy. She'd likely shoot him on sight. Nathan didn't want to turn down the offer outright, though. It could still lead to something. "How about you let us think it over?" he said.

"What's to think? You want the bastard or not?"

"Thanks for the offer. Let's just leave it at that. We know where to find you." Nathan directed Boswell to drive back to his pub, dropping off his passengers a few blocks away.

"Hey, them's ain't your guns!" Boswell complained. "Give 'em back!"

"You're funny, Boswell. Don't push your luck."

When the mobster drove off, Natalia looked at Nathan in disbelief. "We'll think about it? Partnering with that man, a known mobster?"

"It could be beneficial."

"If you don't remember, I'm studying law, Nathan! I can't go running around with gangsters!"

"And yet you're perfectly fine threatening one with a Luger?"

"They came after us first. It was self-defense!"

"Fine, don't blow a gasket."

"I'm trying to stay on the right side of this thing."

"What can I say? Life is complicated."

"Forget it, Nathan. Just forget it." Natalia tucked her gun back into her waistband and marched off to the square, where she unlocked another electric scooter. Nathan took one for himself. As they rode back across town, he half hoped to run into those pesky kids again at the market, just to blow off some steam. Instead, when they reached the liquor store, half of the block was engulfed in flames but no kids were in sight. In their place were residents gathered around to watch helplessly from the opposite sidewalk, waiting for firefighters that might never come. The crews were too busy with the multiple other fires that lit the horizon in various directions, all the handiwork of one Collin Bruce, AKA Dante. He and Natalia hadn't found the man himself yet, but they were learning things bit by bit, including his given name. That meant they were one step closer. Right? He didn't even know where they were headed at the moment. Natalia paused in the middle of the street to watch the unfolding scene, with orange flames lighting the night sky. A woman in a bathrobe paced up and back, holding a small dog in her arms. From across the street, a man unfurled a garden hose and attempted to put some water on the fire, but the pressure was abysmal, barely flowing from the nozzle at all. Groups of locals helped evacuate the buildings up the rest of the block, escorting residents out to the street with what valuables they could grab on short notice. "We ought to help," said Natalia.

"I don't know that there's any more to be done here, not until the fire engines arrive."

Natalia let this sink in. "All because of some petty hooligans, these people are going to lose everything."

"Come on, I think we've had enough for one night. Let's keep moving."

Without another word, Natalia scooted on past. From here it was straight ahead along the Regent's Canal to get to her place. One kilometer further on, the route to Nathan's apartment required a left turn.

"Hey!" Nathan called out as he hit the brakes. "Hang on a sec!"

Natalia stopped a short distance ahead and looked back. "What?"

"Where are we going?"

"I don't know about you, but I'm going home."

"Are we still in this thing?" That was the big, unanswered question and it kept coming up again and again. Were they in this thing, or not? If they were, how much had to do with Dante, and Megan, and the bombings all across the city? And how much with the fact that this quest was the only paltry excuse keeping the two of them together?

"It's not like we learned much, did we?" she said.

"Sure we did. Collin Bruce. We have a name. That's huge." The thought of going back to his Shoreditch apartment all alone filled Nathan with dread, but he was beyond pleading. If she couldn't manage at least a modicum of initiative, he'd just as soon leave it.

"Come over to my place," she said. "We can talk things over." With that, she zipped off down the path. Nathan followed, hot on her heels. Ten minutes later, they were parking their scooters by the curb out front. The former single-family home was divided into three apartments, two downstairs and one up. Natalia's was downstairs and to the right. It was small but cozy, with a fireplace in the living room along with a TV in the corner, one small bedroom and a tiny kitchen. The furnishings looked like those of a starving college student, but all told she wasn't doing so badly, with her own apartment in London, no roommates. "Make yourself at home," said Natalia. "What can I get you?"

"How about a beer?"

"Sure."

Nathan took his place on a threadbare couch and kicked his feet up on a wooden coffee table. Natalia went into the kitchen and opened the fridge, took out two bottles of Bass ale and cracked off the caps with an opener before bringing them out and handing one across. Nathan took his beer and Natalia dropped into an easy chair.

"What do you say we order some food?" said Nathan.

"Are you kidding? Nobody is out, you saw for yourself. Who would deliver? Besides that, the restaurants are all closed."

"Good point. Maybe we ought to see what's going on."

Natalia lifted a remote from the coffee table, turned on her television and switched the channel to the BBC. For the next half hour, they went from there to CNN, to local news and back. All of it painted a grim picture. The terrorists had struck oil refineries, power plants, corporate offices and a shipping terminal on the Thames. All told, twelve targets were struck, with 58 dead and counting. Authorities were tight-lipped on any suspects. The climate conference was spared, but the attacks sent a message. Television pundits were busy debating what that message was, but the prevailing wisdom said that it was meant to tell the world that they weren't doing enough. The fossil fuel industry had to cease operations entirely, the attackers seemed to say.

Natalia shut the television off. "What do you think?"

"Greed makes more sense to me as a motive than ideology. Not that there aren't a whole lot of passionate environmentalists out there, but come on, blowing up an oil shipping terminal on the Thames? That's going to foul the river for years to come."

"You believe that Dante's people are all in it for the money somehow?"

"No. Those people have been sold a bill of goods. Too bad we can't ask Megan Stirling about that angle. I'll bet she could have told us something."

"She was about to."

"Somebody else at that firm of hers might have an insight."

"After what happened to Megan they'd be terrified to come forward. They certainly wouldn't want to speak to us."

"We could always try."

"Who would we ask?"

"I don't know, we look up her colleagues, poke around and see what we find out. You know what they say, if you want to find the truth, *follow the money*. Finance was Megan's business. If anybody knows about money, it's her people."

"Like Suzanne?"

"Forget about Suzanne. Lange Capital, that's our next focus."

Natalia downed some of her beer and leaned back in her chair. "Right now what I need is something to eat and a good night's sleep. How about I make us some pasta?"

"That sounds terrific."

"Don't expect anything special, I'm talking spaghetti with bottled sauce. It's the best I can do."

"You won't get any complaints from me."

For the rest of the evening, Natalia shifted the conversation toward anything other than current events. She didn't want to discuss Megan Stirling, or Finbar Murphy, environmental terrorism or the fact that her city was still on fire. She certainly wasn't going to mention Ammon, or what happened with Nathan up in Cornholme, or anything particularly personal. It seemed that she needed a respite from all that. Instead, they pretended Nathan was just a normal out-of-town visitor as the two of them shot the breeze and let the world go by, entirely unheeded. Natalia had enough veggies in her fridge to add a salad to the meal and they cracked open a bottle of Merlot to wash it all down. Nathan hadn't realized how much he needed a break as well until the tension began washing off him, drifting away into the ether. When they'd finished the meal, Nathan helped Natalia wash up, and then she pulled a half-eaten tub of mint chip ice cream from the freezer. "Dessert?" she asked.

"Why not? A little ice cream won't kill me."

Natalia laughed. "The way things are going, it's got a lot of competition."

Nathan smiled in return. "Indeed."

They had their bowls of ice cream in the living room, he on the couch and she in the easy chair. "Where do you picture your life going from here?" Natalia asked him.

Nathan tilted his head to one side. "That's a very good question."

"You think you'll stay in that little cottage of yours in the south of France? It sounds idyllic, but I have to say, I have a hard time seeing it."

"Why?"

"What do you mean, why? Look at yourself! You're a man in desperate need of a rush. It's in your blood. I can't believe you'll ever give that up. Not for long, anyway."

"Ah, well... you could be right." He took a bite of his ice cream to buy himself some time, thinking it over. "Part of me wants to settle down and lead that quiet life. When I bought the place, I thought I could embrace that. I was going to turn over a new leaf, start this furniture business I'd always dreamed about and embrace it. I do get joy from that, you know. It's not just some kind of ruse."

"But...?"

"You're right, I can't deny it, I'm an adrenaline junkie. I can sit in my shed working on a brand-new wooden table and be perfectly happy for a time, but ultimately I need my fix, to put my life on the line for the greater good, whatever that may entail. To be perfectly honest, I've thought about seeing a shrink, but what would I even tell them? That nothing gets me off more than popping a cap in a bad guy? I don't think that would go over well."

"You have it pretty rough, don't you?"

"I'm not the only one."

"What, me?! Come on! I'm nothing like that, nothing at all."

Nathan smirked and shook his head, then went back to eating his ice cream. It was better to keep his mouth shut when it came to this one.

"I mean, it's not like I get off on it!" she added.

"All right," he conceded. "Never mind."

"I just happen to have a well-calibrated moral compass. Is that so wrong?"

"I didn't say anything was wrong."

"I'd rather fight my battles in the courtroom, but sometimes more is required."

"Absolutely."

When they'd put their empty bowls in the dishwasher, Nathan prepared to call it a night. From here, it would be about 30 minutes on one of the scooters to get back to his apartment. "I ought to get going," he said.

"You're welcome to sleep on the couch."

"I'm not sure that's a good idea."

"Why not? It's not like I'm going to jump you again."

Nathan laughed, though he was wise enough not to say anything more about that, either.

"You never know what craziness is going on out there on the streets," she continued.

"As long as you don't mind."

"Not at all." Natalia made up the couch as a bed, with clean sheets and an extra duvet. She let him take a shower first, then went after, and before long Nathan was lying under the covers, looking up at the darkened living room ceiling. In a way it felt like a storm had passed, on a personal level. What happened between them in Cornholme created a thick, heavy fog of tension that was hard to escape. Both of them shared some blame, but somehow they had worked their way through it. Nathan was intent on not screwing things up a second time around. This detente gave his mind the space it needed to relax. A sense of peace settled over him and Nathan's consciousness faded away to a deep sleep. The rest of the world could get on without him until morning.

Chapter Eighteen

A clock on the living room wall read 5:48 a.m. when Nathan woke up, feeling reasonably well-rested. He rose from the couch and put his pants back on, then went through Natalia's cupboards looking for coffee. Eventually, he found a bag in the refrigerator, boiled some water in a kettle, and used a French press to brew a few cups. All was still quiet in Natalia's room, so he figured he'd let her sleep. Settling in at the kitchen table, he poured himself a mug and gave some thought to the situation. His motivation to follow this thing through to the end, to track down Dante and exact some measure of justice, had not waned. As of the prior evening, Natalia seemed to be back with him on this quest, but he wasn't going to count on it. The whole thing might look different to her in the light of a new day. He would respect her decision whichever way it went. He just hoped she would offer him the same courtesy. In the meantime, there was still a whole lot to figure out. According to Boswell, Dante was in this thing for financial gain, but how would one gain from blowing up oil refineries and power plants? Nathan saw a few possibilities. Either with massive investments in renewable energy, short positions on fossil fuel companies, or both. Then again, so far Dante was only targeting British oil companies. It could be that he was being paid by the Saudis or the Venezuelans or any other big oil producer who wanted to sideline the competition. If money was the goal, then Dante would likely need the help of a financial expert. Hence Megan Stirling's connection? Nathan took out his phone and pulled up the website for Lange Capital.

Peering back at him was a photo of the owner Bertold Lange himself. The man appeared to be in his mid-forties, with prematurely gray hair and an easy smile. He wore a charcoal suit, white dress shirt and no tie. "What do you know about all of this, buddy?" Nathan said to himself. He clicked on Lange's bio, but there wasn't much useful there. He'd grown up in Belfast with a German father and Irish mother. His dad worked the coal mines and died at a young age due to black lung, a traumatic experience that colored the rest of Bertold's life. He vowed to make a living with his mind, not his brawn, and put himself through Trinity College Dublin, the first in his family to get a higher education. The young Bertold got his start working at an investment fund in the City of London, where he prospered as a trader and eventually set out on his own. According to the company website, Lange Capital currently handled more than 450 billion pounds worth of investor funds, specializing in an ESG portfolio, Environmental, Social and Governance. In other words, giving investors with a guilty conscience about the state of the world a place to park their funds: renewable energy, carbon capture, sustainable farming... The world was already heading in that direction, why not speed things up a little bit by funneling capital that way? It certainly might help to partner with a raving lunatic and his cult of environmental terrorists. Nathan knew exactly who he wanted to speak with next, and that was Bertold Lange.

With his phone nearly drained, Nathan located a charging cable in an outlet over the kitchen counter and plugged it in before helping himself to a second mug of coffee. He was searching the refrigerator for breakfast options when Natalia's door cracked open and she appeared in a matching set of flannel pajamas, looking sleepy. "Good morning," she said. "Sleep well?"

"Not bad. You?"

"It seems I needed it."

"Ready for some coffee?"

"Let me put some clothes on first." She closed the door. Nathan found some yogurt in the fridge and granola in the cupboard. He mixed a little of each in a bowl and was sitting at the table when Natalia reappeared, wearing jeans and a pink sweatshirt. She went straight to the French press and managed to get nearly a full cup out of it, added some milk and popped it into the microwave for thirty seconds.

"Ready to face another day of saving the world?" she said.

"I'm getting there. Are you?" Nathan was still not at all sure which way she would go.

"As ready as I'll ever be, I suppose. What's the plan? I'm sure you have one."

Nathan offered a smile. "Same as before, talk to Bertold Lange."

"We can try to track him down, but I'll bet he's not an easy man to see."

"Neither was Oscar Boswell, but we managed that."

Natalia took her coffee out of the microwave, blew across the top and took a sip. "Maybe it's good we kept the guns."

"Definitely."

"I have a Glock of my own, too, but let's keep that between us. It's not like America here, the wild west. It could get me in a lot of trouble."

"Let's just hope we don't need to use them."

"What do you think, then, just head down to the man's office and demand an audience?"

Nathan shrugged. "You have a better idea?"

"Not really. It's worth a try." Natalia took out a carton of eggs and some ham from the fridge. "We might as well start with a decent breakfast." While she cooked the eggs, they watched the BBC to catch up on the latest news. Fires were still burning throughout the city. In the meantime, raids were in progress across the greater metropolitan area as co-conspirators were dragged from their homes in handcuffs. These were everyday people, many of them insiders. They worked for the refineries and the power plants and the offices that were targeted, with the access that came with their jobs. Some had worked in these positions for years, while others were more recent hires who took the jobs for the express purpose of blowing up the premises. Nathan was fairly certain they all had one thing in common, which was membership in Dante's diabolical organization. He may have been behind it all, but there was no sign of him, nor even a mention of his name on the news broadcasts. In financial news, the London markets weren't open yet, but oil company stocks were already taking a hit worldwide.

When the eggs and ham were ready, Nathan and Natalia wolfed them down. Then she changed again into more business-friendly attire, with a white blouse and navy jacket over her jeans. Lastly, she donned a pair of black leather boots. Nathan lifted his Luger from the coffee table in the living room and slid it into his waistband behind his back, then pulled his sweater over the top. Natalia went into her bedroom and came back with her own Glock in a holster. Lifting her shirt, she strapped on the holster, with the gun nestled against her body on the left side.

"You got an extra holster?" said Nathan. "One that might fit a Luger?"

"I have one you can try, sure." She went back into the bedroom and returned with a second holster, handing it over.

Nathan slid the Luger in. Perfect. He attached the holster beneath his shirt, adjusting the straps to fit. "Come on." They headed out the door. Down on the street, the city seemed mostly back to normal with the usual traffic. Public transport was back in operation as well, but Natalia used her phone to order a cab and they rode downtown in silence.

"How is this going to work?" Natalia said as they approached the Lange Capital building. "Just go in and ask to see the man?"

"Maybe if we tell them we have a sizable investment to make? Say, as representatives of a deep-pocket Middle Eastern sovereign wealth fund? That might get us some attention."

"I could just tell them I was Megan Stirling's lawyer, that we have a few things to discuss regarding possible litigation."

"That sounds more convincing. There's nothing like the threat of a lawsuit to get somebody's attention."

When the cab pulled up at the building, they both got out. The address was a 40-story highrise in the heart of the city. Nathan noticed a heavy police presence throughout the area, with heavily armed officers at the corners and an armored police vehicle parked up the block. Walking toward the front door, Nathan spotted several men and women in business attire coming out with cardboard boxes in their arms. A potted plant poked out the top of one box. Inside the lobby was a long desk, behind which sat a concierge. Beside the desk was a security checkpoint, with armed guards manning metal detectors. "Maybe we ought to have considered this," said Natalia as they came to a halt.

Nathan took out his phone and searched for luggage storage in the general vicinity. "Luggage lockers three blocks from here, one pound fifty pence per hour." Five minutes later, they'd stored their guns in an automated locker and were back. Now they just had the concierge to get past.

"We're here to see Bertold Lange," Natalia said.

"And do you have an appointment?" The woman behind the desk peered over the tops of her reading glasses.

"I'm a lawyer representing one of his former employees."

"Either you have an appointment or you don't."

"We believe Mr. Lange might be in danger." Natalia tried a different tactic.

"In that case I suggest you contact the police."

"We think it may be a good idea to notify him personally."

"I can pass along a message. What were your names?"

Natalia looked at Nathan and they both stepped away. "What now?" she said to him.

"I don't know. I'm thinking." More employees carrying boxes came down the elevator and moved through the lobby toward the exit. Nathan stepped across to a middle-aged woman and a younger man. "What's with all of the boxes?" he asked. "Moving day?"

"I wish," said the woman.

"All they were willing to tell us was that we're being shut down," said the man.

"Who is being shut down?" Natalia asked. "Who do you work for?"

"Who *did* we work for, you mean?" said the woman. "Lange Capital. The Financial Conduct Authority is up there right now on the thirty-second floor, seizing everything they can get their hands on. Told us to pack up our personal items and get out."

"Is Bertold Lange up there?" said Natalia.

"Lange? No way. We haven't seen the man in a week."

"Any idea where he might have gone?"

"Probably his private island in the Caribbean," said the man. "Isn't that where you'd be? The rest of us, we've got bills to pay."

"I'll bet he flew off with his beloved Beatrice," said the woman.

"Who is that, his wife?" said Natalia.

"Wife? No. None of us ever laid eyes on Beatrice, but he certainly had a sweet spot for her."

"Why do you say that?" said Nathan.

"Just the things you hear, that's all."

"Thanks for your time," said Nathan. He stood back and watched as the pair made their way out of the building and on down the sidewalk.

"It seems we weren't the only ones following the money," said Natalia. "If the FCA is involved."

Nathan took a last look around. "Bertold Lange must be somewhere. We just need to find him."

"How do you suggest we do that? Fly off to the Caribbean?"

"Right now all I know is that I could use another cup of coffee. You coming?" Nathan started off across the lobby. Natalia shook her head but followed after. Ten minutes later the two of them had retrieved their guns from the locker and were sitting in a coffee shop with fresh cups of joe and a couple of pastries. Nathan was back on his phone, searching for further clues. Nothing about Lange Capital was yet in the news. The outlets were all too preoccupied with the terrorist attacks and nobody, it seemed, had connected those events with the elusive financier. At least nobody in the press. Somebody at the Financial Conduct Authority seemed to know something.

"You know, technically I'm still a law student," said Natalia. "I've got exams to consider. Classes to attend. I'm falling further behind every day. At this rate, I'll never graduate."

"And here I thought you were on summer break?"

"No, summer break is over."

"They can't expect you to go to class when the whole city is under attack. I mean, come on, if that's not a good excuse, what is?"

"What do you think, it's like a snow day?"

"Exactly, but you do what you need to do." Nathan took a big bite of a chocolate croissant and washed it down with some coffee, still hoping that what she needed to do was to see this thing through.

"None of this is getting us very far. I'm sure MI5 is already ten steps ahead. They're the ones with the resources."

"You give them that much credit?"

"Why not? There are some very competent people in that organization."

"All the same, I never trust anybody more than I trust myself."

"Out to save the world, single-handed?"

"Well, with you if you're still game. Let me poke around a little online and see what I come up with. Maybe there's something we've been missing."

"You're lucky I've got a pastry to enjoy."

"You be sure to savor it." Nathan took another look at his phone, where the image of Bertold Lange gazed back from the Lange Capital website. "Where are you hiding, Bertold?" Nathan said under his breath. He remembered a website he'd used in the past for photo searches. PimEyes, it was called. Plug in a person's photo and get results from across the web of the same individual, even in the background, in passing, at any age. Nothing was secret these days if you knew how to search. Nathan copied the pic of Lange, went to the PimEyes site and plugged it in. Moments later he was scrolling through a long list of results, one picture after another of Mr. Lange. A man of his stature had page after page of photos, some from news articles, others from charity events, and more from promotional materials. Here he was at a financial conference in New York, there he was attending a ball for the Cancer Society along with his wife. And of course, he was quite often promoting his brand of ESG investing. Nathan took a moment to look up and see how Natalia's coffee was coming along. Her mug was half full. "Still working on that?"

"If I drink it any slower it will get cold."

"We can get you a refill."

Natalia didn't answer. Instead, she took another sip. Nathan moved to the next page of results. It was more of the same, mostly. One shot that caught his interest was of Lange on the tarmac at a regional airport, with a private airplane in the background. The accompanying story was from a financial magazine, about how investing with a conscience could be profitable, never mind the irony that Lange was flying around the world in a carbon-spewing private jet. The article also showed photos of a few of Lange's residences, including the one on a private island in the Caribbean, another in the French Alps, and Lange's purported favorite of them all, an ancient castle in Scotland, near Inverness on the edge of the North Sea. An accompanying photo showed him with his wife, Alyssa, sitting at a long table in the medieval dining room. Nathan already knew the man was rich, but these shots certainly clarified the point. Lange was very, very rich, or at least he managed to live the lifestyle, by hook or by crook.

The further Nathan went through the list of results, the older were the photos. It was like going through the man's life in reverse, back to when he was just an up-and-coming trader, and before that a university student. Nathan saw Lange in his twenties with an array of different women, pre-Alyssa. He always had seemed to live large, at each stage of the game. Nobody named Beatrice appeared in any of them. The earliest shots were scanned images originally taken with film cameras. One thumbnail from this period caught Nathan's interest. It was a group of men in blue coveralls with hard hats on their heads.

When he clicked on this photo, the image enlarged and he saw that it was taken on an oil-drilling platform. These were workers, four in all, taking time out from the job for a group photo. It was taken by a photographer from the Glasgow Independent newspaper to accompany an article about the oil industry in the North Sea. Even under a blue hardhat, Nathan recognized the young Bertold Lange. Beside him was another familiar face. Nathan had to read the caption to make sure, but there it was plain as day. Third from the left was a young man named Collin Bruce.

"Take a look at this." Nathan held the photo out.

"Well," Natalia replied, still capable of being surprised. "That's something."

Nathan took the phone back and read the article. It didn't say anything particularly useful, but what Nathan did understand was that these two went way back. Whatever their current plan, they'd probably hatched it together. Find one of them and you would very likely find the other. But where were they hiding? Nathan cropped out everything but the face of Collin Bruce and plugged that into the software. A whole new set of results popped up, tracing the adult life of the cult leader.

"What do you see?" said Natalia.

"Nothing much yet." Nathan scrolled through the photos until he saw another shot with Lange's private plane in the background. This one was Collin Bruce and two young women in bikinis, arm-in-arm and smiling on a tropical runway somewhere, with palm trees in the background. He showed it to Natalia. "Here's our man, off saving the world. Maybe at Lange's Caribbean getaway?"

Natalia looked at this photo but had nothing to add.

"Any idea who the women are?" Nathan asked.

"No. What about that plane?"

"It's Lange's."

"How do you know?"

"It showed up before, in another article about the man. Look at the tail number. G-BLNG. G stands for UK registry. BLNG must be Bertold Lange."

"You know this information is public. Flight plans, too. One can track these things."

"Let's see what we can see." Nathan searched the tail number. It didn't take long to find a social media page, run by a bored teenager who posted this kind of information on the private planes of the rich and powerful as a political statement of some sort. This included all recent flight plans along with charts detailing comings and goings of the world's wealthiest people. The most recent listing for G-BLNG was from just the day before. Nathan clicked on a link and was shown the flight path, from Luton just outside London to Inverness in the north of Scotland. "Lange is at his castle."

"Let me see."

Nathan showed her the phone again and Natalia took it in. "A castle will be well defended," she said. "A couple of pistols are not going to do the trick."

"Agreed. We'd need weapons, and we'd need help."

"Or we could pass this information along," said Natalia. "Like normal civilians."

"We aren't normal civilians. You know what will happen. They'll cut us out."

"Is that so bad?"

"What happens if they sit on it? Lange has a private plane. Twenty-four hours from now, he could be anywhere in the world."

"What are you implying we do here, exactly?"

"If we want to have agency, we need to act fast."

"You can't be suggesting we team up with the mobsters?" she scoffed. "I thought you had a moral code!"

"It's a marriage of convenience, sure, but we can help each other."

Natalia didn't like it, not at all, but Nathan knew the one thing he had in his favor on this was the same thing that motivated himself. If anybody was going to take down Collin Bruce and Bertold Lange, neither Nathan nor Natalia wanted to sit idly by on the sidelines.

Nathan leaned back in his chair to finish his coffee. "Just do me one favor, please? Try not to shoot Finbar Murphy until this whole thing is over."

"I'm not making any promises."

"No, somehow I didn't think you would..."

Chapter Nineteen

Nathan had to give credit where credit was due, Oscar Boswell was well organized. The mob boss didn't hesitate to put a team together and by the following morning, Nathan and Natalia were meeting up with their collaborators at a warehouse in the north of London. They arrived not knowing quite what to expect. A ride share dropped them off in the pre-dawn hours under a streetlamp in a commercial district. The area was just coming to life for the day, with delivery trucks rumbling past.

"If this goes wrong at all, my law career is finished," said Natalia.

"Your career is probably the last thing you need to worry about. Just remember, these guys are on our side in this, all right?"

"I'll try."

Nathan wasn't particularly encouraged by this response, but it was too late to argue the point. Instead, they headed up the block until they came to a gate, guarded by two burly men in dark sport coats, dressed as though they shopped at Thugs-R-Us. "We're here for Boswell," Nathan said.

The men looked Nathan and Natalia over, then stepped aside. "He's expecting you."

Nathan held out one hand and Natalia went through first. They passed across a gravel tarmac and came to a large warehouse door, open just a crack. Another man stood here, but he moved aside without a word. No frisking the new arrivals, the mobsters seemed to accept that Nathan and Natalia would be armed. Inside, Nathan saw stacks of crates along with three vehicles, a black Mercedes Sprinter van, a dark blue Jeep Grand Cherokee, and a green Aston Martin. Standing near the van was Oscar Boswell himself, overseeing a small knot of his underlings. Beside him was Finbar Murphy. Nathan half expected Natalia to shoot the man on sight, despite her promises to the contrary, but she behaved herself for now. Busy loading the van were three men and a woman.

"Good morning," said Nathan.

"Is it?" said the mob boss.

"For a hunting expedition? Sure, why not? What supplies have you got for us?" Nathan and Finbar eyed each other with equal parts distrust and disdain. Common enemies made for strange bedfellows. Nathan moved forward to peek into the van, where a pair of long, wooden crates were stored.

"Go ahead," Boswell said to one of his underlings. "Show 'em."

The underling climbed into the van and took the lid off the first crate to reveal a cache of military assault rifles that Nathan recognized as AK-47s. A few of them had grenade launchers attached beneath the barrel.

"Not bad," said Nathan.

"What's in the other one?" said Natalia.

The man smiled and took the lid off the second crate to reveal clips of ammo for the Kalashnikovs, grenades for the launchers and multiple blocks of C4 explosive, along with boxes of detonators. After lifting out one of several plastic cases, the man flipped up a latch and swung open the top to reveal a pair of night vision goggles.

"We got some vests for you boys, too, in case you plan on coming back in one piece," said Boswell.

"Boys?" the other woman said with a sneer.

"Don't take it wrong, Wanda. You're one 'o the boys to me."

Wanda scoffed. She was a few years older than Natalia, maybe late twenties, and wearing a black leather motorcycle jacket with lots of zippers. Her hair was dark and curly, held back in a ponytail. Black eyeliner gave her a Goth appearance, but it was the look in her eyes themselves that suggested a brewing insanity. This woman was dangerous, no doubt about it. With a van-load of assault rifles and grenades? Nathan could only hope she wasn't a loose cannon. As for Finbar Murphy, he hadn't said a word nor did he seem inclined to.

"How long will the drive take?" Nathan asked Boswell.

"Ten hours, give or take. Best to stick to the speed limit, keep a low profile and all. We wouldn't want you stopped along the way."

"You're not coming?"

"Me?" Boswell laughed.

"The boss don't like to get his hands dirty," Finbar finally spoke.

"I can't say I blame you," Nathan said to Boswell.

"Enough o' this gabbin'," Boswell clapped his hands together and looked at his watch. "Time to move it out!"

"You heard the man," said Finbar. The last of the vests were loaded into the van and Wanda took her place in the driver's seat, with Finbar in the passenger seat by her side.

"You two ride with us," said one of the other men before climbing behind the wheel of the Jeep.

"Good luck," said Boswell.

"Thanks," Nathan replied. The last man on the team took the front passenger seat in the Jeep and Nathan got in the back with Natalia. The door to the warehouse was opened wide and they headed out, Jeep in the lead with the van right behind. Nathan checked his watch. It was 4:38 a.m., which meant if all went smoothly, they'd arrive in the middle of the afternoon on a summer day in Scotland, where the sun wouldn't set until close to 10 p.m. They were leaving most of the planning in the hands of a bunch of organized criminals. With his Army officer experience, Nathan was used to calling the shots in these types of combat situations. Trust in these mobsters would be hard in coming, but he did his best to set his anxieties aside. First things first. They'd find Lange, and hopefully Dante. It would all be more or less winging it from there. "Who's in charge of this whole operation, by the way?" Nathan wanted some clarity.

"That'd be Murphy," said the driver.

"Isn't he a contract guy?" said Natalia. "Not a made man, like you say?"

The driver looked her over in the rear-view mirror, tension permeating the air. "The boss says we listen to Murphy. That's it."

"We listen to Murphy, then," said Nathan.

The front passenger switched on the radio, tuning in a pop music station. That was the end of the conversation. The driver navigated to the M1 motorway, north toward Birmingham as the eastern sky glowed with the start of the new day. If all went well, a whole lot would go down before it set once more. Questions answered, retribution delivered. For the time being, however, all they could do was settle in for the ride.

Nathan still didn't know the names of the driver and his partner and didn't plan to ask, but he'd already taken their measure. They both came across as your average, garden-variety thug. That meant they'd probably suffered traumatic childhoods, grown up in poverty and roamed the streets as young men, bullying any kid who got in their way. It was a progression from juvenile delinquent to time in the slammer, until they were effectively unemployable to anybody besides a man like Boswell.

Working for him was a major promotion from penny-ante thievery. This was the life they were born into. Some men in their position managed to escape it, but these were not those men. The driver was stocky and short, bald on top and a little bit older than his partner, maybe late thirties. In Nathan's mind, he dubbed this one *Baldy*. The passenger was tall and thin, with a gold necklace hanging on his chest and black tattoos on the side of his neck. This one was perhaps mid-twenties and Nathan dubbed him *Skinny*. Riding north with them on the motorway felt like some sort of strange field trip. When push came to shove, relying on each other would be the only way to succeed. He looked to Natalia, hoping that she fully accepted this same reality. What he saw beside him was a woman whose life had gone dramatically downhill since he'd arrived. First, her internship ended with a brutal murder, then her relationship unraveled, and now she was heading off on a vigilante crusade with armed mobsters, the man who'd killed her client, and the man she'd cheated on her boyfriend with. The look on her face conveyed it all, but then her eyes narrowed and Nathan saw that steely expression he'd witnessed years earlier, when they'd gone after another hardened criminal together on the Adriatic Sea. That was where he'd seen what she was capable of, and it reminded him that when it came to Natalia Nicolaeva, he had nothing to worry about. There was nobody on earth he'd trust more in the face of danger, and that included some of the extraordinary men he'd served with in the Rangers. This woman was in nearly every way their equal, mentally and physically. Maybe she didn't have their strength, but she knew how to fight, could operate any weapons system that was handed to her, and was smart and determined. Nathan would go into combat with her any time. As for the emotional side of the equation, she'd handle that as well. Ammon, it seemed, was already a thing of the past. Maybe this current excursion was part of the process of moving on with her life.

Four hours into their journey, the two vehicles pulled over for a pit stop outside of Manchester. They parked in front of a roadside restaurant where they could keep an eye on the van. The four mobsters sat at one table, Nathan and Natalia at another. Nobody said much. They ate quickly, downed some coffee, and were on their way. It was on this next leg that Skinny began to get a little chatty. He switched the radio off and attempted to entice Baldy into some conversation.

"You been up this far before?" said Skinny.

Baldy shot him a disparaging glance.

"Scotland, I mean," Skinny was not deterred. "You been to Scotland?"

"Of course I been to fuckin' Scotland, what you take me for? I'm a man of the world."

"I'm just sayin'..." Skinny was ashamed. "It don't mean nothin', just 'cause I ain't been to Scotland."

"You ain't never left the city, have you?"

"Sure, I left the city."

"Where?"

"Pentonville."

"First of all, Pentonville ain't outta the city, and second, lockup don't count."

Skinny was even further discouraged, but then he turned to the rear, hoping for support. "How 'bout you guys, you been up here?"

"Sure," said Natalia. "Never to Inverness. I went to the festival once, in Edinburgh, the Fringe."

"I've traveled all over the world," said Nathan. "But I must admit, never to Scotland."

This answer gave Skinny the confidence he was looking for. "See?" he said to Baldy. "The man ain't never been to Scotland. Just 'cause I ain't been here don't mean nothin'."

"We ain't in Scotland yet," said Baldy.

"Where does it start? I want to know when we get there."

"You'll see the sign," said Natalia. "On the side of the road. We still have a few hours to go."

"This is England, still?" said Skinny.

"Yes, it is."

"Goes a long way, don't it?"

"The empire used to stretch all the way around the world," said Nathan. "India, Australia, Africa, New Guinea..."

Skinny took this information in with awe. Watching his reaction, Nathan's impression of the kid softened. Here was a paid assassin, hired gun for a mobster, yet despite the dreariness of that profession he still hadn't lost his boyish enthusiasm, his joy in the small wonders of life. Nathan envied the kid in some measure. Did Nathan still find that joy? He was struck by how long it had been since he'd considered the question. Life weighed on Nathan, too, but he did find joy. Where? It was the simple things, as well. Working on the renovation project of his little cottage in France, putting the finishing touches on a piece of furniture he'd created from a few blocks of wood, spending time with those friends he had left in this world, and yes, family when he was able to manage it. These were the things that gave his life meaning. Perhaps clearer at this moment were not those things he appreciated in life, but what was missing. He looked at Natalia there beside him and a pang of responsibility hit him. He'd told himself that he was chasing after Dante, and Lange also, because it was the right thing to do. That was true in part, but it wasn't the full picture, not nearly. Nathan was also here because he wanted Natalia Nicolaeva in his life, in whatever measure he could manage. Sharing this vendetta was the only way he currently knew how to keep that going. At this realization, he was hit by a wave of guilt, though she'd made her own decision in the end. Natalia did still have such a thing as free will. Nathan couldn't blame himself entirely. Besides, he needed to put these thoughts aside and keep his head in the game. Nathan needed to focus on the task at hand. He settled back into his seat and did his best to shift to a battlefield mentality. This was war they were heading toward and he had to be prepared.

Two hours later, they crossed the Scottish border south of Gretna Green. Skinny's face lit up as he spotted a large blue sign with a white St. Andrew's Cross. Written across the top were the words, *Welcome to Scotland.* "There it is." Skinny was filled with wonder. Even Baldy seemed taken in by the younger man's innocence, refraining from any belittling remarks.

"There it is," Natalia confirmed.

Despite Nathan's intentions, even Baldy was starting to feel like an actual human being. Mob assassins were people, too, at least this pair. He wasn't sure about the occupants of the van following behind them.

The vehicles stopped again for fuel near Glasgow and the occupants got out to stretch their legs, use the restrooms, and buy some snacks. Walking into the mini-mart, Nathan looked up to see a CCTV camera staring back. If and when this whole expedition went wrong, he'd be directly tied to the organized criminals behind it. His fate was their fate and vice versa. They were all in this together, no doubt about it. Natalia followed him into the store and went to a cooler in the back to pick out a sports drink, then chose a bag of mixed nuts. Nathan grabbed a soda and some crisps. Back outside, they sat at a picnic table some distance from the others as Wanda fueled up the van.

"What's the problem?" Natalia asked as she twisted the cap off her drink.

"What do you mean?"

"Something is bothering you."

Nathan removed his cap and took a drink of soda. "You mean aside from the obvious?"

"You tell me."

Was Nathan so easy to read, he wondered? He seemed to be, at least to Natalia. "I feel like it's my fault that you're here. Tracking these guys down isn't your responsibility."

Natalia laughed. "And is it yours?"

"I guess I wasn't cut out for retirement. I need a little excitement from time to time, to know I'm still alive."

"How's that working so far?"

"I ought to take up a quieter hobby."

"Anything in mind?"

"I don't know, I've been hearing a lot lately about this thing called pickleball. Could be fun, I guess."

"Good luck with that. As far as why I'm here, don't worry, it has nothing to do with you."

"Why are you, then? Do you even know?"

As Natalia sat here at a picnic table in front of a Scottish petrol station off the M73 motorway, she gave her best effort to understanding it herself. "Running away, I suppose."

"From what?"

Natalia shook her head. "Everything the world says we should want."

"What are you going to do, then, throw that all away, everything you've built?"

"I haven't worked that out."

"You'll finish law school, right?"

"Do I have to think about this now?"

"No. Never mind, forget it."

"Live in the present. No future, no past."

"Just make sure you kill the bad guys. Their bad guys, not our bad guys."

"I'll try to keep it straight."

"That's what you keep telling me."

Over at the van, Wanda topped off the tank and replaced the handle on the pump, then looked around and motioned for the others. "Let's move out!"

Nathan finished his crisps, downed the last of his soda and followed Natalia back to the Jeep. Climbing in once more, he checked his watch. Three more hours and they'd be pulling into Inverness. Lange's castle was on the water out past Nairn, twenty minutes further. If all went well, they'd be face-to-face with him soon enough. Until then, Nathan settled in for the ride, thinking about how uncannily similar he and Natalia were, both chasing after intangibles that neither one could ever quite put a finger on, trying to find satisfaction through bending the world to their will through sheer determination. No wonder Ammon Hanan didn't stand a chance. Nathan wasn't likely to fare much better. First, they needed to get through this ordeal and come out the other end, alive and well. The rest could be sorted out later. Tonight it was all about bringing some measure of justice to the world.

Chapter Twenty

A hilltop vantage point roughly one kilometer from Lange's castle complex gave the team an overview. It was more of a large stone manor house than an actual castle, three stories high with a steeply sloping roof and a single square turret extending up from one corner. Paned-glass windows overlooked immaculate gardens on all sides, including a courtyard between two wings. A sloping lawn led down toward the sea, where a single speedboat was tied up to a dock. To the left of the main house were what looked to be a four-car garage, garden house, and storage shed, and beyond them all, a flat section of grass where a helicopter was parked. Somebody was at home, no doubt about that. Nathan eyed it all with a pair of binoculars. He could see two men with rifles on top of the turret. Two more were stationed down below, just outside the front door. The whole complex was surrounded by a six-foot-thick hedge, maybe ten feet high, with one opening for the driveway. Outside the hedge, fallow fields stretched roughly a hundred yards, ending in a wooded area. Nathan handed the binoculars to Finbar beside him. "What do you think?"

"Could be worse."

"Maybe we need a catapult." Skinny tried to make light of the situation.

"With barrels of hot oil," Baldy agreed.

"Come on, boys, don't be glum," said Wanda. "We just need to get creative, that's all."

"You got any ideas?" said Baldy.

"I always got ideas. Send me in there with a torn blouse and I'll have control of the place in ten minutes flat. They'll never know what hit 'em."

"You'd never get a weapon past them," said Nathan.

"Wanda is a weapon in her own right," said Baldy.

"What's your grand idea?" Wanda complained. "We're all of us eager to hear."

Nathan reached out a hand for the binoculars. "Let me take another look." Finbar passed them back and Nathan scanned the property again, focusing on the garage, where one door was open and a blue Lamborghini could be seen poking out. Further over, a man emerged from the garden shed wearing brown coveralls and a wide-brimmed straw hat. He held a long wand in one hand and on his back was a metal canister. The man proceeded to walk the garden, spraying the flower beds with a fine mist. "One of us could impersonate a gardener," said Nathan. "If we could get our hands on some coveralls."

"You lot are brilliant," said Finbar.

"I got another one," said Baldy. "We wait until sundown, shoot out whatever floodlights they got and storm the place with night vision. They'll be blind without it."

"How do you know they don't have it themselves?" said Natalia.

Baldy shrugged. "Chance we gotta take."

"The sun don't set for six more hours," said Finbar. "By then the moon will be up."

"Why'd we bring the goggles, then?"

"Here's the plan," Finbar was fed up. "We sneak up to that hedge, blast our way through, and then full-frontal assault, guns blazing. We'll catch 'em flat-footed and take 'em out before they know what's happenin'."

"I appreciate your boldness," said Nathan.

"What about them two up top?" said Skinny.

"Ain't that what the grenade launchers are for?" said Wanda.

"That's a tough shot," said Nathan. "Lobbing one up and over the wall without over-shooting it. One in a million."

"What do you know?" Wanda continued.

"Eight years in the Army, I know my way around a grenade launcher," said Nathan.

Finbar put his fingers to his chin, trying to determine how much he trusted this American. "I reckon I could make it."

"You expect us to give you a weapons course first?" said Nathan. "Do you even know how to fire the thing?"

Finbar ignored these questions, turning to the others. "We'll leave the Jeep here and park the van off the main road, then make our way through the forest on foot."

"We'd better gear up first," said Natalia.

Finbar swung open the rear doors to the van and Baldy passed out the bullet-proof vests. After donning them, the team divvied up the weapons. Nathan was handed one of the AK-47s with a grenade launcher attached. He picked up a 40mm grenade from a box and loaded the launcher, then took two more grenades and slid them into pockets on his vest. Finbar picked up an identical weapon and looked it over, trying to hide his uncertainty. He lifted one of the grenades and tried to slide it into the launch tube, backward.

"Hey, hey, careful with that!" Natalia called out. "You're putting it in the wrong way!"

Anger burned in Finbar's eyes as he turned to Natalia. "And what do *you* know about it, Missy?"

"What you're holding in your hands is a GP-25 Kostyor. It fires a 40 mm VOG-25 grenade, arming range fifteen meters, fuse self-destruction time fifteen seconds. That's a fragmentation grenade, with a lethal radius of six meters."

"So you know some statistics," said Finbar. "That don't prove nothin'."

Natalia grabbed the weapon out of his hands, took a grenade and properly loaded it before handing the gun back.

"I told you," Nathan said to Finbar. "She knows her shit."

The Irishman looked the weapon over, trying to figure out how it worked. He wasn't about to ask Natalia for a lesson. Instead, he handed it back to her. "I don't need grenades." He took one of the other rifles. "Bullets do just fine."

Natalia slid two grenades into her pockets as well, and then she and Nathan used their third pocket for an extra magazine each.

"We got any comms?" said Nathan.

"What's comms?" said Baldy.

"Radios," said Natalia.

"No comms," said Finbar.

"Let's just try not to shoot at each other, then, all right?" said Natalia.

"You people are a pain in my ass," said Finbar. Everybody piled into the van, with the Irishman behind the wheel.

"You ready for this?" Nathan said to Natalia. Her demeanor was focused, intense, the likes of which he hadn't seen since the last time they'd gone into battle together. She didn't answer his question but he knew that Natalia was dialed in to whatever place she needed to be when the situation called for it. Whatever worries he had about her safety, he had to let pass. They would have each other's backs, as best they could. It only took ten minutes until Nathan heard the tires crunching on gravel and they pulled to a stop.

"Showtime," said Finbar. The doors swung open and everyone exited the vehicle. It was late afternoon in a Scottish summer, which meant overcast and cool. The van was parked right up at the edge of the forest. Everyone made another quick check of their weapons and Baldy grabbed a block of C4 and detonators, just in case. He slid the block into a pocket and handed a second one to Wanda.

"I don't think you want to wear that on the outside of your armor," said Nathan.

"Mind your business," said Wanda.

"I'm just saying..."

"I said shut it, Captain America!" She put the block into her vest pocket and walked away.

"Fine." Nathan raised his hands in the air, then leaned close to Natalia. "Try not to stand too close to those two."

Natalia didn't like this setup any more than he did, having put their faith in a bunch of untrained morons. Nathan worried about innocent bystanders, like the gardener or the servants, but whatever the outcome, he and Natalia were all in. The group set off through the forest with Finbar in the lead. It didn't take long before they'd passed through the wooded strip and were facing the open field. From here it was 100 yards of bare ground between them and the line of hedges. Over the top Nathan saw the roof of the house, along with the square turret rising from the far side. Anybody watching from there could spot them, too, but at the moment he saw nobody. The assault team spread out in a line at the edge of the trees, ten feet apart. On Finbar's call, they started across the field, running at a rapid clip. The fastest sprinters in the world could make this 100-yard dash in less than ten seconds, but in bullet-proof vests and carrying assault rifles, it would take three times that. With every step, Nathan expected shots to ring out. They were halfway across when this expectation was fulfilled. He heard the pop, pop, pop of automatic weapons fire and saw clods of dirt kicking up into the air around him. Continuing forward, it was only a few steps more before he was hidden from view by the hedge. Nathan dove to the ground. Looking back, he saw that everybody had made it this far but Skinny, who was down in the field. The man rolled onto his stomach and began to crawl as incoming fire peppered the ground around him. Inch by inch, he moved ahead until he, too, was hidden from view.

"Yo, man, you shot?" Baldy called to him.

Skinny sucked in air, unable to speak.

"Those mothers got him in the vest," Wanda replied.

Rolling onto his back, Skinny tried to figure out if he was bleeding. What Nathan wanted to know was why the shooting had stopped. Bullets could pierce a hedge, but from this vantage point he saw a ten-foot-high stone wall inside it. They were protected here, but would need to keep moving. Finding a way inside the compound without getting shot was going to be exceptionally challenging.

"You good to move?" Finbar said to Skinny.

"Good..." Skinny wheezed.

More shots rang out as the team scrambled up and to their left along the outside of the wall. Fifty yards down the line, it turned a corner, 90 degrees. They continued along until they came to a wooden door inside the hedge, narrow with an arched top. This would have been installed for gardeners, or field workers, as access to the outer property. Nathan pulled on a heavy iron ring, but the door was locked tight. It would be light work for the AK-47. He aimed his gun. "I'll go through first. The rest of you guys back me up."

"Guys?" said Wanda. "Once again, I guess that leaves me out."

Nathan had no time for pithy jousting. He was focused on what he might find on the other side of this door. Anybody armed would be fair game, especially the men in that tower.

Gardeners would not. He pulled his trigger and fired off a few rounds, blasting an ancient iron lock and splintering the wood around it. One hard kick shifted the door a few feet. A second one and it swung open. What Nathan saw was a short tunnel on the other side leading the rest of the way through the hedge, maybe six feet long. He moved inside, rifle pointed straight ahead. Peeking around the far edge, he had a momentary glimpse of the house, including three men currently in the turret, as well as two more at ground level, all armed with rifles. Those were just the ones he'd spotted. He was met with shouts and gunfire as he quickly backed out, bullets whizzing past him. "Hey Baldy, give me a block of that C4!" he called out.

"You talkin' to me?!" the man replied. Nathan still didn't know his actual name.

"I'm talking to you, toss it over!"

If Baldy was miffed at this nickname, he wasn't in any position to show it. "I told you we might need it," he said instead, pulling out the plastic explosive and throwing it to Nathan. "You know how these detonators work?" He fumbled with a box of them.

"Don't bother."

Nathan heard a handful of adversaries moving across the garden and firing as they went. More were likely to flank them from outside the wall at any time. Nathan reached for the brick, lifted it up and then got to his feet in a low crouch. Taking a step back and lining himself up, he slung the brick through the tunnel as hard as he could with a sidearm toss. It skipped and slid across the lawn and came to a rest in a flowerbed halfway to the house. Lowering himself to a prone position, he pointed the rifle at the block. Lange's men stopped firing. Nathan couldn't tell where they were in the garden exactly, but they'd have seen the brick come through.

208

"We can't stay here!" said Finbar.

"This is our best way in," Nathan countered. "On my lead."

"I say we try the driveway!"

Nathan looked to Natalia. "You with me?"

"Of course," she replied.

He took aim again at the C4, lining the block up in his sights. "Here goes nothing." Nathan pulled the trigger, firing a single shot. The round hit home. The entire block went up in a blinding explosion, shaking the ground beneath them. Nathan ducked his head as debris rained down, but before the smoke cleared he was on his feet, charging through the tunnel and not stopping until he'd raced across the garden to press himself close to the wall of the house in the middle of the courtyard, out of sight from the turret. Natalia was a step behind, joining him against the bricks. Twenty yards away, two adversaries in the garden were splayed out on the ground. Dead? Nathan couldn't tell, but he and Natalia had the same thought. It was best to make sure. Both fired their AKs, first at one of the men and then the other.

"What about our mobsters?" Natalia looked back to the tunnel in the hedge but there was no sign of them.

"I guess we're learning what they're made of," said Nathan. From here, the wall of the house went up three stories to the slanted roof, with the square turret on the opposite side of the building. That meant Nathan and Natalia were shielded from anybody in the tower, but beside them on either side were the wings of the house, with windows on all floors.

"What did you say was the arming distance on these VOG-25s?" Nathan asked.

"I don't actually know," she answered. "It varies, from ten to forty meters, depending on the series."

"I guess we'll take our chances, then." Nathan pointed his weapon at a ground-floor window ten yards away and fired a grenade right through it. He and Natalia moved to press themselves against the stone exterior just beneath it. In his head, Nathan counted down the seconds from fifteen, an eternity in this situation. Three, two one, *boom!* The grenade went off and exploded outwards into the garden, blowing glass and debris past them. Nathan rose to peer through the shattered window. What he saw was a room filled with gilded furniture torn to pieces, one couch on fire, and a man with a rifle on the floor, lifeless in the middle of it all. The sill was four feet off the ground. Nathan hoisted Natalia up and through it first. He handed up his gun and she pulled him in next.

"That's three down that we can confirm," she said.

"But we don't know how many there are. Could be two more, could be ten."

"What about Lange?" she said. "And Dante. We don't even know that they're here."

"They'd better be." Nathan moved to a nearby doorway and peered around the edge. Nobody else was in sight, so he moved through and into a large den, complete with an enormous fireplace. Without a pause, he kept going. The pair of them combed the ground floor, but it was all eerily quiet. On the opposite side of a main entryway, a staircase rose upwards.

"We ought to check the tower," Natalia said.

Nathan agreed and up they went. On the third floor, the stairs continued no further, so they made their way down a hallway until they came to a door, slightly ajar, with another set of stairs visible inside. "This is it," he whispered.

"Who goes first?"

Nathan quickly reloaded his grenade launcher and then led the way up a narrow staircase, pointing his rifle straight ahead, finger on the trigger. Around and around they went until he came to a landing at the top and found the turret… empty. "Nobody is here," he said in disbelief.

"That can't be," Natalia replied.

Nathan moved further inside. Here he was, standing at the top of the turret with a 360-degree view of the property, and not a soul was in sight. Natalia came to his side.

"Where'd they go?" she said.

"Maybe they have a safe room."

"No!" she pointed. "There!"

Nathan followed her arm to see three figures hurrying across the lawn, but only for a split second before they disappeared behind the garden house, too quickly to identify. The helicopter was hidden from view behind a stand of trees, but this group would be headed straight for it. "Come on!" Nathan bolted to the stairway and on down as fast as he could go, to the ground floor and out the front door. They'd only taken a few steps when they heard the whirling of rotors. Halfway to the garden house, they spotted the helicopter rising into the air on the other side. Nathan got a few shots off, but they had no effect on this moving target as the helicopter flew off across the sea, disappearing into the distance along with any hope Nathan had of putting an end to this thing once and for all.

Chapter Twenty-One

With the danger at bay, the mobsters summoned the courage to show themselves again, trying to act as though they'd been in the thick of it all along instead of hiding out like cowards behind the garden wall. With nobody shooting at them any longer, the team broke into pairs and swept the rest of the house, rounding up whoever they could find. In the end, that included four servants in uniform, the gardener, a gray-haired woman in designer clothes and gold jewelry, and the man Dante had referred to as Martin, whom Nathan had seen at the One Tower bombing and then again at the pub, with his hand-made clothing and bowl-cut hairdo. The woman he recognized from photos as Alyssa Lange, the wife of Bertold. Nathan opted to question them in isolation, one at a time. It was less likely that the servants would know anything, so he started with Martin, who seemed to be a trusted assistant to Dante. While the mobsters guarded the bulk of the group in the living room, Nathan peeled Martin away and brought him into a smaller den, seating him in a plush leather chair. Joining the interrogation were Natalia and Finbar.

Given everything that had just gone down, the young man was surprisingly calm. His demeanor was that of a person slightly annoyed by this inconvenience, not somebody in fear for his life. Nathan decided to put a scare into him, pointing his gun at Martin's forehead. "You're going to tell us everything we want to know," he started. "Or this will be the last day of your life on this planet that you're so eager to save."

"Go ahead, shoot me," the young man replied. "I'm not telling you a thing."

Finbar lunged forward, grabbed Martin by the shirt and lifted him up. "I say we beat it out of him. A whiny little shit like this, he'll be spillin' in no time."

"Try it," said Martin.

Finbar shoved him back into the chair and cracked the kid across the jaw with his fist.

"It seems that Dante left you behind," said Nathan. "I guess you didn't make the cut, huh? Tell us where he went."

Blood ran down Martin's chin as he slumped in the chair, looking slightly defeated for the first time, but he said nothing.

"Your boss abandoned you to a pack of hired killers," Nathan added. "What kind of loyalty is that? He left you to die, plain and simple. You owe him nothing."

"Why bother flapping your lips? If you're going to kill me, just get it over with."

This time Finbar threw the kid out of the chair and onto the floor before viciously kicking at him. Martin curled up into a ball, trying to deflect the blows until Natalia stepped in to separate them. "Enough!" she said. Finbar glared at her but backed off, his blood lust only temporarily quenched. Natalia checked the kid, and then lifted him back into the chair. Maybe she could try a version of the good-cop, bad-cop routine. She leaned in close. "Don't make this harder than it has to be," she said. The young man looked at her with his head tilted to one side. It appeared that he might say something after all, but instead he pursed his lips and spat a spray of blood across her face. Natalia stepped back, wiping her cheek with one hand. "Maybe we ought to try the wife."

"Good idea." Nathan dragged the kid to the living room and returned with Mrs. Lange, plopping her into the same leather chair. In contrast to Martin, she was terrified, though doing her best not to show it.

"Good afternoon, Mrs. Lange," said Natalia, trying the soft approach to start with. "We have some questions for you. All we want is answers."

"We store no valuables in this house. I'm afraid you're going to be disappointed."

"We're not after money," said Nathan. "We're after answers. Tell us where your husband went."

"Why, so you can track him down and kill him? What has he done to deserve this?"

"You tell us where he went, we'll let you go," said Finbar. "Otherwise, it's not looking good for you, if I'm going to be honest."

"I can identify each and every one of you. There is no way you'll let me go, under those circumstances. We all know I'm going to die here tonight, no matter what I say."

Mrs. Lange had a point, to a degree. So far only gunmen were dead, while attempting to protect a ruthless cult leader and his putative financier, but it was still going to be difficult to explain this all away. Killing Alyssa Lange, however, would seal their criminal fate. Nathan and Natalia would join the mobsters in going down with this ship. "Look, we're not going to kill you. We're not even going to harm you." As Nathan spoke these words, he glared at Finbar. "We only want to know what your husband is up to."

"You think I know anything about that? I prefer *not* to know. I'm wise enough to steer clear of it all. If he's done something to harm you people in any way, I'm sorry about that, but I have no inside information. No information at all."

"Tell me this," said Natalia. "I know it isn't an easy question, but does Mr. Lange have a mistress?"

Mrs. Lange allowed herself to laugh at this one. "Of course! Many of them, over the years. It's part of our agreement. I don't ask about his mistresses and he doesn't tell me where the money comes from. As long as it keeps coming. That's the deal."

"What about Beatrice?" Natalia pushed. "Who is she?"

"Beatrice?" Mrs. Lange offered a sly smile. "You're kidding, right?"

"Do we look like we're kidding?" said Nathan.

"Beatrice is not a woman! At least not one Bertold ever met."

"What do you mean?" said Nathan.

Mrs. Lange raised a hand and pointed across the room. On the far wall was a map of some sort, framed. Nathan walked across to take a closer look. It wasn't a map, it was a nautical chart. On the left side was the coast of Scotland, with the inlet north of Inverness extending out into the North Sea. Reefs and shoals were marked with numbers indicating water depths. A curving boundary of double lines marked a large section of water, along with symbols that appeared to represent oil platforms. A label was printed in blue text. *Beatrice Oil Field*.

"What does your husband have to do with this?" Nathan pressed.

"That field was his first big investment. He made a killing when it sold to BP a few years later. Where do you think the money for this summer home came from?"

"Summer home?" said Finbar. "It's a damned castle!"

"Tell me, Mrs. Lange, did your husband ever work on those rigs, back in his early days?"

"We never much talked about his early days."

To Nathan, the answer to this question didn't matter. What did matter was that he knew exactly where Bertold Lange was headed, and Dante with him. "They're going for the platforms," he said to the others.

Natalia joined Nathan by the chart. "What platforms?"

Nathan placed his finger on the spot. "Their next target."

Taking it in, Natalia narrowed her eyes. "You think they intend to blow them up?"

"Why not? They've attacked every other piece of oil infrastructure that they can manage."

"But the environmental damage that would cause..." Natalia marveled at the very idea. "This entire coast would be covered in oil!"

"It's all a calculated piece in their grand plan."

Before Natalia could respond, they heard the cavitations of another helicopter, only this one sounded louder and larger than the last. "What is that?"

Finbar moved to the nearest window and peered upwards. "This don't look good."

Nathan joined the Irishman's side to see the familiar shape of an Aérospatiale SA 330 Puma approaching from the southwest. This was a Royal Air Force transport helicopter, capable of carrying up to 20 troops. Instead of the financier they were looking for, they'd find a house full of armed mobsters, a law student, a retired American spy, and a clutch of hostages. The situation was already complicated enough. It was about to get much, much worse. The helicopter hovered over the garden and Nathan saw four lines drop to the ground, followed by soldiers in full combat gear descending onto the lawn. "Everybody, down on the ground, take cover!" Nathan shifted to his left, to one side of the window. Natalia joined him while Finbar took the opposite side. Mrs. Lange just sat up straight in her chair, trying to get a better look.

"They're special operations," Nathan told Natalia. "I think this party is over."

"Not over, no. Just getting started." Finbar raised his weapon in the air, shifted in front of the window and fired off a burst, shattering the glass. Nathan couldn't see what was happening outside from his position, but he heard the sound of a mounted 7.62 mm machine gun opening up with a rat-a-tat-tat. The Irishman was thrown backward, torn to pieces as the rounds shattered everything in the line of fire. Nathan and Natalia ducked even lower, still protected by the stone wall, but there was nothing to do here but throw down their arms and surrender. It was either that or engage a group of British Royal Marines, or whatever these forces were. Taking out any of them would amount to murder in cold blood, treason against the king. A gallows would be their fate, if they survived the battle.

"What do we do?" said Natalia.

"Abandon our weapons and search for some way out."

"What way out? There is no way out!"

"We don't know until we try." Nathan kept his holstered Luger but left the rifle behind as he crawled on hands and knees across the room, keeping low as he headed for the nearest door. On the way, he passed the body of Mrs. Lange, her corpse twisted in a knot on the floor, eyes wide open and with blood running from her nose and mouth. Nathan kept moving as he heard automatic rifle fire and stun grenades exploding in the next room. He reached the far door with Natalia just behind as Wanda rushed in from the opposite side. Spotting Finbar, dead on the floor, she let out a blood-curdling scream. Neither Nathan nor Natalia stuck around to see what came next. Instead, they kept going through the next room before rising to their feet and hurrying deeper into the house. If they couldn't find some means of escape in short order, a very long prison sentence awaited them. But what escape? The helicopter hovered above the driveway, blocking that route. "The garden wall is the only way," said Nathan. "We need to go out the way we came in." They continued through a dining area, past a pair of swinging double doors and into a kitchen, while screams and gunfire echoed through the house.

"The entire east coast of Scotland is going to be covered in a massive oil spill!" Natalia was still fixated on that reality. "Can you picture what that means?"

"It means a bunch of birds and fish are going to meet their demise. I can't see how you and I are going to do anything about that under the circumstances. We need to get out of here, Natalia, right now!"

"We can't just give up! There's still the speedboat."

"Come on, Natalia, that isn't funny."

"Do you see me laughing?" Natalia headed off on her own, through the kitchen and toward the opposite side of the house.

"Where are you going?" Nathan tried to keep up.

"You can come with me or not, your choice."

"Natalia, they've got a helicopter, with a mounted machine gun!"

Natalia didn't answer, she was finished arguing. She was going to get to that boat or die trying. Nathan also understood with a deepening sense of dread that he was going with her. At the back of the kitchen, a door led outside to a small patio enclosed by a six-foot-high wooden fence. On the opposite side of the patio was a wooden gate. All the action was taking place in the front of the house. This gate led to the back, and when Natalia eased it open, they seemed to be temporarily in the clear. No signs of Royal Marines here. They still heard the helicopter but couldn't see it. Nathan did see the opening in the garden wall to his left, only thirty yards from where they were. It was tempting, but if he went that way he'd never be able to live with himself. Instead, he looked to Natalia. "Well?" he said. "You're the boss."

Natalia still had that combat focus in her eyes as she scanned to their right, across the garden and down to the sea where the speedboat was tied up peacefully at the dock. To get there, they'd need to expose themselves to the line of sight of whoever was in that helicopter. Even if they did make it to the boat, the helicopter pilot and his gunner would spot them heading out to sea and make quick work of them. Assuming the keys were in the boat in the first place. The whole endeavor seemed pointless in the extreme, but there was no conveying that to Natalia in the moment. He'd had a good life. If it ended here, he couldn't think of a better person to go out with.

Bending low behind a line of shrubs, Natalia began to crawl in the direction of the water. Nathan followed right behind. The foliage hid them from view for a short distance, but only extended halfway to the dock. That left thirty yards of open ground that they'd have to somehow get across. In the meantime, the mobsters were giving the Royal Marines a fight. Sporadic blasts of automatic weapons fire continued, as well as the mounted gun echoing over the noise of the helicopter rotors. Nathan risked raising his head to the top of the shrubs and peering over. From here he saw the Puma hovering in front of the house at a height of roughly 50 feet. Tracers lit the path of machine gun fire, but he couldn't see what it was aimed at exactly. If anybody in that room survived, mobsters or hostages, it would be a miracle.

"How do you propose we proceed?" Nathan shouted over the racket.

"As fast as we can."

"They'll see us."

"You have a better idea?"

"Yeah, get the hell out of here, through the garden gate."

"Sorry, Nathan. Come with me or not, I'm going to that boat."

"I know." He resigned himself to getting up and running as fast as his legs could carry him. He'd been a running back in high school, but he couldn't outrun a bullet. The one thing going for him, as he saw it, was that they were not visibly armed and would be running away. What soldier would shoot an unarmed man and woman? He would find out shortly. "What do you say, count of three?"

Before Natalia could answer, they heard what sounded like the scream of a wild banshee. It had to be Wanda. Nathan spotted her running from the house and into the yard, firing at the helicopter with her AK-47 as she went. It was a sight of pure unbridled fury. The gunner in the Puma opened up on her and the results were what Nathan had predicted from the start. The exploding block of C4 in her vest rocked the compound, with a bright flash of light and debris bursting up and out, catching the aircraft in a shockwave. The helicopter tipped sideways one way and then the other before the pilot lost control and the craft nosedived into the yard. Nathan ducked back behind the hedge and shielded his face as bits of Wanda's flesh rained down from above.

"Time to go!" Natalia called out. When Nathan looked up again she was off and running. He leaped to his feet and hurried after. They reached the boat but found no keys in the ignition.

"What now?" Nathan asked.

Natalia flipped down a sun visor. A set of keys fell onto the dash. "Get the lines," she said.

Nathan did as instructed, untying the stern and then the bow as she fired up the engine. It was late afternoon as she pointed the bow out to sea and the pair of them ripped off across the water, wind in their hair. Nathan powered up an onboard navigation system and took a few minutes to orient himself, scrolling around on a digital map until he'd located the Beatrice Oil Field, including three marked oil rigs, two of them connected by a short bridge. When he plugged in the coordinates, the GPS estimated their ETA based on current speed. "Forty-seven minutes until arrival," he said. "You think we'll be in time?"

"We'll find out," she answered.

"You have a plan for when we get there?" He managed a smile.

"I'm working on that," she replied.

"I'm sure you are." Beneath his shirt, Nathan felt the weight of his Luger. He'd rather have had the AK and a few grenades, but they'd have to make do. After what they'd just survived, every one of the 47 minutes in transit would feel like a new lease on life. He'd do his best to enjoy these minutes while he could.

Chapter Twenty-Two

Bertold Lange's helicopter made it obvious which platform to aim for. It was parked atop one of the twin structures, with the bridge connecting them. If the plan was to blow them up, it hadn't been put into action yet, though as the speedboat drew close, several figures could be seen running along steel walkways high above the water, stopping to make inspections and then moving on. Nathan saw four men. Even at this distance, he was pretty sure two of them were Lange and Dante. The other two held assault rifles and one of these men raised a hand to point.

"You come up with a plan yet?" Nathan unholstered his gun and held it in his right hand.

"Not exactly."

A few seconds later, the two men on the platform opened fire. Natalia swerved the speedboat from side to side as bullets whizzed into the water around them. "On the left, there's a ladder!" Nathan said.

Natalia took a wide arc, away from the assailants and around toward the outermost support on the opposite platform. With the bulk of the rigs shielding them, they'd have a few precious moments to climb onboard. Nathan holstered his gun once more as they drew close. The steel ladder hung just above the sea. Natalia reversed the engine to slow them down and then cut it entirely. Nathan jumped to the bow and tied a line to the lowest rung before the two of them scrambled up, climbing the support toward the towering platform. Somewhere up above, two men with assault rifles would be making their way across the bridge connecting the rigs, trying to get a bead on the pair. It gave Nathan and Natalia precious seconds to take up positions, if they were lucky. Climbing the ladder, Nathan's focus shifted to what looked like a very large bomb strapped to the inside of the support. It was a block of what had to be explosive material, with a timer attached and counting down from seven minutes, thirty-eight seconds. The device was attached to a strut with duct tape wrapped around and around. He pulled at it gently but there was no getting this off without a knife, and Nathan didn't have a knife.

"What is it?" Natalia clung to the ladder just below him.

"It looks like we've got seven minutes." Nathan peered around at the three other supports holding up the platform, each one roughly twenty yards away across the swirling sea, and all of them with similar packages attached.

"Seven minutes for what?"

"I'm still working on that." Nathan resumed climbing. The ladder led up through a steel walkway on the platform's lowest level. As soon as Nathan poked his head through, he spotted the men with rifles running across the bridge, some four levels higher. They continued forward without pause but they were all on the same rig now. Nathan stood square on the walkway and pulled out his pistol as Natalia joined his side.

"Distance favors them." Natalia took out her Glock. "We need to get them in close quarters. The closer the better."

Nathan moved to his left and went through a hatch that led inside the rig. From here, he passed through empty crew quarters and came to a stairwell leading further up. When he reached the second floor he checked his watch. Six minutes and fifty-seven seconds until she blew. On this level, he saw one door leading to what appeared to be a machine shop, with steel work tables, drills and clamps. Across from that was a storage room, with boxes stacked on shelves. "We ought to split up," he said.

"You take that room, I'll take this one." Natalia nodded toward the storage room. "We'll try to ambush them."

"Right." Nathan went into the machine shop and took up a position behind the door, gun at the ready. If anybody came along this hallway, Nathan would blast them to kingdom come from short range. Natalia would do the same on the opposite side. He checked his watch again. Six minutes and forty-two seconds. Beads of sweat formed on his brow. Every sense was on high alert as he listened for footsteps or heavy breathing. Instead, all he heard was the hum of machinery, and then in the distance, the sound of helicopter rotors beginning to spin. Dante and Lange were preparing their exit, probably leaving their two men behind to die for the cause. Nathan wanted to move forward, to attack, but he was a seasoned hunter. He knew better than to expose himself like that. With six minutes and eighteen seconds to go, he heard a door open. Next, he heard boots approaching, slowly. Here it was. His finger was on the trigger, ready to waste these fools. Any second... and then he heard gunshots, blam, blam, blam! It was a Glock, and Nathan knew they'd gone for the storage room. Bam, bam! Bam! The sound of automatic weapons fire answered as Nathan sprang from his hiding place and emerged into the hallway to find one man dead on the floor and another firing at an unseen target inside the room. Nathan raised his gun and shot the man square in the back. The impact threw the man forward and he crumpled to the ground. Natalia was directly beneath him. This was the first time since this whole thing began that Nathan felt pure panic. He grabbed the man's inert body and pulled him to one side and off. Natalia was on her back, bleeding from a wound in her right hip but alive, eyes wide open.

"Natalia!" was all Nathan could come up with.

"I'm all right," she croaked.

"You've been hit."

Natalia looked down at her torn pant leg, wet with blood. "How bad?"

Nathan took a few precious seconds to further tear open her pants and examine the wound. He'd seen worse, experienced worse, but he had no bandages, no tape, no first aid at all. "Can we get you up? We've got five minutes until this whole thing blows." Nathan helped Natalia to her feet, carefully. When she was standing, they moved into the hall and toward the stairwell, but this was slowing them down, draining away the time.

"Just go," Natalia said. "Leave me."

"I'm not leaving you!"

"Go!" she commanded. "We've come too far to give up!"

"Who said we're giving up?"

"Nathan, don't make me argue with you! There's no time!"

"What am I supposed to do? I can't defuse all those bombs, not in five minutes!"

"You have to try, Nathan. You have to do your best."

To Nathan, it didn't seem possible. He might get to one of them, maybe two, but the simple fact was that there were too many of them and not enough time. What he could do, possibly, was take out Lange's helicopter. After that, he'd come back for Natalia, get the pair of them into the speedboat and escape. That was Nathan's best-case scenario, despite the impending environmental devastation.

"I'll be back," he said. "I won't abandon you."

"Hurry!"

Nathan turned and bolted up the stairs, emerging at the top level of the platform. The drilling tower rose hundreds of feet further still. On the opposite platform, he saw the helicopter still on the pad, with Lange in the right seat and Dante in the left. The rotors spun at full speed and the craft began rising into the air, hovering for just a moment before moving away. Nathan took aim with his pistol, firing off a few rounds. He should have grabbed one of the dead men's rifles, he realized too late. That would have given him a fighting chance. Instead, they were getting away. He watched in frustration for a good ten seconds. The helicopter headed west, back toward the mainland, disappearing into fading light. Nathan turned toward the stairs. He still had time to get Natalia off the rig. As he was heading down, though, he saw the helicopter turn back. With some incredulity, Nathan watched it approach once more. What for? He couldn't say. The helicopter came within 100 feet of the opposite platform and started a slow circle around it. Were Lange and Dante taking one last look at their handiwork? It didn't much matter why, Nathan would have one more chance, as long as they hadn't seen him. He hid himself in the stairwell and waited, channeling all his patience. He heard the helicopter slowly continuing around, sensing its position. When it was only a few hundred feet away, he peeked out from around the door. There it was, right in front of him. Nathan took aim and unloaded every last round he had left, sending sparks flying off the tail rotor. Through the Plexiglas windshield, Nathan saw Dante's horror as he lost control of the craft, desperately yanking at the stick. Around and around, the helicopter began to spin, and then down it went, dropping straight into the sea below. From the platform rail, Nathan made them out clearly inside the cockpit, Lange and Dante, side by side, with terror in their eyes as the craft slowly sank beneath the surface and disappeared, dragging them into the depths. Nathan checked his watch. Four minutes and sixty-eight seconds to go. He hurried back inside the stairwell and down. He was only one level below when he came across Natalia, with company.

"I found them locked in the galley," she said, referring to a crew of three men and two women in greasy coveralls.

"This thing is gonna blow in four minutes," said Nathan.

"We need to shut off the main valves," said one of the workers. "It's the only way to avert a disaster."

"How long will that take?"

Instead of wasting time with an answer, the man turned to one of the others. "Take Buchanan with you and close down platform one. I'll take care of number two."

"Right," said the other man and two of them hurried off.

"The rest of you, get to the escape pod."

"I'm coming with you," Nathan said to the first man.

With no more words to spare, the man headed off. Nathan looked back to the remaining crew. "Take her with you!" He nodded to Natalia and then hurried after the first man, toward number two. They rushed across the bridge between the platforms, the roiling sea beneath. From here, they continued down further, past pipes and machinery. The workman went straight to a series of valves and started to turn one of them. "What can I do?" said Nathan.

The man got the first valve closed, but when he moved to another one it barely turned. He pulled and pulled, and with Nathan's help, they got it to move. Bit by bit the wheel spun until the valve was closed. "That's all," the man said. "Let's go."

They were halfway up to the bridge when the first bomb went off. Both platforms shook and rumbled beneath them. Nathan hung on tightly as flames erupted all around. The bombs weren't coordinated, Nathan realized, as a second blast tore through platform number two. They were halfway across the bridge when number two crumbled into the sea behind them, pulling the bridge down at an angle in a shriek of tearing metal. The sea erupted in flames as Nathan and the crewman hung on, then began to climb, up, up, up.

"We need to make the escape capsule!" the crewman shouted. Nathan's watch still said sixty-eight seconds until the bombs on platform one went off. He looked down at the fiery waters beneath them. Jumping was not an option. Instead, he fought for each foot, higher and higher until they reached the deck on platform one. He gave a hand to the crewman and pulled him the last of the way up before the man led him around to a large enclosed lifeboat mounted at an angle on the opposite side. The door was open. Nathan let the crewman go first and then climbed in after. Inside, Natalia and the rest of the crew were strapped into angled seats, ready to go.

"I thought you'd be out of here already," said Nathan.

"Strap in, hurry!" Natalia replied.

Nathan took the seat beside Natalia and fastened shoulder straps and a seat belt. The last crewman closed and latched the door, took the seat beside it and slammed an emergency release button. Nathan took a quick look at the timer on his watch, with the seconds ticking down. "Four, three, two, one..." Away slid the capsule like a wild roller-coaster ride, free-falling through the air toward the sea below. Moments later, *Bang! Bang! Bang, Bang!* All four struts exploded in sequence, and then *splash!* The capsule hit the water, plunging beneath the surface momentarily and then popping back up. As it bobbed from side to side, the crewman in the rear fired up an engine and steered them through the flaming seas. They were less than 100 yards away when platform one came crashing down, collapsing into the water behind them and creating a giant wave that tossed them around like a toy. When it cleared, both platforms were gone. But for the last traces of burning oil, the sea became calm. Everyone on board the capsule was alive.

"How's your wound?" Nathan turned his attention to Natalia beside him. There was a lot of blood, soaking her clothing and the seat beneath. He didn't see any major damage to the bones, it seemed to be mostly flesh, but he couldn't be sure. "We need to stop the bleeding!"

"I'll survive," she replied, but Nathan was already unstrapping himself and hurrying toward a first aid box in the stern. He unlatched it and pawed through the supplies, pulling out disinfectant, gauze and tape. Bringing these back, he opened a bottle of Betadine and several packets of gauze pads.

"You know this is going to hurt," he said.

Natalia closed her eyes tight and clenched her fists, preparing for it. Nathan pulled her clothing aside, sprayed some of the liquid onto a pad and used that to wipe down her wound, all while she cringed in agony, trying not to scream. When Nathan was satisfied that it was clean, he applied a few sterile pads and taped them in place.

"All done," Nathan said.

Natalia opened her eyes and tried to relax, to become one with the pain, to accept it. Nathan moved the extra supplies out of the way and took the seat beside her again.

"What about Dante? And Lange?" Natalia asked.

"Off to their private place in hell."

Natalia breathed a little easier, relief washing over her. "Fitting."

Nathan felt the same deep sense of relief, that they'd accomplished their goal and eliminated two madmen bent on destruction. These past days had required extraordinary courage from them both, but when it came to saying what he wanted to tell her next, he was all out. How could he admit that he'd been utterly terrified, not about the bombs or the gunmen coming after them, or his own safety at all, but at the prospect of losing Natalia? The prospect that she might not make it had rocked Nathan to his core. He wanted to tell her so, but couldn't bring himself to. If not now, most likely not ever. But then he realized, he didn't have to. Natalia already knew. She reached out and took him by the hand, wrapping his fingers in hers and squeezing before leaning her head against his shoulder. As they motored west toward the coast of Scotland, for the first time in as long as Nathan could remember, all felt right with the world.

Chapter Twenty-Three

Nathan wasn't surprised to find himself in another holding cell. When a coast guard vessel picked up their lifeboat off the coast of Scotland, he was at first treated like any of the other survivors, given a blanket and a cup of hot tea. Natalia was taken to the infirmary where her wounds were dressed by the ship's doctor. Upon docking at Inverness, they were met by teams from multiple law enforcement agencies. Nathan and Natalia were separated out from the oil rig crew, she taken to a nearby medical facility and he locked up. After a day of questioning, he was flown to London in chains. Multiple interrogation sessions followed. Nathan was offered no lawyer. He knew enough to mostly keep his mouth shut, to avoid self-incrimination. "Where is Ms. Nicolaeva? Can I see her?" he asked at one point, but was met with silence. Nathan didn't blame them for their caution. He'd racked up a significant body count in the previous week, from Watford to Inverness to the North Sea. It didn't necessarily matter that it was all in the cause of saving humanity. To the authorities, he was simply dangerous. Maybe he had saved the world, but Nathan very well might end up spending the rest of his life in a British prison as a result. Natalia as well. When his interrogators gave up on prying anything out of him, Nathan was finally appointed a defense counsel, a mousy woman named Gladys Bastian.

"Just keep your mouth shut," his lawyer told him, "until I can work out what the hell is going on here. You can talk to me, but nobody else, got it?"

"Absolutely."

A week went by before Nathan was finally called before a judge, the same one he'd faced after his original run-in with Finbar Murphy at the start of this whole affair. This was the judge who'd confiscated his passport and threatened to lock him back up if he didn't behave. Well, Nathan hadn't quite behaved. Chains bound his wrists and ankles as he faced the judge yet again. Beside him at the defense table were his lawyer, Ms. Bastian, and two other men whom he knew nothing about. These men were better dressed than Bastian, better put together in general, and with a dead-serious air. As Nathan turned to look behind him, he saw that the gallery was empty. No spectators, no press, not a soul in the room who wasn't directly connected to his case. Was he that much of a national security risk? It didn't bode well. The court was called into session. The judge looked over a document on the desk in front of him. A disagreeable expression crossed his face. He didn't much like it, whatever it was.

"In the case of His Majesty the King against Mr. Nathan Grant, I have been made aware that the prosecution would like to make a statement." He looked up at the two prosecuting attorneys, sitting at a table across the aisle from Nathan. "Please proceed," said the judge.

One of the prosecutors stood and cleared his throat. "Your honor, we hereby report that His Majesty has decided to drop all charges. We apologize for wasting the court's time with this proceeding."

Nathan's eyes lit up. He turned to his lawyers, but their faces were impassive. They seemed to have expected this. Only Ms. Bastian offered him a comforting nod.

"May I dare to ask the reason for this decision?" said the judge.

"Lack of evidence, your honor," said the prosecutor.

The judge took a moment to absorb this, then looked over to Nathan. "The defendant is free to go."

Just like that, for reasons Nathan couldn't possibly understand, it was all over. "What about Natalia Nicolaeva?" he asked. "Were her charges dropped as well?" The judge was already moving out of the room. Nathan turned next to Ms. Bastian. "What about Natalia?"

One of the two newcomers on his team responded to this one. "Ms. Nicolaeva is waiting to see you, if you'd care to follow me."

A bailiff approached with a key and removed Nathan's chains.

"Don't ask, just be grateful," said Ms. Bastian. "You're going home."

Nathan followed his lawyers up the aisle toward the courtroom doors and passed through them a free man. His lawyers led him down a long hallway, past some offices, and then up a set of stairs until they came to a conference room.

"All of your questions will be answered inside," said one of the men.

In his gut, Nathan was still uneasy about this whole setup. These kinds of "get out of jail free" situations were rarely "free." They came with strings attached. He didn't know yet what those strings would be, but he was about to find out. If information was all they were after, he'd be happy enough to oblige. After steeling himself, he walked through the door. Inside at a long table, he saw Natalia, all cleaned up and wearing a pair of loose green pants and a baggy blue sweater. A pair of crutches leaned against the table by her side. Across from her was another man he didn't recognize, but with his stocky frame and military bearing, Nathan assumed he was law enforcement of some sort. Beside Natalia was a woman in a blue business suit. This woman he did recognize. It was Marilyn Kearney. He knew her as the recently appointed head of MI6. They'd met once before, years earlier. She'd been Director of Counter-Terrorism for the organization during Nathan's CIA days. Now she ran the whole show. The shock of her presence stopped Nathan in his tracks.

"Welcome, Mr. Grant." Ms. Kearney rose. "I'm Marilyn Kearney."

"We've met." Nathan shook her hand. "Though it's been a number of years."

"I do remember. Marseille, wasn't it? Please, have a seat."

Nathan took the chair directly opposite Kearney, beside the security officer and diagonal from Natalia, who had yet to say a word.

"Ms. Nicolaeva has been filling me in on your latest adventures, Mr. Grant," Kearney went on.

"Adventures," Nathan repeated the word. "You make it sound so pleasant."

"What would you prefer?"

Nathan didn't respond, turning instead to Natalia. "How's the hip?"

"Fine," she said, though the response was muted.

"They were able to patch you up?"

Natalia rose from her chair and pulled her sweater up a few inches to reveal a white bandage underneath. "An inch further over would have shattered it, but I was fortunate."

"Ms. Nicolaeva can look forward to a full recovery," said Kearney as Natalia retook her seat.

"I'm relieved to hear that," Nathan replied. That was true, of course, but he knew something else was coming. "So, why are we here?"

Kearney reached into her pocket and pulled out a blue American passport, then slid it across the table. "You're a free man," she said. "That's all."

Nathan picked up the passport and opened it to see his photo staring back. "I've been around long enough to know," he said to Kearney. "That's never all."

"You have been around, yes," Kearney agreed. "You have an impressive resume and after what you and Ms. Nicolaeva accomplished, our nation owes you a huge debt of gratitude. We couldn't very well lock you up, not after you saved the entire northeast coast of Scotland from environmental devastation."

"You're welcome."

"And you got rid of our Bertold Lange and Collin Bruce problem to boot."

"It was the least we could do."

"And now I'd like to offer you a job."

"No, thank you." Here were the strings. At least they were being presented as an offer, not a demand. So far.

"You haven't heard the details yet."

"You could offer me the crown jewels, my answer would be the same." Nathan clung to his passport, half expecting her to snatch it back.

"That's a shame, but I can't say it's unexpected. I had to try," said Kearney.

At this response, Nathan looked to Natalia. What had her answer been? Based on her demeanor, he was pretty sure he already knew. For Natalia, it likely wasn't an offer. Whatever life she'd planned as a human rights attorney, that was all out the window. Kearney had all the leverage she needed to turn Natalia Nicolaeva into the latest operative in the MI6 arsenal. It would have been that or prison. Nathan felt bereft at the entire prospect, but what could he do? This was the head of British foreign intelligence pulling the strings.

"With the threat of incarceration off the table, we do hope you will answer some further questions," Kearney went on.

"Help us connect the dots between Lange and Bruce. And Oscar Boswell..."

"I'll be happy to tell you what I can," said Nathan. "For what it's worth."

"Good. The thing is, we're still struggling with the motivations. A financier and an environmental terrorist team up to wreck the environment. That's not so obvious on the face of things, now is it?"

"Not hardly, but I suspect you know more than I do. They say it was all about the money."

"Who says?"

"Boswell," Natalia answered this one. "It was certainly about the money for him."

"If this plan had succeeded, the shores of Lange's estate would have been covered in oil. One would think that might lower the value of the place."

"You already know more than you're letting on," said Nathan. "Don't you?"

The director looked a little annoyed, but then conceded. "Lange was broke," she said. "Worse than broke. His entire financial firm was a house of cards, a giant Ponzi scheme. He'd kept it afloat for years by luring in new investors to pay off the old ones, but the whole thing was on the verge of collapse. He was facing complete ruin and a lifetime in prison."

"So he was shorting the market."

"Correct. He and Bruce put every penny they could manage into highly leveraged bets against the very oil companies they targeted. The pair of them would have grossed nearly a billion pounds if they'd gotten away with it."

"What happens to that money now?"

"Those trades will be canceled. What assets Lange had will be sold, but investors will get pennies on the pound at the end of the day."

"Let me get this straight, then," said Nathan. "Lange was broke and cooked up this scheme, then enlisted Bruce to create this Environmental Liberation Front as a way to tank the oil and gas industry, short the market and make a billion pounds?"

"The ELF preceded Lange's plan. It preceded Collin Bruce as well, but with his charisma, he was able to take it over and build it up. What we don't understand is Boswell. What can you tell us about his role in the whole thing?"

"Natalia must have already told you, right?" said Nathan. "Boswell provided the explosive materials. Bruce made a down payment upfront, but stiffed the mobsters on the rest of what was owed."

"What about Megan Stirling, then?"

"Megan was a go-between," said Natalia. "She must have joined the ELF under honest pretenses, believing in its purported environmental mission. Bruce had her hired as an associate at Lange Capital to handle the transfers between Boswell and Lange, money for explosive materials. When she realized what she was involved in, Megan tried to get out. She contacted my firm to help her, but we weren't able to manage. When Collin Bruce realized she'd flipped, he sent assassins after her parents, to keep them quiet."

"I suppose it all makes some perverted sense," said Kearney. "We have to give Ms. Stirling credit. The rest of Collin Bruce's followers were all just dupes. They thought they were changing the world for the better, no matter what it took. Murder, mayhem and destruction. Sadly, all their so-called leader cared about was cold hard cash." Kearney pushed back her chair and rose to her feet. "That will do for the time being. You can expect us to be in touch if we have any further questions."

"Of course," said Nathan.

"Take care, Mr. Grant. I do hope you manage to stay out of trouble from here on," Kearney added. "Though if you want my honest opinion, your track record suggests otherwise."

Nathan stood to shake her hand again, as did Natalia.

"And you," Kearney put her hand on Natalia's shoulder, "you recover well. Our people will be in touch."

"Yes, Ma'am," said Natalia.

Kearney and her man walked out of the room, leaving Nathan and Natalia behind, alone together for the first time in over a week. So much had just transpired that Nathan wasn't sure where to start.

"I don't know about you, but I could use a drink," said Natalia.

"That seems to be our habit," Nathan agreed.

"That's one of the nice things about London. You never need to walk more than half a block to find a pub."

Natalia used both crutches as Nathan held the door. He was still adjusting to the idea of being free and clear, with his passport in his pocket. He passed Natalia as they moved down the hall.

"Hey, slow down!" Natalia complained.

"Sorry." Nathan paused to let her catch up. "I'm a tad eager to get out of here." They took an elevator to the ground floor and then moved through the courthouse lobby and out to the street. Nathan took in the bustling London scene, filling his lungs with air. "We did it." He couldn't mask his incredulity.

"Did you ever have any doubt?" Natalia replied.

"Um... yes," he laughed.

"Come on, Nathan. Second thoughts aren't allowed in this game. You know that." Natalia cocked her head to one side. "I know of a place on the next corner."

"Lead the way."

The pub was called the Laughing Loon, with an image of a tall, skinny bird on the sign. The name was somewhat unconventional, but the establishment itself was a standard British pub, with a dark wooden bar and furnishings. Natalia chose a table and leaned her crutches against a windowsill before taking a seat.

"Any food today?" a server asked.

"Just drinks for me." Natalia looked to Nathan. "What do you think, Scotch?"

"No!" Nathan visibly shook. "I'd rather avoid Scotland altogether."

"Tullamore Dew?"

"Same goes for the Irish. How about we stick to a good old American whiskey?"

"Fine. Two glasses of Jack Daniels, neat. Why don't we make those doubles?" said Natalia.

"Just be careful. We both know where this type of drinking can lead."

"I'd like to think we've grown since then," said Natalia.

"I'll get those right out," the server replied before moving off.

Despite everything having worked out generally for the best, Nathan still felt an air of doom hanging over them. Natalia seemed to share the feeling. This wasn't a celebratory drink, it was a coming to terms with the new reality.

The whiskey arrived and Natalia lifted hers in the air. "What are we drinking to?"

"I don't know... Survival?"

"Sure. Survival, then." Each of them took a good, healthy swig. Nathan felt it hit his stomach, warming his insides. "What happened to the rest of the mobsters?" he asked. "Did Kearney mention anything about that?"

"They didn't make it."

"None of them? What about the hostages?"

"Three survived, four perished. Wanda took out most of them when she blew. You were right, standing near her was a bad idea."

Nathan took another hit of his whiskey. "You don't have to do this, you know. With Kearney. She can't force you to."

Natalia looked at her glass, unwilling or unable to make eye contact. "You think we'd both be sitting here otherwise? She went to a lot of trouble to get us out. An awful lot of strings were pulled."

"Maybe so, but how much is she going to trust an operative who's only in it to avoid prison time? What about your law degree? What about your career? You can't just give all that up!"

"Says who?"

"It's what you wanted, what you've been working so hard for!" What Nathan didn't say, but clearly understood, was that Natalia wasn't merely choosing between espionage and law, she was choosing between espionage and Nathan Grant. The life of an intelligence operative did not leave room for relationships. He had his own experience on that side of things.

"This isn't easy for me, either."

"I never said it was easy. I just want to understand."

"But you already do. If anybody on earth understands, it's you."

Nathan let this truth sink in. He remembered the thrill of it all when he'd signed up himself. Even now, chasing after bad guys was an addiction that was hard to quit. His brother was a lawyer, working as a federal prosecutor back home. Nathan had always looked upon that existence with dread. He didn't blame Natalia for avoiding that sort of fate, but those weren't the only options. He could offer her a third. "Come with me. You'll love the south of France. We'll fix up my cottage, plant a garden..."

"Admit it, Nathan, you miss the life yourself. I know you do, you told me so."

Nathan couldn't argue, she was right to a degree. The thrill of it he certainly did miss, from time to time. What he didn't miss was working for somebody else, letting his bosses in an office in Virginia call the shots. That was what he'd outgrown, and there was no going back. Natalia was still young, though. For her it was different. She'd carve out a place for herself on her own terms, as best she could. Marilyn Kearney was lucky to have her. Nathan lifted his glass once again. "To your new career."

Natalia tapped her glass to his and they drank. Neither one was ready to part just yet, to let this moment slip past. Instead, they ordered steaks with potatoes and broccoli, switched to red wine, and ended a few hours later with coffee. Nathan wobbled only slightly on his feet this time. Natalia was doing better, as always. He insisted on paying and she retrieved her crutches before they moved out to the street. Here they were, saying goodbye all over again. As they stood on the sidewalk, he tried to push aside the gravity of their imminent parting.

"We'd better get you a cab," said Nathan. "We could share one if you'd like."

"No, it's the opposite direction. I'll be fine on my own."

"You're sure?"

"Come on, Nathan, you don't have to baby me."

Nathan laughed. "No, heaven forbid." He held up a hand and flagged down a passing taxi. When it pulled to a stop, Nathan knew perfectly well that he might never see her again, for real this time. She'd made her choice, and he wasn't it. "Goodbye, Natalia."

"Goodbye, Nathan." She switched both crutches to one hand and wrapped her arms around him in an awkward last embrace.

Nathan inhaled and squeezed her tight, taking in every last bit of it before letting go. "Try not to be a hero."

"Look who's talking." She leaned forward and kissed him on the cheek.

Nathan opened the door and helped her into the back of the cab.

"Camden," she said to the driver.

As the car pulled away, he gave her one last wave and then watched the black London cab move off up the street until he could it no more. Every now and then there came these crossroads in life, moments where one decision could change a person's entire trajectory. This was one of those moments. Nathan could have tried getting down on one knee. He could have begged and pleaded, but that wasn't his style. Besides, Natalia had to chart her own path. Picturing her as an MI6 operative in training, he had to smile. "We are two peas in a pod, you and I," he said quietly. "I wish you the best of luck." Nathan headed up the sidewalk, fingering the passport in his pocket as he went. In the morning he'd catch the first plane bound for France. After that, he'd have the rest of his life ahead of him, whatever he cared to make of it.

Thank you for reading
London on Fire!

Congratulations, you made it to the end of this latest episode in the Nathan Grant Thriller Series! I hope you enjoyed this one. For those who want another fix of Nathan and Natalia right away, you can check out the fourth book in the Natalia Nicolaeva series, *Mystery Girl,* if you haven't read it already. That was the book where this pair first met, chasing after a notorious arms dealer, each for their respective reasons. If you're interested in reading the entire four-book Natalia series, you can start with *Russia Girl,* in which she comes into her own as an international crime fighter.

As for Nathan Grant, his saga will continue, with book number five on the way and expected sometime in early 2024. For a free Nathan Grant prequel novella about Nathan's first assignment with the CIA, you can download *The Vienna Assignment* by signing up for my newsletter at kennethrosenberg.com.

I also love hearing from readers, so if you have any comments feel free to write to me at kenneth@kennethrosenberg.com. That's it for now, but again, I hope you liked the book and if so, don't be shy about leaving a review! Until next time…

Kenneth Rosenberg

Printed in Great Britain
by Amazon

27901723R00142